WHITE FRIGHT

SID DE BEER

To my wife Nadine, thank you for being a fantastic mother to our three daughters, an incredible grandmother and for always being available to offer any help that our daughters may ask for.

To my three daughters Odette, Shi-Anne and Kim, thank you for growing up to be the mothers you are today, with the values your mother and I instilled in you and for giving birth to a grand parent's most prized possession, their grandchildren.

To my three sons in law, Terence, Gary and Danny, who thanks to the many passionate nights you spent with my daughters gave me the gift of my precious grandchildren.

Thought you slept in separate bedrooms after marriage!

'I forgive you.'

To my seven grandchildren, Blake, Kegan, Shayna, Logan, Hunter, Ryder and Sienna who I love more than they will ever know.

Always remember what I have taught you -'Knowledge is Power.'

Acknowledgments

Thank you to Jan Scherpenhuizen for his assessment.

A special thank you to my youngest daughter Kim for diligently correcting spelling errors, grammar and for the numerous suggestions and input she offered.

Thank you to my family for the encouragement.

A special thank you to Dani Streay of An Altered Aspect, www.analteredaspect.com for the design of the cover and his guidance and input into various aspects of the novel.

I am grateful for his contribution.

Life is trying things to see if they work

-Ray Bradbury

Contents

The President turned to his aides seated around the table in the situation room.

His face white with fright!

Chapter 1

Zurich

Switzerland

It was snowing heavily as the Range Rover that the CIA had hired earlier in the day made its way up the ramp leading to the entrance of The Grand Hotel.

Yonti bid the two agents farewell and slipped out of the Range Rover before it had totally stopped, flicking the rear passenger door closed as he exited.

He quick stepped around the rear of the vehicle and was undercover at the main entrance to hotel moments later, brushing the snowflakes from both shoulders of his chic camel coloured cashmere designer coat.

Nimble underfoot for a young man, allowing himself a rear smile of confidence that he has what it takes at the tender age of twenty two.

He ran his hand over his crop of dark brown hair to smooth away any remaining snowflakes and glanced at the Range Rover as it made its way down the ramp on the other side from the hotels entrance until it was out of sight, then turned and made his way towards the entrance of the hotel.

The Range Rover parked opposite the entrance to the underground parking on the lower level and the driver and his fellow agent waited patiently.

The Grand Hotel, set in a stately building dating back to 1899 offering sweeping views of the Alps and Lake Zurich and a short walk to the Kunsthaus Zurich museum.

Accommodation in this exclusive hotel was completely booked out as it offered a secure location that could easily be guarded on all sides.

The doorman opened the side door rather than the main doors as he approached, to minimize the cold draft wafting into the hotel.

The evening was extremely cold with the temperature at a chilly 26.6 degrees Fahrenheit which felt much colder in the 10 knot breeze.

Zurich had not experienced a cold spell like this for years, possibly due to global warming.

The smartly dressed doorman smiled broadly as he rubbed his hands offering a courteous greeting. 'Good evening sir and welcome to The Grand Hotel.'

'Thank you, I am expected in the ballroom on the second floor for the cocktail party hosted by The Three Sixty Degrees Group,' replied Yonti.

'Kindly proceed to the concierge on the right hand side of the entrance,' instructed the doorman indicating the way.

'You can register your coat for storage at the kiosk situated outside the entrance to the ballroom on the second floor,' continued the doorman.

Yonti acknowledged the doorman's instruction with a nod of the head and made his way towards the concierge who stood behind his desk observing him as he approached.

Quickly scanning the layout of the room, he noted the cameras positioned to the left and right hand side of the desk and those discreetly hidden amongst the décor.

The training he had received from the CIA and the experience he had gained in the field, ensured that he followed a procedure of awareness. The greeting from the concierge was cordial.

'Good evening sir, your name please?' asked the concierge smiling politely.

'Aaron Armando.'

He was travelling under cover as the CIA had taken all necessary precautions possible to disguise its operatives and agents, ensuring that there would never be a trail to follow for any person wishing to discover their true identity.

They had created a complete new person for Yonti in all the American databases, passport, social security card, driver's licence, identity document and schoolbook photographs to give him the appearance of being an authentic American citizen.

Yonti had several aliases which he had used on many missions for the CIA and the alias that had been allocated to Yonti from the first day he was recruited by the CIA was Rafael Dujon on the instruction of Director Barnaby Heathcott.

Within the CIA, he was known as Rafa as his real name was known only to Director Heathcott, Stanley Noble, the CIA station chief in Paris and his assistant, Lieutenant Johnston.

His real identity and passport had been locked away in a safe within the Director of the CIA's office since the day he started working for the CIA.

Yonti was born of French parents Marcel and Brielle Barre from the Provence-Alpes –Cote d' Azure region on the French Riviera in the South of France, famous for its chic elegance, high living and the playground of the rich and famous and was the older of two brothers.

His parents owned and ran a luxury three story, fifteen bedroom exclusive apartment block namely Appartements vue mer (Sea View Apartments) on the Promenade des Anglais in Nice. The exclusive establishment was famous for its breathtaking panoramic views of the beach and ocean.

Sought after by the beautiful rich and famous sun loving people of the world. Each apartment was lavishly appointed featuring its own balcony and set back from the others to afford maximum privacy, catering to the every whim and needs of the beautiful people who sought the sun in the region every year and sported a price tag to match.

The property had been acquired by Yonti's grandfather Jean-Pierre shortly after the Second World War. Updated and modernised over decades by the ever energetic Marcel, it had become one of the most sought after holiday residences in Nice.

Pierre the younger brother by two years had a keen interest in the family business and was clearly the heir to his father's throne.

Having done his daily chores in the complex which involved any repairs and painting rather than mundane chores, Yonti would spend his spare time studying science, computer engineering and counter-intelligence, subjects that interested him.

Unbeknown to Yonti, this was to set the course that he would follow later in life. His mother, a talented culinary executive chef created scrumptious meals daily for guests to enjoy.

Most guests chose to dine in rather than dine out in case they missed one of Brielle's speciality created meals. She specialised in a delicious seafood Mornay.

Patrons helped themselves to drinks at the bar overlooking the swimming pool as there was no barman in attendance noting down what they had taken in an honesty system, which was most popular with the guest as trust far outshone the need for a barman to be present.

Marcel took care of marketing and the management of the complex and any requests for cocktails were made to Marcel, who obliged and created whatever the guests desired.

Yonti was fluent in English having realised that large parts of the commercial world conversed in that universal language and had taken English as a second language at school, passing with a distinction.

Having completed his schooling as a top student he went onto university at the Sorbonne University in Paris. The university had a reputation of academic achievement and was founded in 1257.

With no fewer than 32 Nobel Prize and Fields Medal Winners amongst its past students, the university had a long tradition of academic excellence.

Yonti graduated 'Cum Laude' with a master's degree in Economics (PSME), Computer Systems Engineering and Management (IKSEM).

His father Marcel wanted him to follow in his footsteps and eventually take over the family business continuing his legacy, a thought he had long forgotten, opting for his younger son Pierre to be the heir to his throne.

Yonti's interest lay elsewhere, leaving it up to Pierre to continue the family tradition.

Chapter 2

Langley

Virginia USA

Yonti had come to the attention of the CIA station chief in Paris in his first year at the Sorbonne University. He graduated 'Cum Laude' at the age of 22, having spent some four years studying when the CIA station chief, Stanley Noble based in Paris drew Barnaby Heathcott's attention to this exceptionally talented student.

Barnaby Heathcott was The Director of the CIA stationed at their head-quarters at Langley in Virginia in the USA.

Yonti was a fit 22 year old athlete who had excelled in triathlon at university and martial arts, sporting a first Dan in the Japanese Shito-ryu style karate with an array of gold medals confirming his prowess.

Handsome with a slightly olive tanned complexion, standing over 6 feet tall and weighing 187 pounds, his muscular frame was an imposing sight and was popular with the ladies with a reputation to match.

Stanley Noble, arranged to meet with Yonti at Café Floret situated at 170 Boulevard at Saint Germaine in Paris

The meeting was cordial as the station chief chatted casually with Yonti praising him about his academic and sporting achievements over coffee, when they were suddenly joined by a well-groomed-tanned suave looking gentleman with neatly styled grey hair confirming his ageing years.

Sliding into the seat alongside Yonti, Barnaby Heathcott extended his hand in a greeting without introducing himself.

'I have a job offer for you,' said Barnaby.

Yonti was taken aback with the sudden appearance of this stranger as Stan Noble leaned back in his chair and watched the interaction with interest.

Pointing to Stan Noble, Barnaby said, 'Stan will give you all the details and you are expected to meet with me tomorrow at 10.00 a.m.'

'Don't be late,' and with that, Barnaby was gone as quickly as he had arrived.

A former navy seal, Stan had moved from Seal Team Six to accept a safer job within the CIA as station chief in France years previously.

This was instigated by his close friend Barnaby Heathcott due to the fact that he was ageing and the injuries he had sustained in the many campaigns he was involved in.

He had done his time defending America on the front line.

Barnaby needed somebody of Stan's calibre in the CIA as his unique skill at ferreting out ideal recruits and his analytical skill proved invaluable.

Yonti shot an enquiring look at Stan Noble who in turn shrugged his shoulders and tilted his head but offered no response.

Standing Stan said, 'be there and be on time,' dropping a hand written note with the address detailed on it and twenty francs for the coffee in front of Yonti and he too was up and on his way.

Yonti picked up the note, studied the address on it for some time which was familiar to him and put it in his pocket.

He sat back in his chair, hands behind his head wondering what on earth had just happened and whether these two strangers were in fact from the USA embassy.

They had appeared mysteriously in his life, one had introduced himself as Stanley Noble, who seemed to know a lot about him and the other who had not introduced himself by name at all, however expected to meet with him the next morning.

Very mysterious indeed thought Yonti as he gazed at the patrons enjoying their meals and coffee in the early afternoon sun.

Yonti knew he would make the appointment out of curiosity as he was keen to find out more about these two mysterious people and he in turn found himself staring at his empty cup of coffee.

Bewildered by not knowing a thing about the two people he had just met, where they were from or who they worked for, he wondered why they would possibly want to meet him.

Stan and Barnaby had forged a close relationship over many years, working closely together at the Pentagon.

Stan had personally saved Barnaby's life in the corridors of the Pentagon when the hijacked plane crashed into the western side at 09.37 EDT on that fateful day in September.

The eleventh of September 2001 was etched in the memory of all Americans forever.

Both were on their way to a meeting in the Pentagon and had just rounded the corner of one of the polygons when the plane crashed into the complex.

Barnaby and Stan had been thrown against the wall by the ensuing blast, with Barnaby taking the brunt of the impact against the wall and Stan falling behind him, which cushioned him from any serious injuries.

Barnaby was unconscious from the impact and Stan realising that something awful had happened sprung to his feet instantaneously, dragged Barnaby towards a door close by and punched a security code into the panel of the fireproof door.

He opened the door and dragged his friend into the secure room with moments to spare.

Stan had quickly closed the door securely behind him as he was aware of a possible fireball careering down the passageway towards them.

This saved both their lives as the ensuing fireball careered down the passageway of the Pentagon and past them moments after they had entered through the fireproof door.

Thankfully they were both safely inside.

Barnaby suffered a broken leg, broken arm, two broken ribs with a severe cut on the top of his head.

Stan sustained minor bruises mainly due to Barnaby taking brunt of the impact.

Thankfully the overhead sprinkler system was intact and activated in the secure room thus saving both from severe burns and certain death due to the extensive heat in the passage which eventually eased as firefighters fought the blaze.

Barnaby was in pain, moaning constantly and complaining of the heat and Stan did his best to stop the bleeding on top his friend's head whilst comforting him, ensuring him of just how lucky they had been to escape and evade the fireball that followed them down the passage.

Drenched and dehydrated from the sprinklers and sweat from the heat in the stuffy hazy room they waited patiently to be rescued.

Eventually, after what seemed like several hours, Stan could hear the first responders in the passage.

He banged on the heated door and they were rescued when the firefighters hacked the door open.

Both were rushed to hospital dehydrated and in need of urgent medical attention.

This forged a lasting relationship between them for life.

Having been released from hospital Barnaby ignored the doctor's orders to take time off and recuperate for a few weeks.

He was back at his desk the same day he was released a week later albeit in a new part of the Pentagon, feeling extremely uncomfortable and still in a great deal of pain, Barnaby buried himself in his day to day analytical chores of CIA business.

His committed focus to the tasks at hand, helped pass the days and weeks easing the pain until he had fully recovered.

The years passed by as the hunt for Osama Bin Ladin continued 24/7 and finally President Obama announced to the American public and the world at large, that the USA had conducted a covert mission in Pakistan that killed the leader of Al-Qaeda on the 2nd of May 2011.

The republicans won the election and President Ronald Trent took office on the 20th of January 2017.

The Director of the CIA, Jean Hammond retired after 3 years in the role and Barnaby was summoned to the White House to meet with President Trent.

'Good morning Barnaby,' said the President extending his hand in a greeting.

'I am pleased to see that you have recovered well from your experience at the Pentagon all those years ago,' continued the President.

President Trent was not a man of many words and could be as direct as any person could ever be and was similar in persona to Barnaby.

'As you are aware Director Hammond is retiring and I have invited you here to offer you the role of Director of the CIA,' said the President.

'Your credentials are outstanding and I'm positive that you will be an excellent choice,' continued the President.

'Of course the nomination is subject to congressional approval, however I have it on good authority that your appointment will receive bilateral support,' said the President.

'I trust that you will accept the role and get to work tracking down the impending threat of the recent coalition between Russia and China as a matter of urgency,' stated the President.

'You'll be afforded whatever support you need and I will throw all our resources behind finding out whether this threat has any creditability,' said the President.

Although Barnaby was rather surprised by the appointment, he accepted it without hesitation.

'Excellent,' said the President standing and taking Barnaby's hand.

'Time to get to work Barnaby and ferret out all the information possible as this poses a significant threat to America and the world at large,' said the President.

'This is most urgent Barnaby,' reiterated The President.

'I'll make the announcement of your impending appointment as soon as congress ratifies it,' continued the President as he stood and bid Barnaby farewell.

'Good luck Barnaby, we need to ensure immediate success in finding out what the Russians and Chinese are up to,' stated the President.

As the secret service agents drove Barnaby from the White House to Langley a short distance of some nine miles, Barnaby found himself deep in thought about his career to date affording himself a rare smile of satisfaction at his achievement.

He wondered what his wife Mandy would think of his promotion, albeit that whilst she knew that he was married to his job, she could not even contemplate that the demands of the job would take him away from the family for extended periods, leaving her with more responsibility to raise the children.

A family man with 10 year old identical twin boys Chase and Chance, Barnaby had married Mandy two years his junior twelve years previously and lived in a double storey house in Stone Ridge, a middle income suburb twenty seven miles from Langley.

The identical twins were enrolled at Marbletown Elementary School in Stone Ridge.

Teachers and fellow students often could not tell the twins apart, even their mannerisms and sporting achievements made it extremely difficult to separate them.

Even at this tender age, their best friends had difficulty telling them apart.

Things would move very rapidly for Barnaby as he moved into the office as CIA Director at Langley in Virginia.

His appointment had been ratified by congress at record speed due to the danger being posed to America and westernised countries by Russia and China and proved to be a popular choice amongst the rank and file at the firm.

Chapter 3

USA Embassy

Paris

The morning after his meeting with the two mysterious individuals, Yonti cycled from his studio apartment to the address on the piece of paper, the American Embassy at 2 AV Gabriel, which was eight miles away and took around ten minutes at a steady pace.

He dressed warmly to minimise any draft, donning a jumper, gloves, riding goggles, backpack with his laptop in it, a bottle of water and a lock and chain to be used to securely lock his bicycle to a street pole at the designated address.

Yonti arrived at 9.50 a.m. ensuring he was on time. He chained his bicycle to a tree outside the embassy fence and reported to the security booth at the entrance announcing that he was there for a meeting with a person whose name he did not even know.

'Name and identification please?' came the instruction from the security officer inside the bullet proof booth.

'Yonti Barre,' he said producing his photo I.D. card.

'I have an appointment arranged by Stanley Noble scheduled for 10.00 a.m.'

'Thank you,' replied the security officer, as he held up the I.D. card for comparison to his persona, then turning to his computer punched in details and finally gave Yonti a visitors badge to pin to his lapel.

A second security officer appeared inside the perimeter fence as the gate swung open and enquired whether Yonti had any weapons in his possession.

'No weapons officer,' replied Yonti as the security officer stepped aside allowing Yonti entry to the embassy grounds. The guard then proceeded to scan the wand over all parts of his body, satisfied, he turned and indicated that he should follow another security officer who would escort him to front door.

The gate creaked shut automatically once Yonti was inside the perimeter of the fence.

The trees rustled in the morning breeze blowing the scent from their flowers in his direction and he looked towards the canopy of the trees noting the European Starlings chirping merrily in the canopies.

Feet crunching on the gravel, Yonti followed the security officer to the entrance of the embassy entering through a metal detector and into the foyer.

The security officer stationed inside the embassy offered a courteous, 'Good morning sir, kindly remove any valuables, watch, mobile phone and any other items from your pockets including your wallet and place them in the tray.'

'Please place your backpack in a separate tray and put it onto the conveyor to be scanned,' instructed the officer.

Yonti placed the items into the two trays, rolling them forward on the rolling conveyor belt until the security officer took control and pushed them towards the x-ray machine.

'Please step through the detector sir,' ordered the security officer.

Second detector Yonti thought to himself as he stepped through the metal detector.

Having cleared the detector he waited for both trays to exit the X-ray machine on the other side.

'Identification please,' asked the security officer on the other side and Yonti obliged by once again producing his photographed student card from his wallet that he had retrieved from one of the trays.

Having carefully examined it the security officer politely thanked him and returned his wallet to him.

Very thorough Yonti thought to himself.

The security officer indicated that Yonti needed to return the wallet to the tray and he followed the instruction, placing it back into the tray.

The security officer mentioned to Yonti that all his belongings including his wallet would be housed in a security locker until he exited the building.

Certainly a world of espionage and intrigue he thought to himself.

The security officer escorted Yonti into an elevator and they took the short ride to the basement on level two.

The unmistakable dinging sound and sudden stopping of the elevator announced their arrival at basement level two.

Exiting the elevator, Yonti was again subject to the wave of the magic wand and through yet another detector and was met by a smartly dressed female naval officer who was waiting for him to clear the detector, offering her hand in a greeting as he approached.

'Good morning Mr. Barre, my name is Lieutenant Johnston, follow me please.'

Smartly dressed in her crisp white naval officer's uniform, her blonde hair tied neatly into a ponytail and sporting the two golden stripes and a star on each of her lapels, Lieutenant Johnston looked absolutely stunning.

Nice legs, Yonti thought to himself, as he followed the lieutenant through a door that led to a conference room, all the while admiring her beautiful backside as he followed, biting his lower lip.

The Lieutenant knocked on the door, opened it, revealing two gentlemen seated side by side at the table with their backs to the door, stooped in what appeared to be a whispered conversation.

'Mr. Barre sir,' announced the Lieutenant as the two gentlemen swung around in their chairs revealing their identity to face Yonti.

'Thank you Lieutenant,' replied the man who had suddenly appeared at the coffee shop only to disappear shortly thereafter.

The Lieutenant closed the door as she exited the room.

'Ah Mr. Barre, thank you for being prompt,' said Barnaby.

'Stanley and I are pleased you made it,' continued Barnaby.

Both men extended their hands in a greeting.

'My name is Barnaby Heathcott.'

'I am the Director of the CIA and you remember our station chief Stanley Noble,' said Barnaby.

'Pleased to meet you Mr. Heathcott,' replied Yonti taking a quick glance at Stan Noble and was now more than curious why the CIA Director wanted to meet with him.

Both Barnaby and Stanley returned to their seats on the opposite side of the table and pointed to a seat offered to Yonti opposite them.

Barnaby stated that he had studied Yonti's academic and sporting achievements which were both very impressive indeed.

Not a man of many words and getting directly to the point, Barnaby confirmed his interest in Yonti.

'My understanding is that you have an interest in intelligence,' said Barnaby.

'I am offering you a job at the CIA,' continued Barnaby.

'It is a job that comes with certain risks, is clandestine and can be dangerous. If you accept the job, you will be put through a rigorous training regime for nine months, be based in the United States and then possibly be posted somewhere outside of the United States,' said Barnaby.

Barnaby continued, 'I re-iterate that this job comes with certain risks, however the training you will receive, will adequately arm you with the necessary skills to counter any threat you may encounter.'

Shit, how the hell do these people even know of my interest in the intelligence field, thought Yonti to himself?

Unbelievable.

What Yonti did not know was that the CIA had tracked his every move and followed his academic achievements from the first year he entered university as his marks indicated an extraordinarily talented student.

His academic achievements at university had been carefully monitored by the CIA's French station chief Stanley Noble, a close friend of Director Heathcott.

Yonti accepted the job offer immediately as this was exactly what he dreamed of his whole life.

'You need to make arrangements to clear your belongings out of your university apartment, pack up your things and report back here to Stan a week from today at 12.00 noon at which time Stan will finalise your appointment,' continued Barnaby.

'Bask in the sun, screw your arse off and be ready to leave France immediately,' said Barnaby.

'Oh and by the way, you cannot tell anyone that you have joined the CIA including your father Marcel, mother Brielle or brother Pierre,' continued Barnaby.

Jesus Yonti thought to himself, what the fuck else do they know about me.

'Oh yes, bid Jacqui, the piece of arse that you have been screwing at university farewell too,' said Barnaby.

'Tell your family and friends that you have accepted an appointment with an investment bank in New York and stick to that story,' stated Barnaby.

'Stan will bring you up to date with the details when you next meet,' said Barnaby.

'One final thing, as of right now you will assume the name of Rafael Dujon.'

'You will forget your real name and only use the alias when you land in the US,' continued Barnaby.

'Make sure you never forget this Yonti as this will be the last time either myself or Stan will refer to you by your real name,' said Barnaby.

Barnaby stood shaking Yonti's hand and bid him farewell, leaving Stan to see him to the front door.

Fuck me tenderly pondered Yonti to himself.

Shit, this really is a clandestine world I will be entering Yonti thought to himself.

Stan and Yonti rode the elevator from basement level two to the ground floor and Stan also bid Yonti farewell at the detector passing him onto the security officer who returned his belongings and passed him onto another security officer that escorted him back to the main gate.

'Good day sir,' offered the security guard at the gate and with that he turned and briskly returned to the main entrance of the embassy.

Yonti returned the visitors card to the security officer in the booth who then buzzed the gate open allowing Yonti to exit the embassy grounds.

As he unchained his bicycle Yonti glanced back at the embassy.

Fuck, I hope I have done the right thing thought Yonti to himself, however entering this new clandestine world of the gooks intrigued him.

Can't wait to see what is waiting for me in America Yonti thought to himself.

Yonti packed his belongings, notified the university authorities that he was vacating his apartment, gave his bicycle to a friend, gathered up his trophies and a picture of himself, packed them up and mailed them to his parents.

Well hung, he spent time with Jacqui making love each day and called his parents to notify them of his decision to accept a job offer to join a merchant bank in the USA.

Bidding farewell to Jacqui proved a lot more difficult as she burst into tears at the thought of losing him.

Their love making had been intense, especially over the past week.

Yonti never saw the relationship with Jacqui as anything other than convenient, however there was no doubt that Jacqui saw it differently and did not want lose her lover.

Women found his athletic build, lightly tanned olive skin and his husky French accent irresistible.

He called and spoke to both his parents a second time, conversing with them on speaker phone and both parents expressed their disappointment that he was not returning to the family business in Nice.

He bid them farewell promising to call regularly.

Yonti's father had long come to realise that his son would fly the coup as his interest lay elsewhere.

Having Yonti's younger brother now entrenched in the family business made it a little easier.

Chapter 4

Le Bourget Airport

Paris

A week later Yonti cabbed it to the US embassy and reported for duty at 12.00 noon at the security booth dragging his meagre belongings in a suitcase and a backpack where he was met by Stan in person inside the security gate.

'Hello Yonti,' said Stan.

Having greeted Stan at the gate he was buzzed into the grounds by the guard in the security booth.

Stan led the way to reception in silence.

'Good afternoon sir,' said the security agent at the door.

'Hi,' responded Yonti.

Once again Yonti was put through the rigorous security checks as he made his way through the embassy's front entrance and through the detector. The security officer repeated the procedure that Yonti had to follow being that all his belongings would be scanned and housed in a security locker until he exited the embassy.

Having cleared the detector and into the inner echelons of the embassy, they rode the elevator to the second basement level and Yonti was put through the same regimented security procedure once again.

Stan ushered him into a conference room, presented Yonti with the employment and waiver contracts to read, firmly placing the forms in front of him.

Stan excused himself and left the conference room allowing Yonti time to read over the two contracts.

The waiver agreement was very onerous indeed, taking away any rights an individual had which was expected.

All that he had read about intelligence agencies was now confirmed.

They would deny any knowledge of a person's existence or any knowledge of citizenship of the country they worked for if ever caught, so it was no surprise whatsoever that he was expected to sign a waiver document.

Yonti stared at the salary detailed in the employment agreement for some time.

Not much for being a CIA agent and possibly putting your life on the line he thought to himself and he wondered whether there was ever an annual salary review, pension and medical insurance.

'I take it that you have read the employment and waiver contracts,' said Stan as he opened the conference room door some thirty minutes later.

'Do you have any questions Yonti?' enquired Stan.

'No sir, it all seems to be in order,' he replied.

Excellent and with that Stan dialled a number on the internal phone system asking for Lieutenant Johnston to join them in the conference room in order to witness Yonti signing the agreements.

Lieutenant Johnston knocked on the door and entered on Stan's instruction.

'Good afternoon Mr. Barre,' said Lieutenant Johnston.

'Hello Lieutenant, good to see you again,' responded Yonti.

'Thanks for joining us Lieutenant Johnston,' said Stan.

'Would you kindly witness Mr. Barre signing his employment and waiver agreements please,' said Stan.

'Certainly sir,' replied the Lieutenant.

Yonti signed the two agreements initialising each page as expected.

'Please make a copy for Mr. Barre Lieutenant,' instructed Stan.

'Certainly sir,' said Lieutenant Johnston leaving the room.

Yonti found himself gazing at the Lieutenant's beautiful backside as she exited the room, wondering if he would ever see her again.

Following Yonti's gaze, Stan simply smiled.

'Out of bounds my friend,' said Stan.

'Stick to your day job from now on,' continued Stan.

'Yes sir,' replied Yonti, all the while fantasizing to himself.

'Oh, by the way, as of now you need to assume your new identity and you will be known as Rafael Dujon within the agency,' said Stan.

'You need to forget the name Yonti Barre ever existed from now on,' stressed Stan.

'Director Heathcott will formally present you with your new identity when you get to the States,' continued Stan.

There was a tap on the door and Lieutenant Johnston returned the documents to Stan and excused herself from the room.

Stan offered one copy of each of the agreements to Rafael.

Geez, got to remember my new name he thought to himself.

As Lieutenant Johnston exited the room Rafael thought to himself, got to get posted here to the US embassy in my native France.

Need to put my hands on that bare backside for sure.

Stan and Rafael entered the elevator and rode it to the ground level exiting at reception.

Stan waited for the security officer to retrieve Rafael's belongings and wished him farewell and bon voyage with a handshake before introducing agent Richard d'Avray who had been waiting patiently at the reception desk for Yonti.

He firmly took Rafael's hand in a greeting.

'Pleased to meet you Mr. Dujon.' 'Welcome to the club my friend,' stated Richard.

Yonti flinched slightly. Better get used to the new name very quickly.

Before Stan turned and departed, he said, 'Richard is your handler until you reach the USA, swap contact numbers in case you need to speak with him within the next 10 hours,' and with that Stan bid Rafael farewell again, turned and walked away.

Rafael gave Richard the visitors badge as Richard reached out and took his backpack leading the way towards an elevator in the foyer that took them down to the basement parking lot with him dragging his meagre belongings along in his suitcase.

In the basement Richard indicated for Rafael to follow him to the black bullet proof Jeep Grand Cherokee that was ready to depart as soon as they were securely buckled up.

Rafael stowed his suitcase and backpack in the rear cargo compartment and jumped into the rear passenger's seat and buckled up.

Richard introduced the driver, Alex Van Der Jong as he got into the vehicle.

Turning towards Rafael, the driver offered his hand and greeted him by name.

'Hello Mr. Dujon.' 'Welcome to the club my friend.'

Well at least my name is French Yonti thought to himself.

The driver meandered his way through the garage basement driving up the ramp from the lower level, stopped to scan his security card, waited for the gate to open and joined the traffic on their way from the embassy to the airport.

The ride to the airport was in silence as Rafael pondered whether he had in fact bitten off more than he could chew.

The roads were busy on the drive to Paris Le Bourget Airport, Europe's busiest business aviation airport dedicated exclusively to private aviation situated on the outskirts of Paris and some 6.9 miles from the city centre taking around thirty minutes in the busy Parisian traffic.

The airport was ideally situated for CIA's operations in and out of France, with more private jet charter terminal (FBO) facilities than any other European Airport, as it is a top choice for private flights in and out of Paris.

This busy hub was ideal for the CIA to use at a moment's notice and the CIA had a long standing arrangement with the French government not to enter through the main gate, rather using a maintenance gate thus avoiding security and passport control.

The driver pulled up next to the streamlined Gulfstream Aerospace G700, a US$75 million plane which was the latest in the CIA's fleet, sporting an attractive blue and grey livery.

Richard assisted with Rafael's backpack retrieving if from the rear of the SUV, handed it to him at the bottom of the stairs and bid him farewell, watching as he climbed the short staircase into the belly of the jet where he was met by the Co-Pilot.

'Good afternoon Mr. Dujon and welcome aboard sir,' said the Co-Pilot in a courteous manner.

The Gulfstream seats up to nineteen passengers, allowing sleeping facilities for ten people, offering five spacious living areas, he found himself alone as the sole passenger traveling to Langley, VA USA a distance of some 3,838 miles

The aircraft has a service ceiling of 51,000ft and is powered by twin Rolls Royce Pearl 700 engines, with a high speed cruise of Mach 0.90 for 6,400 nautical miles or at its long range cruising speed of Mach 0.85 for 7,500 nautical miles.

The flagship of the CIA.

Having been greeted by the Co-Pilot as he boarded, Rafael stowed his suitcase and backpack in the locker cupboard near the door and made his way to a window seat on the port side.

Geez, this is the life Rafael thought to himself as he buckled up and made himself comfortable lying back in his seat and putting his feet on the ottoman conveniently positioned between the seats facing each other as the jet taxied towards the runway.

The Pilots increased the power to full throttle and off they went careering down the runway and into the sky. Rafael took his last look at Paris as they climbed towards the cloudy sky.

Shortly after take-off Rafael started to explore the galley for something to eat and drink.

He discovered three meals, one for each of the Pilots and one for himself in the warmer drawer just as the Co-Pilot appeared in the galley.

'I see that you have found your way to the galley,' stated the Co-Pilot.

Placing two of the meals and two diet sodas onto a tray, the Co-Pilot returned to the cockpit.

Rafael followed suit, released the latch on the fridge extracting a diet soda and retrieved the meal from the warmer drawer. Placing both on the tray, he made his way back to his seat.

Having enjoyed his meal of salmon and vegetables he settled back in his seat, activated his mobile phone and checked for any messages and to his disappointment the phone was devoid of any.

He switched his mobile phone off, leaned back and thought to himself, fuck I hope this forms part of the lifestyle waiting for me in the US.

It could not have been further from the truth.

Some 7 hours later Rafael was awakened by the Co-Pilot announcing their impending arrival into Virginia.

OK, we are here. Let the games begin he thought to himself.

I wonder what's waiting for me.

Chapter 5

Williamsburg

Virginia USA

The Gulfstream taxied towards a hanger reserved for the CIA and the Pilots parked the plane inside the hanger killing the engines.

The CIA had years previously acquired a private airfield near the Biglers Mill site which is close to Williamsburg in Virginia that was most convenient, as it was around thirty miles from their headquarters at Langley

The Co-Pilot bid Rafael farewell and wished him good luck as he exited.

Never got to see or meet the Pilot Rafael thought to himself.

As Rafael disembarked, he was met by a secret service agent by the name of Giles Hammond, waiting at the bottom of the staircase.

'Hello Mr. Dujon,' said agent Hammond offering his hand.

'Hi,' replied Rafael as he took his hand.

'Here let me help you with your back pack,' said agent Hammond.

'Thank you,' replied Rafael handing the backpack to the agent as he reached the bottom of the staircase.

Indicating towards the parked black SUV, Giles said, 'this way please.'

Having stowed his suitcase and backpack in the rear of the SUV, Rafael assumed his usual position in rear of the vehicle.

'Meet Oliver Jacobson,' said agent Hammond pointing to the driver.

'Howdy,' replied agent Jacobson with a wave of his right hand eying Rafael in the rear view mirror without turning around.

'Hi,' replied Rafael.

With that Oliver started the SUV and navigated his way out of the hanger with the hanger door closing behind them as they exited.

They joined the traffic for the thirty mile drive to Langley.

Oliver pulled up at the front gate to the CIA headquarters at Langley, stopping to present his security card to the guard in the booth and was waved through a short while later.

The SUV pulled up at the main entrance and Rafael thanked the two agents and debussed from the vehicle.

Giles retrieved Rafael's backpack offering his hand in a farewell gesture as he made his way to the back of the SUV.

'Welcome to the club and good luck,' said Giles as he walked back to the SUV.

'Thanks pal,' responded Rafael as he made his way towards the entrance.

Rafael was greeted by a secret service agent at the entrance, proceeded through the detector and was ushered towards the conveyer and instructed to place all his belongings into the trays, following the same procedure as in the embassy in Paris.

Retrieving his belongings after it had cleared the scanner, the secret service agent notified Rafael that his belongings would be stored in a security locker until he departed.

Another secret service agent was waiting for Rafael introducing himself as Peter Gainsford.

'Hello Mr. Dujon,' said the agent. 'Welcome to the club sir.'

Some club Rafael thought to himself. I wonder what's waiting for me.

As agent Gainsford led the way to the elevator, Rafael noted the words inscribed in the lobby, "And ye shall know the truth and the truth shall set you free."

That's a little rich Rafael thought to himself.

Nobody ever knows the truth when it came to this secretive organisation he thought.

They rode the elevator to the top level and agent Gainsford led the way to the personal assistant of the Director of the CIA's office and knocked on the door.

Opening the door agent Gainsford said, 'Mr. Dujon for Director Heathcott Miss Marple.'

'Thank you Peter, I will take it from here dismissing the agent.'

'Hello Mr. Dujon, a moment please.'

Miss Marple tapped lightly on the door announcing the arrival of Mr. Dujon.

'Thank you Gizelle,' said Barnaby rising from his chair and rounding his desk, extending his hand in a greeting.

Miss Marple closed the door and returned to her desk.

'Hello Rafael, please take a seat,' said Barnaby pointing to a seat at the conference table.

'I trust that you had a pleasant flight Rafael?' questioned Barnaby.

'Thank you, I did Mr. Heathcott,' replied Rafael.

'OK young man let's get down to business,' said Barnaby.

'Firstly, I will need you to accompany Miss Marple to reception and retrieve your personal belongings and return here,' continued Barnaby.

Barnaby buzzed Miss Marple and instructed her to accompany Rafael to reception to gather his personal belongs and return to his office.

A short while later Miss Marple announced that Rafael had returned and Barnaby instructed him to put all his belongings onto the table and Rafael complied.

'Your personal belongings and your mobile phone will be securely locked up in a safe in my office,' said Barnaby.

'You will be given a new mobile phone at the appropriate time,' continued Barnaby.

Rafael obliged, handing over his belongings.

Barnaby opened a file on the desk and gave Rafael some documents to peruse that detailed his new identity and additional CIA information.

He gazed at his new identity for some time. Rafael Dujon, reminding himself of the need to get used it very quickly.

'The name is appropriate and fits perfectly with your French accent,' stated Barnaby.

'Tell anybody you befriend here to call you Rafa and stick to that religiously,' continued Barnaby.

OK, but what about the people that greeted him by his real name when he arrived at the embassy in Paris as well as Lieutenant Johnston, the lady with the sexy backside he thought to himself. They know my real name he pondered to himself.

They must have been sworn to secrecy he thought, however soon came to the conclusion that their paths were unlikely to ever cross again.

Somehow I've got to get to see Lieutenant Johnston again, Rafael thought to himself.

Having met with Barnaby for well over an hour and having been briefed about the CIA's expectations, Rafael found himself wondering yet again if he had done the right thing by joining the CIA.

Barnaby buzzed Gizelle on the internal line and asked her to accompany Rafael to reception, then stood indicating that the meeting had ended, offering his hand in a farewell gesture.

No bullshit here, simply right down to business Rafael thought to himself.

'You will be met at reception by agent Wilfred Conte and driven to our training facility at Camp Peary,' said Barnaby.

'Good luck Rafael,' offered Barnaby shaking his hand.

Camp Peary was situated on 9,000 acres and is within a US military reservation in York County near Williamsburg in Virginia.

Rafael stood as Gizelle tapped lightly on the door and entered.

She motioned for Rafael to follow her and they made their way to the Directors private elevator situated outside his office.

Dragging his meagre belongs in the suitcase minus his mobile phone and student identification card he followed Gizelle towards the elevator.

Rafael found himself staring at Gizelle's backside which was firm for a middle aged lady and wondered whether the Director was somehow sexually involved with her, but soon enough regained his composure as they entered the elevator and rode it to reception on the ground floor.

Gizelle bid him farewell as they exited the elevator on the ground floor offering her hand in a farewell gesture, turned, re-entered the elevator and rode it back to the executive level.

Agent Conte was waiting patiently at the front entrance for Rafael to exit reception.

'Hello, my name is Wilfred Conte Mr. Dujon.' 'Welcome to the club.'

'Pleased to meet you,' responded Rafael again wondering why everybody referred to the place as a club.

Agent Conte led the way to the waiting black SUV.

Having stored his suitcase and the backpack in the rear of the SUV, Rafael hopped into the rear passenger's seat with agent Conte getting into the front passenger's seat and introduced the driver.

'Meet Marcel Rodriguez,' said agent Conte tapping the driver on the shoulder.

Marcel turned and offered his hand in a greeting.

'Hello Mr. Dujon.' 'Welcome to the club,' he replied.

Jesus here we go again. What the fuck is this club thing Rafael pondered.

'Hi, pleased to meet you,' replied Rafael.

This really must be some fucking club, he thought to himself.

As they exited the Langley complex and drove towards Camp Peary, Rafael stared at the passing country side and was deep in thought.

Fuck me, this joint is so regimented, everything follows a very strict protocol, from the way they greet you, to the way you are checked by security, to the black bullet proof SUV's they use and even to the cordial "welcome to the club" greeting.

Jesus, I'm in at the deep end now as his thoughts drifted back to Lieutenant Johnston's sexy legs and backside.

Got to somehow find my way back to the embassy in Paris he thought. I really want to make love to her for sure he thought to himself.

The drive from Langley to Camp Peary known as The Farm to those within the CIA took around forty minutes.

As they arrived at the camp Rafael noticed the security fence that surrounded the entire complex as well as security guards with guard dogs off in the distance on either side of the main gate.

The security fence seemed to be electrified with CCTV cameras strategically placed at intervals along the fence.

The drive from the front gate seemed to take forever as the barracks were situated some distance from the main gate and deep into the undergrowth.

Finally the gravel road rounded a corner revealing a complex consisting of three buildings and they stopped in front of what appeared to be some sort of an office.

Rafael crouched and leaned forward between the two front bucket seats so that he could get a better view of where they were headed, noticing a muscular hulk of a man leaning against a pillar on a veranda drinking what appeared to be a cup of coffee.

At a distance this hulk was dressed in army fatigues and was an imposing figure. His long blond hair tied back in a ponytail and balding slightly with massive biceps that made him look like Arnold Schwarzenegger in his heyday.

Agents Conte and Rodriguez walked up the Hulk offering their hands in a greeting.

Taking both agents hands he simply nodded without saying a word and stared rigidly in Rafael's direction as he retrieved his belongings from the cargo compartment of the SUV.

'So what do we have here?' asked the Hulk pushing himself away from the pillar on the veranda.

'This is Rafael Dujon,' said agent Conte.

Agent Conte turned to face Rafael. 'Meet Jose Hernandez,' he said as Rafael approached.

Rafael held out his hand as he reached the top of the stairs on the veranda.

'Good afternoon,' he offered.

The Hulk was unresponsive and merely stared at him not returning the gesture.

Jesus, who the fuck is this monster Rafael thought to himself.

This monster reminded him of Sebastian Chabal a French Rugby Union player Rafael thought to himself.

Also a fearless fucking wild man.

'Agent Hernandez will be your handler from here on in,' stated agent Conte.

Both agents turned to Rafael, bid him farewell and then said their goodbyes to Jose and made their way back to the SUV.

Once safely inside the SUV, agent Conte turned to face his partner and said, 'poor bastard does not know what he is in for.'

Both agents had completed their training under the guidance of the Hulk as he was known within the CIA and had suffered through the rigorous six month basic training course coming out of it fully equipped for the challenges that faced them in the future.

'Pick up your things and follow me,' ordered the Hulk forcefully.

He turned and made his way to the adjoining barrack, opened the door and entered, pointing to a bunk with a rolled up mattress on it.

'Unpack your belongings, make your bed and be on the parade ground in 30 minutes,' instructed the Hulk walking away. Rafael noticed the fatigues neatly packed on the side table next to the bed.

Rafael rolled out the mattress, made his bed, unpacked his belongs and made his way to the parade ground waiting for the Hulk to appear.

After waiting for ten minutes, the Hulk appeared.

'Now follow me' ordered the Hulk walking towards the office.

He made his way up the stairs and into the office, where the Hulk had positioned himself at the white board that detailed Rafael's daily activities.

'This is your daily routine,' explained the Hulk.

Rafael stared at the white board.

05:00 Hour	Wake up & make your bed
06:00-08:00 Hours	Fitness training & obstacle course training
08:00-08:30 Hours	Shower
08:30-09:00 Hours	Breakfast
09:00-09:15 Hours	Toilet break
09:15-10:15 Hours	Hand to hand combat
10:15-10:30 Hours	Toilet break
10:30-13:00 Hours	Weapons training
13:00-13:30 Hours	Lunch
13:30-14:00 Hours	Toilet break
14:00-15:00 Hours	Counter terrorism training
15:00-15:15 Hours	Toilet break
15:15-17:00 Hours	Explosives training
17:00-17:30 Hours	Shower
17:30-18:00 Hours	Free time
18:00-18:30 Hours	Laundry
18:30-19:00 Hours	Dinner

19:00-20:00 Hours   Lectures & combat movies

20:00 Hour   Free time

'This will be your training regime each and every day of the week for the next six months,' said the Hulk.

Rafael stared at the white board thinking to himself, sweet Jesus, not even a day off.

This fucking monster is going to kill me, he thought to himself.

At 06:00 not wanting to be on the wrong side of this monster, Rafael presented himself on time and ready for his first fitness training session.

He was fit and ready to go and found the run of around 14 miles relatively easy due to the triathlons he had competed in at university.

Then came the obstacle course which was significantly more difficult, climbing up, over and crawling under various obstacles, through mud, up and over ladders, rope climbing and abseiling typical of the military obstacle courses used for basic training.

This was extremely taxing as he had to complete the course within a designated timeframe whilst the Hulk barked orders and yelled abuse as he drove in a golf buggy alongside him.

It got easier in time as his fitness to this type of rigorous training improved.

The Hulk often heard Rafael whispering 'ce salaud va me tuer' to himself in French, this bastard is going to kill me.

He found the hand to hand combat most difficult.

Trying to match the physical strength of the Hulk was impossible.

This guy had enormous strength and power and Rafael did his best to avoid any stronghold that the Hulk could gain on him.

Agile and too quick for the Hulk, Rafael was quick to evade his attempts at getting a stranglehold on him, thanks to his martial arts training.

Rafael found the counter terrorism most interesting and enjoyed the weapons training as it allowed him to learn a new skill. He honed his accuracy over time and perfected the art of grouping his shots in tight formations.

This training regime went on day after day for six months and whilst Rafael was drained and totally exhausted from the rigorous training regime after it had finally ended, he was ready to face any threats he may encounter in the field.

The Hulk secretly admired Rafael's agility, tenacity, determination and endurance as he too had experienced the French stubbornness and never surrender attitude previously.

Finally the last day of his six month training course had arrived and the Hulk invited him to a late afternoon sit down and offered him a beer.

Clinking beer bottles the Hulk said, 'à votre santé,' to your health.

'Alors je t'ai tué,' so did I kill you? Asked the Hulk.

Holy shit, this monster can understand French, Rafael thought to himself.

He never let on that he could speak French at all.

Unbeknown to Rafael the Hulk had served in The French Foreign Legion years previously and really liked and admired the French.

The next day agents Conte and Rodrigues pulled up at the main office to collect Rafael.

Turning to face Rafael both agents offered their hands in a greeting.

Both agents greeted the Hulk with a handshake and waited as Rafael loaded his belongings into the rear compartment of the SUV.

'Hello Rafa, glad to see that you survived.'

Rafael bid the Hulk farewell, shaking his hand saying, 'adieu et toute le meilleur,' farewell and all the best.

'Oui,' yes replied the Hulk.

Agents Conte and Rodrigues bid the Hulk farewell and jumped into the SUV with Rafael assuming his usual position in the rear for the ride back to Langley.

As they drove off agent Conte turned around to face Rafael, raised his eyebrows and said, 'and so?'

'Geez guys, you could have warned me,' responded Rafael.

'Yeah right,' laughed agent Conte.

'You may have jumped out of the vehicle my friend,' continued agent Conte.

Thank the good Lord, that's over Rafael pondered to himself.

'So what now guys?' asked Rafael.

Turning to face Rafael, agent Conte handed him an airline ticket to San Antonio airport.

'You will be met by agents Chas O'Brien and Harrison Brown outside the terminal, just look for the usual black SUV and they will drive you to Camp Stanley, the CIA's weapons training facility where you will undergo a further three months of intensive weapons training,' said agent Conte.

Touching agent Rodrigues on the shoulder, agent Conte said, 'believe me, whilst rather tiring, you will thoroughly enjoy this part of the training.'

'Not even a weekend off boys,' said Rafael shaking his head.

'Nope straight into war games I'm afraid,' replied agent Conte.

As they drove from The Farm directly to Washington Dulles International Airport, Rafael again found himself staring blankly at the passing scenery wondering what awaited him.

Agents Rodrigues and Conte dropped Rafael off at the domestic terminal and bid him farewell.

The training is conducted in secret focusing on hand gun basics, advanced techniques, consisting of control drills in the stationery position as well as on the run, rolling and shooting whilst in the air.

Awareness of ones surroundings is critical, to their survival skill.

This advanced training equips all agents with the necessary skills to eliminate any adversary as well as to protect themselves.

Rafael made his way to the gate for his flight to San Antonio, sat and waited for the boarding call which came thirty minutes later.

He boarded the flight and found his usual window seat on the port side, buckled up resting his head against the headrest and was sound asleep before they had taxied to the runway.

Shortly before landing he was startled awake with the purser announcing the need to fasten seat belts.

Rafael, extracted his small suitcase from the overhead locker and disembarked through the front door and out of the domestic terminal making his way towards the black SUV.

Agent Chas O'Brien was leaning with his back resting on the side of the SUV when Rafael approached.

Extending his hand in a greeting agent O'Brien offered, 'hello Rafael, I'm Chas O'Brien.'

'Hi, pleased to meet you Chas, please call me Rafa,' he said.

Rafael loaded his belongings into the rear cargo compartment and jumped into his usual seat in the rear of the vehicle and was introduced to Harrison Brown, the driver.

Turning to face Rafael, Harrison took his hand in a greeting.

'OK boys, let get out here,' said Rafael.

Harrison eased out of the parking spot, joined the traffic and pointed the SUV towards Camp Stanley.

Rafael, deep in thought reminded himself that he had not called his parents for six months.

Wonder what they must be thinking he pondered.

They finally arrived at the security booth at the gate to Camp Stanley.

Stopping at the main office, agents O'Brien and Brown exited the SUV and accompanied Rafael to the main office introducing him to Sergeant Benson Blackadder.

'Hello Sergeant, meet Rafael Dujon,' said agent Chas O'Brien.

Turning from a white board, Sergeant Blackadder offered a courteous, 'hello Rafael.'

Rafael returned the courtesy and replied, 'pleased to meet you sergeant.'

The training consisted of counter insurgency training, tracking and identification of terrorists and an extensive weapons training course.

Rafael found himself exhausted after each daily session, forcing himself to do a five mile run and a thirty minute session in the gym ending with an intense fifteen minute solo martial arts training session every day.

His instructor was a mature aged person and was very different in persona to that of the Hulk at Camp Peary.

Each session focused on shooting in the stationary position, on the run as well as rolling and jumping whilst taking a shot.

Rafael spent dozens of hours on the shooting range perfecting his grouping which over time resulted in very tight formations.

He reflected on the comment made by agent Conte that whilst this part of the training would test him, it would be thoroughly enjoyable.

Rafael, enjoyed this part of the training as it taught him new skills.

Rafael struck up an excellent working relationship with sergeant Blackadder and the atmosphere was far more relaxed and focused on honing Rafael's marksmanship skills.

The Final day of his training arrived and he packed up his belongings as agents O'Brien and Brown arrived to pick him up.

Having bid sergeant Blackadder farewell, the agents drove him to San Antonio airport.

Rafael was booked on a flight to Washington Dulles International Airport and was met by agents Conte and Rodrigues at the domestic terminal on his arrival.

Jumping into the rear passengers seat Rafael offered a courteous greeting.

'Bloody hell, not you two again,' said Rafael as he took both agents hands.

'Did you miss us?' questioned agent Conte.

'I really need to get a chauffeur job like yours boys,' said Rafael.

'Yep if only,' said agent Rodrigues looking at Rafael in the rear view mirror.

'So any other surprises?' questioned Rafael with a raised eyebrow.

Turning to face Rafael, agent Conte said, 'the boss is waiting for you at the club my friend.'

They drove to Langley in relative silence, his mind wondering back to the stunningly beautiful Lieutenant Johnston.

Got to date this stunner. He afforded himself the fantasy of bringing her flowers.

Barnaby watched from the window of his office as agent Rodrigues pulled up at the security gate in the distance at Langley.

A short while later they stopped at the main entrance and Rafael bid the two agents farewell and entered through the front door.

Once again, passing through the security protocol he was met by Gizelle, Barnaby Heathcott's personal assistant.

'Hello Rafa, glad to see that you survived those nine months,' she said.

'Oh hi Miss Marple,' he replied.

'Follow me,' she said, turning to make her way to the private elevator.

Miss Marple, tapped gently on Barnaby's door.

'Rafael sir,' she said.

'Thank you Gizelle,' replied Barnaby.

'Good to see that you are alive and still in one piece Rafa,' said Barnaby taking his hand in a greeting.

Indicating to a seat at the conference table, Barnaby said, 'take a seat young man.'

'OK, let's get down to business,' continued Barnaby.

Barnaby picked up a package and handed it to Rafael.

'This is your mobile phone, drivers licence, two credit cards, your wallet and a few passports in various names,' continued Barnaby.

'Memorise the mobile number detailed in the notes and then destroy it,' said Barnaby.

'I want you to use the passport with the alias of Jon Jones' name on it for your first mission,' stated Barnaby.

'Store the other passports in the security locker as you exit,' stated Barnaby.

'Agents Conte and Rodrigues are waiting for you at reception,' he continued.

Barnaby handed Rafael a small bag to store all the other passports in and instructed Rafael to hand it to agent Harper at reception.

'When you get back, you will be driven to an apartment that I have rented for you in Hampton Harbor that has all the amenities you will need,' stated Barnaby.

Rafael opened his wallet and stared at the bundle of cash in it.

Must be a few dollars in here he thought as he rolled his fingers over the notes.

'There's three thousand dollars in it and here's a ticket to fly to Paris,' said Barnaby.

'Go and visit your parents and remember not to tell anybody that you work for the CIA,' expressed Barnaby.

'Remember that you are an investment banker,' continued Barnaby.

'Take a week off and blow off some steam and report to Stan at the embassy at 12.00 noon a week from today,' said Barnaby.

'You can retrieve the other passports when you return to the States,' continued Barnaby.

Rising, Barnaby took his hand and bid him farewell and said, 'Au revoir Rafa.'

'Miss Marple will see you to the front door where and agents Conte and Rodrigues are waiting to drive you to the airport,' continued Barnaby.

'You have earned the rest and your flight leaves in two hours Rafa,' said Barnaby.

Brilliant thought Rafael, I will get to see Lieutenant Johnston again.

Can't wait pondered Rafael.

The place is so regimented he thought to himself as he entered the elevator, reminding himself that he had not called his parents in nine months.

Everything seems to start at 12.00 noon.

As he exited the private elevator, Miss Marple bid him farewell.

The agent at the detector took possession of his bag containing the passports and stored them in a secure locker.

Agent Conte was waiting for him as he retrieved his belongings and made his way out to the waiting SUV.

'Hi boys, I'm back,' he said as he jumped into the rear passenger seat.

'Long time no see,' said agent Conte.

'Right, let's get out of here,' said agent Marcel Rodrigues as he pointed the SUV in the direction of the gate.

Exiting they joined the traffic to the Ronald Regan Washington National Airport.

'See you boys,' said Rafael as he exited the SUV retrieving his belongings and quickly entered into the international departure lounge.

He boarded American Airlines flight AA202, a non-stop flight to the Charles de Gaulle international airport in Paris which was a 13.55 hour flight.

Back in cattle class, he thought to himself as he found his way to his seat on the port side of the aircraft.

The CIA does not spend an extra cent on travel expenses.

The plane landed in Paris a little after 2.00 p.m. the next day and having cleared passport control, Rafael made his way to the internal flight terminal and boarded a flight to Nice International airport on the French Riviera.

Arriving late in the afternoon, Rafael grabbed a cab for the ride to his parents apartment block.

Walking in unannounced, his father looked up from his laptop computer and was totally surprised to see his son, hugging and kissing him on both cheeks, his father Marcel said, 'Bonjour mon fils,' hello my son.

Shit, better remember to use my real name, thought Yonti.

His mother Brielle and brother Pierre were busy in the kitchen and heard Marcel's raised voice when he greeted his son.

They came out of the kitchen, his mother hugging and kissing him on both cheeks.

'Regarde toi', look at you, said his mother.

Pierre shook his hand, hugged and embraced him.

'Ça fait longtemps mon frère,' it's been a long time my brother, said Pierre.

'This calls for a glass of champagne,' said Marcel as he popped the cork of a bottle of Dom Pérignon.

'À votre santé, cheers, said Marcel with all clinking glasses.

'Why have you not called us for nine months Yonti?' asked his mother.

'Sorry papa and mama, I have been on an extensive training course,' he answered trying his best not to lie.

Having gotten used to the alias of Rafael, it seemed rather odd to hear his real name again.

Yonti unpacked his belongings in his bedroom which was one of the three bedrooms in the family apartment section of the apartment block and went to work doing the odd jobs that needed immediate attention.

In desperate need of some rest, he made his way onto the beach and soaked up some late afternoon sun for a few hours, taking a dip in the sea to cool down.

Need to work on my sun tan tomorrow, as his thoughts drifted back to Jacqui and he wondered what had happened to her.

No point in trying to look her up. I don't want to go through the farewell again.

Chapter 6

Anvin

Pas de Calais

Rafael reported to the embassy as instructed by Barnaby Heathcott and was met by agent Greg Smith.

'Hi Jon, I'm Greg Smith,' he said offering his hand.

'Hello,' replied Jon.

'Where's Lieutenant Johnston?' he inquired.

'She's on honeymoon and will be back in two weeks,' responded agent Smith.

You have got to be fucking kidding he thought to himself, his shoulders drooping visibly in disappointment. I was so looking forward to seeing her.

Agent Smith escorted Rafael to the conference room.

Rising from the conference table, Stan offered his hand in a greeting.

'Hello Jon, good to see you again,' he said.

I'm Jon Jones now he reminded himself.

'Meet Capitaine Bastienne Petit of the DGSE, the French equivalent of the CIA and the British MI6 that operates under the French Ministry of Defence,' said Stan.

'Bonjour Monsieur Jones,' hello Mr. Jones offered Capitaine Petit extending his hand in a greeting.

'Bonjour Capitaine,' said Jon taking his hand.

'OK Gentlemen, let's get down to business,' replied Stan.

'Capitaine Petit and I have reviewed all the intelligence we have gathered on two terrorists over the past two weeks and Bastienne and the French authorities are comfortable that we have one terrorist that escaped the Charlie Hebdo massacre in Paris firmly insight,' said Stan.

'We have been tracking a terrorist by the name of Rafiq Zahida that has been responsible for the deaths of hundreds of American soldiers in Syria which has led us to where we are today,' continued Stan.

Unbeknown to the French authorities, the identity of a fourth terrorist namely Abdul Sinai was never discovered and he was the fourth member of the terrorist cell that carried out the attack on the French Magazine Charlie Hebdo on the 27th of January 2015, in which seventeen people lost their lives.

Abdul Sinai became known to the CIA as they intercepted communications between himself and the terrorist they had been hunting by the name of Rafiq Zahida.

Rafiq Zahida was guilty of killing numerous American soldiers in the Syrian conflict and had escaped to France on board a container ship posing as a stevedore and slipped into the port of Calais.

He was met by Abdul Sinai one of the brotherhoods jihadists and whisked away to the village town of Villeneuve-d'Ascq and Dunkerque in Nord-Pas-de-Calais. He became part of a new terrorist cell planning another attack on French soil.

Unbeknown to the French authorities, this was where Abdul Sinai had masterminded the attack on the Charlie Hebdo.

Police arrived at the scene as the attackers were leaving the building, however the brothers opened fire on the officers and were able to drive away in their own vehicle.

While fleeing from the scene, the Kouachi brothers stopped to kill their 12th and final victim, police officer Ahmed Merabet, who was on patrol in the area.

After the terrorists abandoned their getaway car and hijacked another one, the police were thrown off their track, but an identity card left behind in the abandoned vehicle allowed authorities to identify the attackers.

Molotov cocktails and two jihadist flags were also found.

The police were able to take up the trail of the Kouachis again the following day after the brothers robbed a service station near the commune of Villers-Cotterêts, roughly 45 miles (72 km) northeast of Paris.

The chase continued until the morning of January 9, when the fugitives were forced off the road by a police roadblock near Dammartin-en-Goële, about 22 miles (35 km) northeast of Paris.

An exchange of gunfire ensued, and the brothers then entered an industrial park, where they holed up in a print works and took its owner, Michel Catalano, hostage.

Catalano was later released together with Lilian Lepère, an employee of the company who had been told by Catalano to hide.

She took refuge under the sink in the upstairs canteen.

Lilian's presence was unknown to the Kouachis during the eight-hour siege that followed.

During that time Lepère was able to relay information to the police via text messages.

In a short phone interview with BFM TV, Chérif Kouachi referred to himself and his brother as defenders of the Prophet Muhammad and said that he had been sent by al-Qaeda in the Arabian Peninsula (AQAP).

The brothers told police negotiators that they were ready to die as martyrs, and just before 5:00 p.m. they emerged from the building and were killed in the ensuing shoot-out.

The French police had killed the Kouachi brothers Saïd and Chérif Kouachi and the third terrorist namely, Hamyd Mourad handed himself into the police after having seen his name circulating on social media.

Despite having searched the premises of the Kouachi brothers and Mourad as well as having interrogated Mourad, the French authorities were unable to establish whether there were any other terrorists involved and finally concluded the investigation.

Stan turned on the television set and inserted a USB stick into the set.

The screen blinked to life with images of an old barn house in the rural village of Anvin Pas De Calais.

The barn house was in a remote part of the village, an ideal hideaway with few immediate neighbors, renovated to house up to six people with four beds, two toilets, two bathrooms, a kitchen and TV room.

Ideal for these jihadists to hide in.

'OK gentlemen, we have been monitoring this site for some time and we can confirm that there are four people living in the barn house, two males and two females,' said Stan.

'The owner has been away in Paris for an extended period so these terrorists have chosen well,' continued Stan.

'The occupants leave the barn house every Friday at around 11.00 a.m. and go to a house in Monchy-Cayeux, which is 1.3 miles away and around a 5 minute drive,' stated Stan.

'There is no Mosque nearby so it appears that they attend prayers at a friend's house,' continued Stan.

'They drop the two women off at a supermarket and collect them after prayers, then make their way home and return around 1.00 p.m.' said Stan.

'The women then make lunch and the men sit down on the carpet in the lounge area and eat their meal on a low floor table around 1.30 p.m. every day,' he said.

Continuing Stan said, 'they have followed this routine since we have been monitoring them.'

Traditionally women eat separately in the Muslim religion, thus eat in the kitchen.

'From what we can gather the women are not involved in any terrorism activity at all,' stated Stan.

'There is a lot of activity in the garage attached to the barn house and we suspect that they may be preparing some sort of car bomb,' continued Stan.

'Here's what I am proposing.' 'You wait for them to leave the barn house on Friday, then move into the premises and place an explosive device under the table where these two terrorists eat their meals that can be activated by a remote when the time is right,' said Stan.

'You can activate the remote when you have confirmation of the men sitting at the table,' he said.

'Capitaine Petit will be in charge of the operation,' said Stan.

'OK, so what we will do is the following,' said Bastienne.

'We will use a van that has the EUC, Electricity Utility Company logo on it and park it at the end of the street, just before the intersection,' continued Bastienne.

'This is the only route that the terrorists can take as their road is in a cul-de-sac,' he stated.

On Friday Bastienne and Jon arrived at around 10.00 a.m., parked their van on the nature strip and set up a long ladder against a power pole at the end of the street pretending to be repairing a faulty power line.

They placed the ladder facing towards the direction of the barn house and continued this charade for an hour until finally they saw the old dilapidated van exit the driveway of the barn house and drive towards them.

Jon was on top of the ladder taking great care not to touch any live wires and keeping his focus on the wires above him, whilst Bastienne leaning against the ladder at the bottom was able to glance in the direction of the oncoming van to ensure that all four occupants were inside the vehicle.

Bastienne was careful not to turn around and look at them as they passed and continued looking up the ladder at Jon working above.

They waited for a further fifteen minutes to ensure that the terrorists did not make a U-turn and come back and check on them.

Comfortable that the terrorists were not returning, Jon and Bastienne jumped into the van and drove into the driveway of the barn house.

Bastienne quickly picked the lock on the front door while Jon retrieved the explosive device from the van. Placing an old towel on the floor he turned the table on its side and attached the explosive device to the underside of the table using a drill and screws.

Jon rolled up the towel returning the table to its exact position and placing the four legs in the indentation marks on the carpet, careful not to let any wood shavings fall onto the carpet after he had attached the explosive device to the underside of the table.

Bastienne and Jon exited the barn house, locking the door behind them and drove back to where they had left the ladder at the end of the road and sat down to a lunch of sandwiches and coffee and waited patiently for the terrorists to return.

Bastienne had placed a mini spy camera on the mantelpiece discretely hidden amongst some artificial flowers, giving them an excellent view of the table where the two terrorists sit and eat their meals.

Finally the van turned into the road and made its way past Bastienne and Jon sitting and eating their lunch.

Neither Bastienne nor Jon looked their way as they passed, however Bastienne had positioned himself facing the barn house, thus was able to watch the van driving away from them towards the house while Jon had his back to the road careful not to look in their direction.

The mini spy camera would give them a clear picture of the lounge area.

The terrorists drove up to the front door, parked and entered the barn house.

Images of them entering the lounge flickered to life on the laptop in the van.

It appeared that the men had visited the toilets and after some time, entered the lounge and seated themselves on the carpet at the table just as the two females came into the room with plates and food in a bowl.

The two agents packed up the ladder securing it to the roof of the EDF Utility Company van and were watching the activity on a monitor from the back of the van.

The terrorists were chatting away and started eating after the two females had departed the room.

A huge explosion rang out from the barn house after Jon had activated the remote control and set off the bomb.

'Au revoir et bons riddens,' good bye and good riddens, said Jon.

'Oui,' yes said Bastienne.

Bastienne and Jon drove off in the direction of Café Floret, Stan's favourite coffee shop, called ahead and arranged to meet Stan there.

'Gentlemen, travail bien fait,' said Stan offering his hand to Bastienne and Jon. Job well done.

The reporter on French Television interrupted the mid-afternoon program reporting a massive explosion at an old barn house in Anvin Pas De Calais, a remote country village, just as their coffees arrived.

'French police have confirmed that a fourth terrorist by the name of Abdul Sinai that escaped capture in the Charlie Hebdo massacre has been eliminated together with an accomplice by the name of Rafiq Zahida who was wanted by the CIA for the killing of hundreds of American soldiers in Syria,' said the reporter.

'It is believed that these two terrorists were planning further attacks on French soil,' she reported.

'The police have confirmed that an operation took place in Anvin Pas De Calais earlier in the day, however investigations are continuing and they are therefore unable to comment any further,' said the reporter.

'Two females were also in the house at the time and were injured in the explosion.' 'They have been taken to hospital and are under police guard,' continued the reporter.

Stan ordered a bottle of Dom Pérignon champagne, clinking glasses he said, 'à votre santé,' cheers.

Having celebrated for a while, Stan stood shaking their hands and bid Bastienne and Jon farewell.

'Au revoir gentlemen, job well done,' said Stan.

'See you at the embassy tomorrow at 12.00 noon Jon,' continued Stan and with that he was on his way.

'Jon, you should come and work with us,' said Bastienne as he stood to leave a little later.

'Maybe someday,' replied Jon thinking of Lieutenant Johnston.

Sipping the last of his champagne, Jon thought to himself, geez, I have become a real killer now.

I'm an assassin, comfortable in the knowledge that he had eliminated the last remaining terrorist in the Charlie Hebdo massacre in the country of his birth, justified his participation in the operation.

Chapter 7

Charles de Gaulle Airport

Paris

Next day Jon found his way to the US embassy and once again found himself seated in the conference room, fantasizing about the beautiful Lieutenant Johnston when his train of thought was broken as Stan Noble opened the door.

'Hi Rafael, sorry for the delay,' said Stan.

Oh shit, here we go again, I'm back to my CIA name of Rafael he thought to himself.

Need to remember that he reminded himself.

Really confusing he pondered.

'Job well done Rafa,' continued Stan.

'Thank you sir,' responded Rafael.

'We got rid of a terrorist that we have been chasing for a number of years Rafael, so the President is really pleased, an excellent job,' said Stan.

'We have another mission for you,' stated Stan.

'You are booked on a flight back to Washington leaving tomorrow at 11.25 a.m.,' he continued.

'I have booked you into hotel Montblanc at 35 Rue Pascal, 5th arr, Paris for the night and you will be picked up at 09:00 at your hotel by agent's d'Avray and Van Der Jong and driven to Charles de Gaulle Airport,' said Stan.

'On arrival in Washington you will be met by agents Rodrigues and Conte who will be parked directly outside terminal and driven to Langley,' stated Stan.

'You must then report to Director Heathcott,' continued Stan.

'Take the time to reenergize yourself this evening and stay out of trouble Rafael and keep your magic wand in your pants,' continued Stan.

Standing and taking Rafael's hand Stan gave him the airline ticket and said, 'Au revoir Rafael, job well done my friend.'

Rafael booked into the hotel and did not bother to unpack his meagre belongs.

He ambled downstairs to the bar and ordered a beer, then made his way outside and found a table on the sidewalk.

Having taken a mouthful of beer, he activated his mobile and checked for messages.

A moment later a lady screamed for help as two males attempted to kidnap her ten year old daughter and bundle her into a waiting car.

Rafael, was on his feet in an instant and ran towards the corner, noticing one of the males had his hand gripped around the child's mouth and was ushering her towards the waiting car.

Hopping on one leg, he extracted the Glock from his ankle holster and raced down the sidewalk towards the car.

The mother was hysterical, screaming for help and noticed Rafael as he approached the corner with his weapon aimed at the kidnapper.

Two quick shots on the run found its mark and the kidnapper fell to the ground.

His accomplice revved the car and drove off in the opposite direction with the rear door still ajar.

Rafael bent down on one knee and aimed at the driver through the rear view window of the car and fired.

The first shot shattered the rear window and was followed by a second shot an instant later that hit the driver in the back of the head.

The driver slumped forward over the steering wheel as the car careered sideways and smashed into a parked car.

Moments later, two policemen were alongside and had trained their weapons on Rafael ordering him to lie flat on the ground with his face facing the pavement and his arms spread wide.

Rafael complied and one of the officers took possession of Rafael's Glock and cuffed him.

Pulling him to his feet one of the officers radioed their control centre and a short while later a police van arrived and Rafael caught a glimpse of Bastienne.

'Hello Jon,' said Bastienne.

Oh shit here we go again, best remember I'm Jon not Rafael he thought to himself.

'Geez, you again Capitaine,' said Jon.

'You seem to appear out of thin air Capitaine,' continued Jon.

'Oui, yes I am everywhere my friend,' replied Capitaine Bastienne Petit.

'Un cuff this gentleman,' instructed Bastienne.

The policemen un-cuffed him and handed his Glock back to him.

'Who taught you to shoot that accurately?' enquired Bastienne.

Just then the mother and her daughter appeared alongside Jon and gave him a hug and a kiss on the cheek.

'Merci beaucoup, tu as sauvé la vie de mes filles,' thank you very much, you saved my daughters life, said the mother.

'We have uncovered a paedophile ring in Paris that are kidnapping young girls and using them as sex slaves,' said Bastienne.

Continuing Bastienne added, 'I believe that the one you shot on the sidewalk, is in fact the ring leader, so well done Jon.'

People had gathered around the scene with many filming the event on their mobile phones.

Jon did his best to hide his face as he did not want his parents to get a glimpse of his face in the evening news.

Later that evening, his father was watching television and called out to his wife, 'Brielle, come and see this,' he said.

'This looks like Yonti,' he said, using his real name, continued his father Marcel.

'I thought he was back in America,' said Marcel.

'Let's wait to hear from him,' said Brielle.

Sitting in the hotel lounge the next day Rafael noticed the black SUV pull up at the entrance. He picked up his jacket and pulling his suitcase made his way towards the exit and jumped into the rear seat.

'Hi guys, nice to see you once again,' he said to both agents who turned and took his hand in a greeting.

'Well boys, how do I qualify for a job like yours?' enquired Rafael.

Turning to face Rafael agent d'Avray said, 'wish it was that easy mate.'

'OK boys, to the airport please,' said Rafael.

'Sweet, we are on our way,' said agent Van Der Jong as he eased into the morning traffic and drove towards Charles de Gaulle International Airport.

As they drove, Rafael found himself deep in thought with his mind wandering back to the beautiful Lieutenant Johnston.

It's a real waste of time even thinking of her he reminded himself.

Agent Van Der Jong pulled up at the drop off point and lifted his hand in a goodbye gesture whilst looking at Rafael in the rear view mirror and agent d'Avray turned and shook his hand, 'Au Revoir Monsieur Dujon.'

'See you next time guys,' said Rafael as he collected his suitcase from the rear baggage compartment of the SUV.

Chapter 8

Zurich Guest House Hotel

Zurich

The CIA make up agent had discreetly entered Aaron's room at the Zurich Guest House Hotel, a modest 4-star hotel that was situated a few kilometres from The Grand Hotel late in the afternoon posing as a room service employee.

Entering late in the afternoon, their Intel assured the CIA that all room service activities had been completed for the day and therefore it would be easy to extract a room service trolley from the service storage room adjacent to staircase.

This minimised the possibility of anybody seeing the make-up agent extracting a room service trolley and moving towards Aaron's room.

Another agent approached the reception desk posing as a person enquiring about the rates to distract the receptionist while the make-up agent made her way down the hallway to Aaron's room with the service trolley in tow.

The CIA knew that there would only be one receptionist on duty in the late afternoon, thus it was imperative to take the receptionist away from the CCTV coverage of the first floor where Aaron's room was located.

The make-up agent had changed her appearance earlier in the day by donning a blond wig and had booked into a room opposite to Aaron's room under a false name, paying in cash thus ensuring there was no paper trail.

The agent insisted on the room opposite Aaron's stating that a friend of hers had stayed in that room some time ago and that her friend had mentioned that the room was nice and quiet as it faced towards the rear of the building and away from the street.

This gave Aaron a possible escape route as the balcony was adjacent to an overhanging portico allowing for an easy quick getaway if needed.

Aaron's room overlooked the front of the hotel with a view of the road below.

The secret service agent changed Aaron's appearance by slightly darkening the colour of his complexion and changed the colour of his eyes with faintly tinted green non reflective contact lenses.

The CIA had perfected a new set of thin pearly white false teeth fitting perfectly over his own teeth which could not be detected by security surveillance nor by highly trained security personnel.

The make-up agent lightly tinted his hair grey on the temples giving him a sophisticated suave mature look.

Aaron was careful not to touch anything in the apartment and prior to leaving his room he loaded a magazine into his Glock, cocked it and clicked the safety to off. He then placed it under the pillow closest to the window.

He also placed two full magazines alongside the gun and checked a second time to ensure that the safety was off and ready to fire before he left the room.

As he left the room he placed the 'Do Not Disturb' card on the outside of the door and made his way downstairs to a waiting Range Rover with two agents seated in the front seats.

He hopped into the rear passenger's seat and was driven a short distance to The Grand Hotel.

The elevator ground to a halt on the second floor and he rounded the corner towards the conference room, which revealed a short, thin, wiry looking man seated at a desk sporting a pair of John Lennon style round spectacles.

He was surrounded by muscular security personnel blocking any direct access to the ballroom ahead.

'Good evening sir, your name please, came the courteous response from the little man behind the desk.'

'Good evening,' responded Aaron in an equally courteous manner.

'Aaron Armando,'

'Identification please,' responded the wiry balding man who seemed rather out of place amongst the bevy of muscular security personnel.

His glasses clearly indicating that he was some sort of a computer nerd gifted and skilled at his craft.

Aaron extracted his wallet from the rear pocket of his suit pants and provided his photographed drivers licence as identification.

The man punched the details into the laptop, compared Aaron's face to an image on the computer screen for what seemed like an eternity, finally punching in a security clearance, smiled at Aaron and nodded his approval for him to proceed to the security person positioned alongside him.

His arm indicating the way to proceed.

'Thank you sir, enjoy your evening.'

Aaron afforded a courteous nod and proceeded to the man with the security wand, extended his arms and waited patiently for the security sweep to be completed.

'Thank you sir, please proceed to the kiosk to store your coat and then to the door on the right hand side,' said the man with the wand.

Aaron made his way to the kiosk removing his coat as he approached, registered it for safe storage, then proceeded towards the ballroom door which automatically opened as he approached, revealing a room filled with people socialising and drinking.

He noted the four burly armed security guards positioned on the landing which surrounded most of the ballroom as he entered.

His eyes took in multiple security cameras around the room, some openly displayed to give guests reassurance of the importance to provide adequate security, whilst others were discretely hidden at various locations around the room.

He made his way towards the bar at the far end of the room.

'Good evening sir, what would you like?' asked the bar tender.

'Good evening, a double Johnny Walker Blue on the rocks please,' replied Aaron.

'Certainly sir,' replied the bar tender.

Aaron tentatively watched as the bar tender drew a double tot of Johnny Walker Blue Scotch whisky from the optic tot measure and placed it on the bar counter in front of him.

'Thank you,' said Aaron picking up the tumbler and turning around to face the room with his back and elbow leaning on the bar counter.

He scanned the room for the connection he was to meet at the function.

Suddenly Joseph Diamond appeared out of nowhere alongside him to his left.

'Hello Rafael, how are you stranger?' came the jovial greeting.

'Long-time no see old boy,' continued Joseph.

Joseph knew Aaron by the name of Rafael Dujon, the alias that the Director of the CIA Barnaby Heathcott had given him the day he started at the CIA and was unaware that he had assumed the alias of Aaron Armando for the evening's cocktail party.

His real name of Yonti Barre was long forgotten as all his identity documents had been securely locked up in a safe in Director Barnaby Heathcott's office.

'Yes, long time no see,' replied Aaron.

'How the hell are you Joe?' questioned Aaron.

'All good thank you,' said Joseph taking his hand firmly in a greeting.

'How's life in the land of the brave?' enquired Joseph.

'Usual day to day bullshit,' responded Aaron in his husky French accent.

'How's life in the land of the Crown Jewels?' asked Aaron.

'Outstanding my friend,' came the reply from Joseph Diamond as they moved away from the bar and closer towards the outer circle of patrons.

Neither agent knew the others real name and were unaware that both were using an alias.

Aaron had befriended Joseph when the CIA and Mossad came together in a covert operation to eliminate Ali Darwish a known terrorist in the Jihad Council of Hezbollah in Lebanon a few years previously.

The CIA had tracked Ali Darwish to an apartment block where he was living months previously, keeping tabs on him and then shared the information with Mossad, which was how the two organisation became involved in the operation.

The CIA needed Mossad's guidance as they were familiar with the area and far better acquainted with the surroundings than they were.

Joseph and Aaron posing as Jihadi fighters had entered an apartment building attached to the building where Ali Darwish lived in the early hours of the morning when most of the jihadists guarding the area had fallen asleep.

Mossad had acquired the apartment months previously, having paid the owner, an old man in his late 80's a handsome sum of money to vacate, which he unduly did, leaving all his belongings behind.

The new occupant, an elderly Mossad agent fluent in Lebanese, posing as the previous owner's brother, told neighbours that his brother had returned to the village of his birth where he wanted to spend the last days of his life.

Mossad had followed the old man after he vacated the apartment onto a bus taking him to a remote village on the outskirts of Beirut and followed him as he headed towards the household of an old friend. They assassinated him in the foothills of a valley near his friend's house.

Mossad did not want to risk the old man telling his friend that he had sold his apartment to a stranger and retrieved the pile of money paid to him before disappearing into the surrounding hillside.

Mossad had meticulously planned this operation for six months leaving a rope that could be used to abseil into Ali Darwish's apartment hidden in the ceiling.

The apartment was in a ten storey block that Mossad had acquired from the old man that was attached to the apartment block where Ali Darwish lived and one storey higher which proved to be invaluable.

The apartment that Mossad had acquired was on the top floor and the only apartment with a balcony overlooking the rooftops of the attached neighbouring buildings.

This allowed Aaron and Joseph the privacy to go about their business unnoticed.

Abseiling down to Ali Darwish's apartment was the only option of getting into his apartment as the entrance to his apartment was heavily guarded by armed jihadists.

Fortunately the manhole in the ceiling was close to a wall and Aaron let Joseph get onto his shoulders, then hoisted him up with Joseph leaning against the wall for support.

This allowed him to reach the manhole, open it and remove the rope.

He passed it down to Aaron who slowly squatted allowing Joseph to get off his shoulders.

Both agents made their way to the rooftop of the building that Ali Darwish lived in around 21:00 hours and tied the rope to a pole.

Aaron and Joseph peered over the side of the building, looking down to ensure that people were not on their balconies below. Having satisfied themselves that it was safe to proceed, the agent's abseiled down to the balcony below.

Luckily there were no guards on the rooftops of any surrounding buildings which allowed the agents to abseil unseen.

Joseph and Aaron quickly entered through a doorway that had no door attached.

Ali Darwish was seated on a carpet eating his evening meal, while his wife and kids ate in the kitchen unaware of the presence of Aaron and Joseph.

Two quick shots to the head from Aaron's Glock fitted with a silencer ensured that the popping sound of the rounds going off was muffled.

The terrorist had lived his last moment.

Aaron and Joseph quickly made their way to the balcony, climbed back up the rope and onto the roof of the apartment block, retrieved the rope, dropped it onto the rooftop floor and proceeded to make their way along the rooftops of the adjoining buildings and into a stairwell of a neighbouring building which lead to the ground floor.

They exited into the waiting getaway car driven by the elderly Mossad agent.

A guard noticed their hasty retreat and shouted a warning to other militant jihadist who opened fire as the car raced down the road and turned into the back streets of Beirut.

Aaron and Joseph ducked to avoid the hail of bullets following them remembering that as a daring mission with a lucky escape.

It was most unusual for these two agencies to work in concert as both were suspicious of each other and each held closely guarded secrets, only sharing vital information when it suited either party.

This was the beginning of a long friendship between these two agents.

A real who's who that were gathered here this evening thought Joseph to himself as he looked around the room.

Aaron noted the presence of various Foreign Affairs Ministers as well as the Russian Minister for Foreign Affairs Damir Lacrov, who seemed to be surrounded by a bevy of security personnel.

A host of government dignitaries from various countries were also in attendance.

Wonder why Lacrov is here Aaron thought to himself, after all they are the enemy.

Joseph Diamond a Mossad secret service agent also traveling incognito, whose real name was in fact Lev Zaslavsky, however Aaron only new him by the name of Joseph Diamond.

Born in Eilat of Jewish immigrants from Morocco who left the country of their birth for the Promised Land of Israel in 1987.

The young married couple had fallen in love and married at the tender age of 17. His father Abel Zaslavsky worked as a baker in Tangier, a coastal city living in a small room above the bakery with his wife Sami.

The rent for the room formed part of his modest salary and his mother cleaned the homes of the wealthy Moroccan elite. Both saved as much money as possible for the day they would try the reach the Promised Land of Israel.

Abel and Sami barely had enough money saved when they finally left Morocco and made their way to Israel where Abel believed he would start a new life with Sami and start a family.

He wanted any children that he fathered to be born in the Holy Land.

Lev Zaslavsky had grown up in Eilat and was an only child of Abel and Sami Zaslavsky.

Having settled in the southern coastal city of Eilat in Israel, Abel loaned enough money from a person he befriended and started a bakery in an old shop, which he modernised and expanded over time to be the largest and most popular bakery in town.

Sami tended tables and served behind the counter.

Having completed his homework each day, Joseph spent the remainder of each day and the evenings working in his father's bakery.

This was a seven day a week job for Abel and Sami and their proud son Joseph was there every day dutifully assisting his parents, baking, serving tables and cleaning as required.

Having completed his schooling and finishing top of his class, Joseph was invited to apply for entry into the prestigious Weizmann Institute of Science in Jerusalem.

He registered for a course in computer science and engineering.

His skill and academic achievements came to the attention of Mossad, the secret intelligence service of Israel.

Mossad put Joseph through a rigorous six month basic training course, then proceeded to school him as a diplomat and finally seconded him to the Israeli embassy in London.

He was tasked with gathering strategic information from foreign countries, specialising in terrorism in order to safeguard the Jewish holy land and was sent to London posing as an attaché at the Israeli embassy.

It was believed in Jerusalem, that many terrorists had infiltrated the UK and were clandestinely planning attacks on Israel from there.

Joseph's mission was to identify any terrorist cells in the UK and gather intelligence.

As a front, he would actively arrange fund raising campaigns, something that Joseph had become highly successful at doing which he extended to the USA, hence his relationship with Chaim Benowitz who in concert with Joseph had raised millions of US dollars for Israel.

Chaim Benowitz was Jewish and an extremely influential senator. He was a great friend of Israel and was the chairman of the U.S. House Committee on Armed Services, thus able to influence arms decisions in favour of Israel in the US senate.

Aaron and Joseph made their way closer towards the outer fringe of the throng of people. Aaron noticed the beautiful blond, her back facing towards them, elegantly dressed in a stunning tight fitting emerald green off the shoulder evening gown.

The back of the gown cut open to just above her buttocks displaying her silky smooth tanned skin and her athletic build.

Aaron immediately recognised her. Who could ever forget a body like that?

Hmmm, Aaron thought to himself, definitely no underwear. She did not wear them.

Her hair cropped short in a 70's David Bowie style which made her even more attractive.

Aaron looked longingly at her beautiful figure, pursing his lips in anticipation of touching her once again.

They had made love once, a few years ago which rekindled his desire to once again take her in a loving embrace.

With her back to Aaron, she was the centre of attention with a bevy of admirers that surrounding her with one suiter sticking close to her attempting to block the other admirers.

Nadia was unaware of Aaron's presence.

Joseph was waffling along about the Islamic threat to Israel.

Aaron took great care to ensure that he was interested in what Joseph was saying, however his eyes were constantly scanning the room for the contact he was to meet.

His eyes eventually making contact with his connection who was positioned near the Russian foreign minister Damir Lacrov in the centre of the room.

The contacts eyes fixed on Aaron as they made eye contact, then a subtle scratch of the forehead confirming that he had seen Aaron, who responded with the same gesture.

Aaron had positioned himself facing his contact in the centre of the room, shuffling slightly from side to side occasionally and moving in such a way that Joseph's back was facing the centre of the room and unaware of Aaron's focus on his connection.

He was conscious to keep looking at Joe and still be able to follow his contact in his peripheral vision.

Glancing occasionally at his contact to ascertain when he would decide to move towards the toilet, Aaron rubbed his chin, a sign to meet at the urinal.

The contact whispered something into one of the body guard's ears, moved slowly around the people that had encircled the Russian Foreign Minister, appearing to be checking the perimeter and slowly made his way inconspicuously towards the toilet.

Aaron excused himself and left Joseph standing alone. 'I need to take a leak my friend.'

'No problem, off you go,' responded Joseph watching as Aaron placed his empty whisky tumbler onto a roving waiter's tray and made his way towards the toilets located outside the ballroom.

Joseph took time to scan the room to see who was in attendance and noticed Chaim Benowitz, the senator from Ohio, an old and dear friend to Israel.

As Aaron opened the door to the men's toilet, his contact approached him on his way out extending his hand in a greeting.

'Hi, I'm Victor Portnorsky,' offering Aaron his hand.

'Pleased to meet you, we should catch up for a drink,' said Victor in broken English.

'I'm Aaron Armando, pleased to meet you,' he replied.

'Look forward to having a drink with you shortly,' continued Aaron.

In the handshake, Victor passed on a USB stick that he had clasped firmly in his hand, tilting the palm of his hand downwards to ensure the secure transfer of the stick to Aaron.

Taking Victor's hand in a firm grip Victor continued in his broken English Russian accent, 'yes I look forward to chatting a little later,' he said as he departed the toilet.

With the USB stick in his possession, Aaron clasped his hand into a fist securing the stick firmly in his hand, then placed his hand in his pocket, releasing the stick and proceeded towards the urinal to relieve himself.

Victor was seconded to the security detail of Damir Lacrov to provide protection for the Russian foreign minister for this conference by Pushkin himself.

The USB contained sensitive information about a meeting between the Russian President Pushkin and Xiu Jaoping the General Secretary of the Communist Party of China.

Whilst Aaron relieved himself, he retrieved the USB stick from his pocket and placed it into a slit in the top of his belt behind one of the loops in his pants, ensuring that it was securely positioned.

He washed his hands, taking care to check each toilet booth to ensure that they were unoccupied as he made his way out of the toilet.

The CIA had recruited the personal assistant to the chairman in The Three Sixty Degrees Group and ensured that Aaron's name appeared on the guest list posing as a French entrepreneur within the IT industry.

Victor Portnorsky, a young lieutenant in the FSB had been recruited by the CIA years previously by Stan Noble in New York.

Years previously Stan had passed a note to Victor when their paths crossed at the United Nations enquiring whether he would act as a spy in return for a safe passage to the USA.

Victor had been careful and extremely cautious to follow the instruction detailed on the piece of edible paper that Stan had passed onto him detailing the procedure to follow when passing on secret information to a CIA contact in Russia.

The information that the CIA had gathered from Victor over the years had proven to be invaluable, as he passed on various sensitive Russian secrets to the CIA.

Victor long held a closely guarded personal desire to escape the draconian regimented authoritarian system in Russia.

He never married and when the time came to make his move and escape to the West, he did not want to be burdened with a wife and kids.

There was no way possible for him to escape with a family in tow as it was guaranteed that when the time came and he did leave Russia, Pushkin would round up his parents, wife and any children he may have fathered and have them all killed in the most horrific way.

So now in his mid-forties and a senior FSB officer with the rank of colonel, his parents deceased and no wife or children, he could start planning his exit.

He always harboured a secret desire to go to America and held this closely guarded secret for many years, dreaming of a life of freedom, free to roam around unhindered.

He dreamed of the freedom to go fishing, hunting and hiking, activities he was unable to do in mother Russia.

Victor had been part of Pushkin's Russian security detail for the secret meeting with the Chinese leader Xiu Jaoping at the Russian/China border city of Blagoveshchensk in Russia which is the administration centre of Amur Oblast located at the confluence of the Amur and Zeya rivers opposite the Chinese city of Heihe.

He was a trusted cadre to Pushkin and had been selected to have total control over the Russian security detail for this highly secretive meeting between these two communist leaders.

Victor had saved Pushkin's life years previously in an assignation attempt in Moscow as he exited his Aurus Senat limousine. He threw himself in front of the Russian President, taking three bullets, one in the leg, the shoulder and in his left arm.

This heroic act, similar to that of Secret Service Agent Timothy McCarthy who spread out his body to act as a human shield in 1981, thus saving President Ronald Regan from being assassinated, left him with a slight limp.

Pushkin acknowledged his heroism and had honoured Victor with the Hero of the Soviet Union award.

The CIA had cautiously used information passed on by Victor in such a way that the Russians would never suspect Victor of treason.

Aaron left the gents toilet, turned left away from the ballroom towards the elevators which were situated around the corner, made his way to the staircase door, opened it and inserted a tiny plastic card similar in thickness to a credit card into the groove of the strike plate stopping the ball from securing itself in the groove and sealing the door when the door is shut.

He did this to ensure that the door would not seal and that he would be able to get back into the elevator foyer.

Taking the staircase to the basement he followed the same procedure at the basement door and found his way to the grill gate which opened for vehicles when entering into the underground parking.

He flicked his lighter and the secret service agent climbed out of the Range Rover and approached him.

Carefully removing the USB stick from the opening in his belt, he passed it through the grill to the secret service agent who turned and made his way back to the Range Rover, taking his seat next to the driver.

They departed slowly ensuring that they did not draw any attention to themselves as they exited the parking area opposite the entrance to the underground parking garage.

Aaron made his way back through the basement garage door removing the plastic lug from the strike plate and made his way up the staircase to the second floor and followed the same procedure at the door leading to the elevator.

Aaron passed the security detail who merely afforded him a glance as they were familiar with his persona and made his way into the ballroom, his eyes seeking out the stunning beauty that he had seen earlier.

Noting Joseph, who now seemed deep in conversation with the Senator Chaim Benowitz, Aaron skirted around Joe and made his way towards the smorgasbord ensuring that he joined the queue on the opposite side of the table to this sexy lady.

He made sure that he would be directly across the table from her as she selected some hors d'oeuvres for herself.

Nadia Baciu had just finished selecting a couple of hors d'oeuvres when she glanced up and was rather startled to see Aaron opposite her on the other side of the table.

She admired his well-tanned skin and noticed that his hair was greying slightly at the temples.

Taken aback, her eyes fixed firmly on Aaron, she twitched slightly, however remained calm, ensuring that the suiter that had latched onto her earlier in the evening, standing next to her wouldn't notice that she had recognised someone she knew.

Chapter 9

Croydon South

South London

Nadia meaning hope in Russian and Baciu derived from the Romanian word baci meaning shepherd, this stunning Romanian beauty had met Aaron a couple of years earlier, after she had almost shot him in a Brixton mosque.

Aaron and Nadia's paths crossed when both had entered the Brixton Mosque early one Friday evening after prayers, neither aware of the others presence.

Aaron dressed in a traditional male Islamic Thoube long sleeve Kaftan with a taqiyah, a close-fitting prayer cap and Nadia, dressed in black and sporting a Niqab face veil hiding her real identity.

She had chosen a black colour Abaya cloak, which would not be easily seen in the moonless night.

Both had entered the mosque within minutes of each other and were oblivious of each other at the time. The streets around the mosque were deserted as all people had made their way home and were indoors long after evening prayers had finished.

The Imam was about to lock up and head home himself.

He was actively involved in recruiting people to join Al Qaeda and raising funds for their cause.

His lectures were well attended and militant in nature, clearly advocating his hatred for America and its infidel partners.

The CIA wanted him eliminated as he was responsible for recruiting jihadists that caused the deaths of hundreds of American and allied soldiers.

It was unclear who Nadia was working for, however whichever government it was, it was clear that they too wanted the Imam eliminated.

Aaron hid himself behind the Hussainia, where the speaker normally stands as he lectures the congregation and was aware of the shadow cast on the wall coming from a dimly lit street light depicting something moving in the mosque.

Frozen behind the Hussainia he was now aware, that he was not alone in the mosque and would need to be extremely cautious and lightning fast when he made his move to eliminate the Imam.

Ensuring that he remained dead still, he watched for any further movement and wondered who else would be in the mosque and why.

Having entered the mosque Nadia had hidden behind the minbar, the pulpit where the Imam stands to deliver his sermon.

All Aaron's sensors were on high alert as he looked for any further signs of movement or shadows being cast on the mosque wall, confirming that whoever else was in the mosque was also hiding somewhere out of sight.

A slight clicking and tapping noise coming from the Imam's shoes on the floor confirmed that he had closed a door and was possibly heading towards the exit.

Aaron peeped around the corner of the Hussainia as the Imam passed close by.

He had already assumed a crouched position, coiled and ready to spring into action, however he was conscious of the fact that there was somebody else in the mosque and with lightning speed moved quickly across the floor covering the few feet between himself and the Imam in an instant.

Aaron had earlier removed a syringe from a plastic container and held it firmly in his hand careful to ensure that the needle protruded away from his hand. He did not want to prick himself and reached the Imam a moment later without him even being aware of his presence.

Aaron cupped his hand around the Imam's mouth silencing him, whilst holding him in a sleeper choke hold, spun him around to position himself behind the Imam covering himself in the line of sight from where he thought the other person may be hiding in the mosque.

The Imam struggled and wriggled for a while, however did not have the strength to counter Aaron's grip.

Aaron felt the Imam's body starting to go limp a minute later as he struggled to breath and passed out.

Aaron quickly injected the deadly substance into the carotid artery that travels up the side of the neck and into the skull behind his hair.

He had practiced this multiple times at Camp Peary and had been well taught by his instructor. His precision paid off bringing a quick death to the Imam.

Aaron placed the Imam's body gently on the floor as he crouched and dodged moving rapidly from side to side towards where he thought the other person may have been hiding in the mosque.

The sudden whizzing sound of a bullet passing near his ear followed by another closely missing his torso confirmed the presence of the other person as they moved towards a pillar close by.

The silencer used by the assailant ensured a muffled suppressed sound that was hardly audible as both bullets embedded themselves into a mosaic on the wall, hiding any obvious sign of damage to the mosaic which appeared to have been a natural ageing process.

Aaron's athletic agility and evasive action had saved his life as he covered the distance between himself and the other person in a flash, just as the person made a run for the next pillar.

Aaron tackled the person, grabbing the hand that held the gun, twisting it and disabling it, ensuring that he had secured the persons left hand, he now had excellent fulcrum control with his right hand to bend the gun backwards forcing the person to release the weapon onto his foot ensuring that any sound of the gun falling to the floor would be suppressed.

Aaron dropped his body to his right hand side positioning his right leg behind the person's legs and twisted causing the person to fall to the ground with him positioned on top.

He pushed the gun away with his knee positioning the same knee on the person's elbow preventing the person from retrieving the gun.

Techniques that came naturally to him, having been taught that as a martial arts student.

He dropped the syringe and ripped the veil from the persons head, revealing the identity of a stunning blond with blue eyes staring rigidly back at him.

'Who the hell are you and who do you work for?' insisted Aaron.

'Jesus, I could have killed you,' he continued.

Aaron frisked the assailant all over, running his hand up the inside of her thigh ensuring that there were no other hidden weapons. He picked up her gun and placed the syringe back into the plastic container and pulled her to her feet.

The blond beauty said nothing at all, merely glaring at Aaron through those icy blue eyes.

Aaron instructed her to put the veil back on and positioned her in front of himself with his Glock firmly positioned against her back as they made their way towards the exit.

Moving her to his left with his Glock pointing at her rib cage, he peered out of the front door searching the surroundings and ensuring that nobody would see them as they exited the mosque.

The street in front of the mosque was deserted at this hour.

Tugging the blonds arm, they quickly made their way down the road and around the corner to the small parked commercial van he had stolen earlier in the day.

Thankfully the dilapidated courier van was full of dents and scratches devoid of any signwriting making it less conspicuous to people living in the area.

'Keep your hands where I can see them,' instructed Aaron as he drove off, heading onto the A23 motorway towards South Croydon where he had rented an apartment a couple of days previously.

He donned a peak cap and pulled the visor down to cover his eyes ensuring that any CCTV cameras placed at intervals along the motorway would not get a clear view of his face.

Traffic on the motorway was light.

The rain had increased to a downpour by the time he had parked the van near the entrance to the apartment that he had rented.

They both made their way through the front entrance, up the stairs and into the apartment that was small and sparsely furnished.

Satisfied that she had no more weapons in her possession Aaron picked her up throwing her on the bed and instructed her take off the veil.

The blond removed her veil staring at Aaron revealing her true beauty in the brightly lit room.

Leaning over her, Aaron was clearly attracted to her.

God, she is a real looker, he thought to himself.

'OK, who the hell are you and who do you work for?' asked Aaron.

'My name is Nadia and I work for myself.'

'Don't fucking mess with me lady,' said Aaron in an agitated voice.

'In case you don't remember, you tried to kill me a short while ago, so don't give me that bullshit,' said Aaron raising his voice slightly.

'OK, I am Romanian and work for the Russian Government,' replied Nadia.

'So what the hell were you doing in the mosque?' inquired Aaron.

'I was instructed to kill the Imam,' said Nadia.

'He was responsible for recruiting Islamic fighters to go to Syria and as you know, these fighters have killed hundreds of their people,' she said.

'I was unaware of your presence in the mosque and was waiting for the right opportunity to shoot the Imam,' she continued.

'That was until I saw you make a move and kill him,' she said.

'I was instructed to ensure that nobody knew I was there,' stated Nadia.

'That's why I tried to shoot you,' she explained.

Aaron crouched over her, staring into her eyes and wondered if this story had some truth to it or not.

'So you are Romanian?' enquired Aaron seeking further confirmation.

'Yes I am Romanian,' she nodded.

Getting more complicated by the minute Aaron thought to himself.

Why would she be working for Ivan he thought?

On impulse he leaned down and kissed her passionately. Nadia did not resist and responded by embracing him in a hug.

Fuck it, Aaron thought to himself as he tore off the Abaya that covered Nadia's naked body revealing her athletic curves.

This bitch could have killed me, now I'm going to fuck her.

The leg holster was still strapped to her upper thigh, now devoid of the weapon that Aaron had wrestled from her hand in the mosque.

Skirting on the edge of not knowing precisely who she was, he threw caution to the wind and made passionate love to her.

Nadia did not resist Aarons advance and found herself immersed in fantasy spiralling into ecstasy as their lovemaking reached, crescendo after crescendo.

Live dangerously Aaron thought to himself.

Life's way too short.

Finally spent, Aaron rolled off her and watched her slowly gather her breath.

'OK, so what now?' asked Aaron.

'Take me back to the mosque,' she said.

'I have a parked car there,' continued Nadia.

They both got dressed back into the same attire that they donned for their missions, returned to the panel van and drove back to the mosque.

Aaron was somewhat concerned that somebody may have discovered the Imam's body, which proved invalid as they drove slowly past the mosque.

The door to the mosque was still slightly ajar, just as Aaron had left it when they made their way out and onto street earlier in the evening.

Seemed that nobody had noticed it and Aaron gave a sigh of relief and relaxed a little more.

Nadia pointed out the car she had hired further down the road from the mosque and Aaron pulled up alongside it and let her out without bidding her farewell. He drove slowly down the road, glancing in the rear view mirror to see Nadia's car make its way out of the parking spot, make a U-Turn and then drive off in the opposite direction.

Wonder if I will ever see her again he thought to himself.

Aaron drove back to the apartment in Croydon South and parked the van a couple of blocks away.

He entered the apartment and removed his clothing, stowed it in a black garbage bag which he disposed of the next day when he vacated the apartment, leaving the stolen panel van where he had parked it the previous evening.

He walked a few blocks and hailed a cab taking a ride to the airport.

As he sipped his coffee waiting for the boarding call, the leading story on the afternoon television news channel displayed on a large screen was full of reports of the death of the Imam.

'It is believed that the Imam suffered a heart attack,' stated the BBC reporter.

Crowds had gathered at the mosque and were boisterously condemning America and Israel in their usual demonstration.

Chapter 10

Kontororu Think Tank

Airborne Virus

Having made eye contact at the buffet table, Aaron afforded Nadia a gracious smile in return just as the lights dimmed slightly and the tinging sound of a spoon against a glass announcing the attention of the crowd towards the person on the stage, ready to make a speech.

The noise simmered to mere whispers amongst the patrons in the ballroom.

'Good evening ladies and gentlemen.'

'Thank you ever so much for attending this evening's cocktail party.'

'My name is Doctor Goodfellow.'

'I am the chairperson of The Three Sixty Degrees Group and it is my pleasure to warmly welcome you all here this evening.'

'This evening is a celebration of a number of new developments for The Three Sixty Degrees Group primarily the formation of our Kontororu Think Tank.'

'A Think Tank that is actively exploring world anarchy, ill-discipline and ways and means to counter the changing world,' continued Dr. Goodfellow.

The Think Tank had amongst its elite membership of 250, various world leaders, the mega rich, scientists, captains of industry, financial experts and leading academia.

The ideas presented to the G7 leaders of their countries as well as Russia by the Think Tank had been widely welcomed.

The world including the USA and Russia had experienced anarchy, with unruly citizens taking matters in their own hands, constantly ignoring warnings from authorities.

Seemed the only time that America and Russia had agreed on anything.

Both major powers had embraced the ideas put to them by The Three Sixty Degrees Group to investigate ways and means of curtailing the activities of these anarchists.

'A special thankyou to our new members present here this evening,' said Dr. Goodfellow.

'I look forward to personally meeting each and every one of you in the near future,' stated Dr. Goodfellow.

Unbeknown to patrons, the Kontororu Think Tank was actively exploring many other options including the implementation of microchips into the human anatomy, which would allow for authorities to track a person's every move and had perfected an identification process by digitising images from a person's cornea, the front of the eye.

This would allow authorities to create a database of a person's identity without them even knowing and be in a position to cancel a person's records in all databases if need be, ensuring that a person no longer existed. People would have no access to their bank and would simply disappear from the face of the earth.

They had secretly developed a new airborne virus which they called the D3B Virus, however had not yet released it.

The virus would make people extremely ill when inhaled and the masses would hastily seek to get inoculated against the virus causing mass hysteria worldwide.

Unbeknown to the world population, the antivirus vaccine that they had developed would kill people within a twelve month period.

The antivirus vaccine, when administered would ensure the elimination of half of the world's population, achieving their worldwide goal of mass population reduction.

The world population would be duped into believing that this antivirus vaccine would save lives and they would arrange for mass inoculation worldwide within a six month window thus ensuring that they would achieve their goal of halving the world's population.

The vaccine hid its true intention- The death of three billion people, hence the name D3B-Death to three Billion.

The wealthy ruling elite's way of culling the world's population starting in the impoverished continent of Africa where the majority of people are uneducated and live in poverty.

This was the new world orders way of countering the anarchy that had raised its head in the world recently as well as culling half of the world's population.

The Kontororu Think Tank had secretly developed a separate effective vaccine for selective elite people, academics and world leaders in order to ensure that these people were able to survive the pandemic.

The speech was short, sweet, succinct and to the point without revealing anything to those present.

Concluding his speech Dr. Goodfellow stated, 'enjoy the hospitality and the rest of the evening ladies and gentlemen.'

As Nadia left the table and made her way towards the centre of the room, she knew she had to shake off the suiter, who seemed to stick close to her most of the evening.

Having eaten the morsels of hors d'oeuvres she had dished up for herself she excused herself from the suiter and made her towards the ladies toilet.

She emerged a while later and found Aaron waiting outside the ballroom door for her. Taking her arm he guided her back into the ballroom towards the bar.

A glass of champagne and a double Johnny Walker Blue on the rocks please.

Aaron assumed that she drank champagne as he had seen a flute glass in her hand earlier in the evening.

The bar tender went about preparing the drinks and Aaron turned to Nadia and said, 'You look very beautiful this evening.'

'Meet me in half an hour outside the front entrance, I can't wait to hold you in my arms and make love to you again,' said Aaron.

'It's been a long time ma beaute,' continued Aaron in his irresistibly husky French accent.

Nadia felt the tingle run through her body and the hairs on her body rise in anticipation at the thought of making love to this extraordinarily handsome man again.

She recalled the memory of their lovemaking very clearly and had longed for another love making session, however had long come to the conclusion that she would never see Aaron again.

Aaron threw back his scotch and departed the ballroom as Nadia turned and made her back through the throng of people towards the suiter and the guests that had surrounded her earlier.

Aaron retrieved his coat from the kiosk attendant and took a ride in the elevator to the ground floor.

'Please excuse me gentlemen, I need to make a call,' said Nadia and with that she turned and headed towards the ballroom door.

The suitor and the other guests stared admiringly at her as she made her way through the crowded room disappearing an instant later.

Nadia headed for the kiosk, retrieved her coat and headed for the hotel exit.

The CIA had hired a car and parked it in a reserved parking area adjacent to the entrance earlier in the day ensuring that the handsome tip given to the doorman would guarantee that nobody questioned why it was parked there.

The keys were left under the dashboard on the right hand side of the steering wheel.

Easy to find for somebody who knew where to feel for it?

'Good night sir,' came the farewell greeting from the doorman as he opened the side door.

'Enjoy the rest of your evening sir,' he continued.

'Thank you,' replied Aaron as he made his way through the open door and towards the parked car.

Once inside, he felt for the keys under the dash and started the car, warming it in anticipation of Nadia's arrival.

He needed to warm the inside of car because it felt like the inside of a fridge and eventually he felt the warm air waft over the interior of the vehicle.

He removed the false teeth veneer that the makeup artist had fitted earlier and put it in his pocket.

Glancing at the doorway, he noticed the doorman looking his way casually saluting him, in gratitude for the handsome tip he received earlier in the evening.

Aaron returned the gesture with a wave of his hand and patiently tapped the top of the steering wheel in anticipation of Nadia's arrival. Finally he caught a glimpse of Nadia as she exited the elevator and made her way towards the exit.

The doorman politely opened the side door, ushering her outside and bid her farewell.

'Good night madam, enjoy the rest of your evening,' said the doorman.

'Thank you,' replied Nadia having noticed Aaron sitting in car across from the entrance, as she made her way towards him.

The doorman stared lovingly in her direction.

Aaron was waiting patiently.

'Bonjour mon pigeon,' he said kissing Nadia as she entered the car.

Aaron drove the short distance from The Grand Hotel to the Zurich Guest House Hotel pulling Nadia closer to him as they drove.

His eyes darting from Nadia to the road repeatedly, steering the vehicle with one hand and running his hand up her inner thigh with his other hand.

I cannot wait to get her into bed, he thought to himself.

Glancing occasionally in the rear view mirror to ensure that they were not being followed, he parked the car on the road near the entrance to the hotel.

They made their way up the stairs to the first floor, opting not to take the elevator and Aaron extracted the room card key card from his wallet, carefully removing the card key on the top and not take the card key housed behind it which was the card key to the room over the way in the passage that was reserved by the blond agent earlier in the day.

The room was booked as a backup in case there was a need for a hasty escape as the room's balcony was situated above a portico making a quick exit somewhat easier.

CIA seemed to think of every possibility.

They hardly made it into the room and having closed the door, Aaron threw his coat and jacket over the chair and proceeded to remove Nadia's coat, rubbing his hands over her shoulders and dropping her evening gown to the floor revealing her naked body.

Like a man possessed Aaron ripped his clothes off leaving them scattered around the room.

'Doux Jésus Mon Cher,' sweet Jesus my dear, Aaron whispered in Nadia's ear.

'I have never wanted you more.' 'Let's make love, my pigeon,' whispered Aaron.

Nadia tilted her head backwards inviting Aaron to take her.

Kissing Nadia, he swept her off her feet and laid her gently on the bed, feeling under the pillow closest to the window with his left hand taking great care to ensure that she did not notice.

He needed to be sure that the Glock was still where it was supposed to be.

Passionately kissing her he moved his lips to her bosom and took hold of her right hand ensuring that she did not feel under the pillow or move it in a moment of passion.

Taking her nipple in his lips, he ran his tongue around her nipple now fully erect whilst steadily stroking the bottom of her stomach in a slow swirling manner, then allowing his hand to caress her pubic hairs.

She started moaning as he separated her legs moving his head towards her naval.

Kissing her naval and then moving down towards her vagina, still holding her right hand.

Taking her clitoris gently in his teeth, then using his tongue he probed for her G Spot.

Nadia stretched her neck backwards on the pillow slightly arching her back as his tongue moved in a rhythmic circular motion from side to side over her vagina.

Memories came flooding back to Nadia of the time he had taken her in the apartment in Croydon.

Aaron felt her arch her back and her buttocks moved slightly off the bed as she started to reach an orgasm squeezing his hand tightly, she spiralled from one orgasm to the next.

He tightened his tongue against his lips and teeth moving it in an upward and downward motion adding more pressure as she reached each orgasm, then easing the pressure as he felt her body go limp.

He added more pressure each time as she moaned in the pleasure of reaching another orgasm.

Nadia had taken the pillow from under her head and put it on top of her face to subdue the screaming sounds of pleasure coming with each orgasm.

Aaron moved to her right hand side close to her body and positioned himself between Nadia's body and the pillow that hid the Glock and magazines ensuring that her right hand would not move the pillow and discover the weapon as she reached another orgasm.

Using the middle finger of his right hand he immediately found the G-Spot and proceeded to use a circular motion driving her to reach an even higher crescendo as the increased pressure driving her to another climax.

Her passionate screams increased with every orgasm.

Aaron could make out her muffled pleas from under the pillow, begging him to insert his penis and fuck her.

Ahhhhhh-Nadia's muffled screams seemed to reach a new crescendo each time.

Changing periodically from a circular motion to an up and down motion over her G-Spot and increasing the pressure took it to another level.

Finally Aaron mounted her and without inserting his penis into her vagina, rubbed it up and down over her clitoris time and time again, causing her to beg him to insert it until he finally inserted his penis into her wet vagina pulsating in and out slowly at first then increasing the rhythm.

He positioned her legs over his shoulders in a shoulder hold position ensuring a deeper penetration and sucked her toes as he increased his rhythm with ever stroke.

Aaron expertly flipped her onto her stomach and proceeded to make love to her dog style for some time positioning his thumbs on the dimples of Venus on her lower back with his hands firmly clasping her hips.

He admired the beautiful contour of her buttocks before rolling over and positioning her on top of himself allowing her to ride him in the splits position.

He caressed her firm breasts and moved her one last time back into the missionary position and she finally felt him ejaculate and pushed him off.

'I can't take anymore,' she panted.

She must have had twenty orgasms Aaron thought to himself.

Fuck me I'm good, he pondered.

My magic wand is so hot, I can weld with it, he thought to himself.

Aaron allowed himself one of his rare smiles.

Should have been a gigolo he thought to himself. A far safer job no doubt.

Nadia's panting eventually subsided and she lay motionless for some time whilst Aaron lying on his back appeared to have fallen asleep.

Nadia slowly and gently slid off the bed ensuring that she did not wake Aaron, got dressed, put on her coat and moved to the balcony door. She drew the curtain slightly and quietly slid the balcony door open slightly ensuring that she did not make a noise that could wake Aaron.

The slight change in temperature and a feint ray of light coming from a street lamp that had found its way onto the ceiling confirmed what she had done.

Lying on his back, a position he never assumed when sleeping as he always slept on the side facing a bedroom door or passage, Aaron was not asleep, however pretended to be fast asleep whilst watching Nadia's every move through slit eyes.

It afforded him a one hundred and eighty degree view of the room.

Nadia extracted a cigarette from the box in her clutch handbag and lit it near the door, took one puff blowing the smoke through the slightly opened door, nipped the ash onto the balcony floor then placed the remainder of the cigarette back into the cigarette box.

She picked up her clutch handbag and turned towards the door.

Aaron heard a car door close somewhere in the street below.

The sudden brightness of the passage light into the room confirmed that Nadia had opened the door and then the fading of the light on the ceiling indicated that she had closed the door.

Nadia removed the cellophane wrap from the box of cigarettes and placed the box on the floor ensuring that no fingerprints were not left on the box.

A feint ray of light remained on the ceiling in the passage leading to the bedroom indicating that she must have placed the cigarette box on the floor between the door frame and the door preventing it from closing.

Aaron quickly gathered up the pillows and placed them one behind the other rolling them up under the blankets to make it look like a person was snuggled up in bed and fast asleep. He retrieved the Glock and the two magazines from under the pillow and lay down naked alongside the bed with his head facing the bottom of the bed.

He peeped around the end of the bed with his Glock aimed at the passage waiting for what he believed would be an attempt on his life.

The training afforded him by the CIA and numerous field operations had honed his sensors making him aware of every possibility and to ensure that he was ready to face whatever threat confronted him.

A short while later the intensity of light from the passage filtered into the room confirmed that the door had been opened and a moment later the dark figure of what appeared to be a man rounded the corner.

As the darkened figure rounded the passage wall, the popping sound of the rounds being fired confirmed that the person had a silencer fitted to the weapon.

The person had fired five shots into the rolled up blankets assuming that Aaron would be tucked up and sound asleep in the bed.

A moment after the person had fired the rounds into the bed, Aaron fired two head shots in quick succession.

The person fell onto the floor.

Aaron was quick to his feet, checked to ensure that the person was dead which was confirmed by the pool of blood spreading across the carpet.

Aaron moved quickly to the door, removed the cigarette box from the bottom of the door frame and gently closed the door using a tissue on the door handle and put the cigarette box next his suitcase.

Time was of the essence now.

Aaron quickly got dressed in the darked room, put his dress shoes into the suitcase and donned a pair of Nike runners and went around the room wiping down any areas of the room that may have fingerprints on it ensuring that he checked every possible area in the room.

He had taken great care not to touch anything earlier that afternoon, thus minimising the possibility of leaving any trace of his DNA.

He removed the pillow slips and sheets, rolled them up and put them into his empty suitcase hoping that all his DNA had been removed.

Checking that his wallet was safely in his rear pocket, Aaron put the cigarette box into his suitcase, picked up it up, donned a peak cap and pulled the visor over his eyes.

He placed his suitcase close to the door before he left the room and walked down the passage towards the elevator looking downwards to hide his features.

As he walked down the passage towards the elevator, he passed the CCTV security camera and extracted a small spray can that he had removed from his suitcase earlier and put into his pocket, turned around returning towards the direction he came from.

He positioned himself so that the camera was unable to record a view of his face and then proceeded to spray black paint onto the glass cover of the camera.

This ensured a total black out of vision from the camera.

He had to move quickly before the night manager had noticed the blackened screen of the security camera on his level and came to investigate.

He quickly returned to the room and opened the door, keeping the door ajar with his foot, picked up his suitcase, closing the door quietly behind him as he exited, he wiped the door handle to remove any sign of finger prints with a wet tissue and moved across the passage way to the room adjacent to his.

He opened the door with the card key given to him by the secret service make-up agent earlier that afternoon placing his back on the door as he pushed and opened it and placed the key card back into his wallet ensuring that there were no trace of any fingerprints on the door.

The feint low pitched click of the door closing was hardly audible and confirmed that the door was shut minimizing the possibility that other guests could possibly have heard.

He immediately made his way to the balcony door, opened it slowly ensuring that there was no noise and made his way onto the balcony.

Clutching his suitcase tightly in his arms, he jumped onto the portico porch which was around six feet below landing as quietly as possible on his Nike runners ensuring that he did not wake up any guests.

The CIA really thinks of everything he thought to himself.

Still clutching his small suitcase as tightly as possible, he jumped from the portico porch onto the road below which led to the rear of the hotel, a drop of around 15 feet and rolled onto his side as he landed, thus minimising any noise and damage to his ankles.

Hope I have not damaged my favourite coat he thought to himself.

He was on his feet the second he hit the walkway, quickly making his way around the hotel towards the front entrance and into a bush of shrubs on the other side of road leading to the hotels entrance.

Hidden amongst the bushes, he scanned the area in front of him.

His eyes fixing on a vehicle he thought might have been the vehicle that the noise of the car door closing had come from earlier.

He stared at it for some time when he suddenly noticed the red glow coming from the tip of a cigarette which was evidence that there was a person sitting in the front passenger's seat of the car.

Whilst Aaron could not make out who the darkened person was sitting in the passenger's seat at this late hour, he was convinced that it could possibly Nadia waiting for the assassin to return.

It had been a short while since her partner had made his way into the hotel, thus Nadia thought that he may have encountered resistance from the night manager and had to eliminate him before proceeding to Aaron's room.

So she was not unduly worried that it had taken some time and was confident that the assassin would succeed in killing Aaron.

Sitting quietly and reminiscing about their love making, she felt sad that Aaron would be dead and that she would never again and have love made to her the way he did.

Aaron gripped his Glock tightly feeling the silencer and reminding himself that he had only discharged two rounds from the fifteen round magazine.

He left his suitcase in the bushes, quickly, quietly and stealthily moved towards the rear of the car keeping himself hidden by the rear panel between the rear door and the back window from the occupant in the car.

He moved like a leopard about to strike its prey and rounded the back of the car quickly, minimising the opportunity for the person sitting in the passenger's seat to get a glimpse of any movement in the external rear view passenger side mirror.

He opened the door finding Nadia seated in the passenger's seat and popped two rounds into her temple. She slumped forward her head coming to rest on the dashboard.

Fucking bitch he thought to himself.

What a waste.

Would have been nice to have made love to her a few more times.

He knew that he had to eliminate her because the next time their path's crossed, she would most certainly kill him.

She must have placed a micro GPS chip into her clutch bag allowing the assassin to track her he thought to himself.

Chapter 11

Biglers Mill

Virginia USA

The agent that retrieved the USB stick from Aaron at the underground parking garage door of The Grand Hotel made his way back to the Range Rover.

The driver put the Range Rover into gear and pointed the vehicle in the direction of the Paris Le Bourget airport.

The Gulfstream G700 was waiting for them, ready to leave the moment they arrived.

The Pilots were seated in the cockpit and fired up the Gulfstream's engines as the headlights of the Range Rover approached the hanger and they watched as the driver parked the vehicle next to the hanger.

The Pilots were anxious to get going and waited as the agents walked towards the aircraft and were happy to finally be on their way.

The Pilot's backside was numb from sitting for a few hours waiting for the agents to appear and the Co-Pilot opened the door to the aircraft as the agents approached and greeted both agents as they climbed the staircase leading to the inside of the aircraft.

'Good evening gentlemen,' offered the Co-Pilot.

'Hi my friend,' answered the first agent as he climbed the staircase.

The second agent responded with a simple, 'hello.'

The Co-Pilot closed the door securing it and made his way back into the cockpit just as they started taxiing towards the runway with the hanger door closing automatically behind them.

The agents felt the surge of the engines as the aircraft turned onto the runway and the Pilots engaged full throttle.

They were up and into the clouds minutes later.

The flight time would be around seven and a half hours so the agents made themselves comfortable enjoying a few a few beers and a scrumptious dinner of garlic prawns and salad.

The Director of the CIA waited patiently and watched as the Gulfstream Aerospace G700 was on its final approach to the runway at Biglers Mill near their headquarters at Langley.

The information on the USB stick was far too precious to allow any agents to safely transport it to Langley.

Barnaby wanted to take care of this himself.

The agents disembarked from the belly of the Gulfstream, greeting Barnaby in their usual manner.

Both agents offering a courteous 'hello boss,' to Barnaby.

One of the agents extracted the USB stick from his pocket and gave it to Barnaby.

'There you are sir,' said the agent.

'Thank you,' replied Barnaby taking the stick and placing it in his pocket.

Barnaby turned and made his way towards the SUV, jumped in and they departed with a security detail in front and at the rear as they sped towards the White House.

The President was expecting Barnaby and had cleared his schedule for the rest of the day as he anxiously waited for Barnaby's arrival.

He was desperate to view the information contained on the USB stick in Barnaby's possession.

Barnaby's entourage entered through the security gate of the White House and he was quickly out of the vehicle, past the security detail at the door and into the building.

President Trent's personal assistant tapped on the door of the oval office announcing the arrival of the Director of the CIA.

'The Director of the CIA Mr. President,' she stated.

'Thank you Alecia,' responded President Trent rising from his seat.

'Hello Barnaby,' said President Trent offering his hand in a cordial greeting.

'Good afternoon Mr. President,' replied Barnaby taking the President's hand.

Barnaby greeted Vice President Miles Tippence, Secretary of State Neville Pompello and the President's National Security Advisor Michael O'Rourke.

'Would you like some coffee Barnaby?' enquired the President pointing to a seat.

'Thank you Mr. President I could use a cup right now,' said Barnaby.

'OK Barnaby, what do you think we have?' inquired the President as he passed the cup of coffee to Barnaby.

'I have no idea Mr. President,' said Barnaby.

'I have come directly here from the airport sir,' offered Barnaby.

'We have been tracking both Pushkin and Xiu Jaoping by satellite and I can confirm that both met at the Russian/China border city of Blagoveshchensk in Russia,' said Barnaby.

'OK, bring your coffee and let's make our way to the situation room,' said the President.

'I want this contained to the five of us for now,' continued the President.

'Once we have established what secrets this USB stick holds, I will decide whether or not to involve the Joint Chiefs of Staff,' stated the President emphatically.

Barnaby was aware that the 64 megabyte USB stick could only record around one and half hours of video footage and prayed that there was enough footage on the stick to ascertain what the Russians and Chinese were up to.

They made their way to the situation room, Barnaby inserted the USB into the hard drive and the monitor on the wall blinked to life.

Images of Pushkin and Xiu Jaoping were displayed on the monitor as they took their seats with their respective delegations seated alongside them.

The audio was not clear to begin with and a little scratchy, however seemed to improve a little as time moved on.

Nothing that the CIA could not fix.

After the usual cordial greeting between the two leaders and their respective delegations both parties seated themselves and got comfortable.

The Russian and Chinese security details were excused with the exception of Victor Portnorsky head of Russian security and Heng Zhao the head of Chinese security.

Both these agents positioned themselves on the wall behind their respective leaders.

Their security agents were positioned outside the doors behind each of the leaders.

Pushkin was the first to speak in English, a universal language understood by both parties.

'Mr. Chairman, we both have issues with imperialist America,' said Pushkin.

'They have blamed your country for the COVID 19 outbreak when we both know that it was the Americans that released it in your country,' stated Pushkin.

'Trent imposed sanctions against us for what they allege is the poisoning of a former Russian spy and his daughter in the UK in March 2018 and US banks are banned from providing loans to Russia and Washington will also be opposing any loan extension to us by international institutions,' continued Pushkin.

'Trent has also imposed sanctions on China,' said Pushkin.

'A way to distract the world's attention away from issues in their own country as well as Trent's effort to gain support from their allies as they continue to move manufacturing away from your country to India, Vietnam and Cambodia, which has had a devastating effect on your economy,' said Pushkin.

'So what are you proposing?' asked Chairman Xiu Jaoping.

'Well, before we get into bed together, we need to come to an agreement on a number of issues,' stated Pushkin.

'In the new world order dominated by both of us, we will take control of Europe and you take Africa,' suggested Pushkin.

'Yes we want Africa as well as Australia,' stated Xiu Jaoping emphatically.

'I'm sick of these imperialists controlling the world and continually undermining us,' continued Pushkin.

'If we agree to you taking Africa and Australia, then I want an ironclad agreement with you that you will supply us with any minerals we may need at a significantly reduced market price,' stated Pushkin.

Xiu Jaoping simply nodded.

'So what are you proposing?' Asked Xiu Jaoping.

'The world is reeling from the effects of COVID 19 and world economies are in freefall and it seems that this will continue for the foreseeable future.' 'The west are therefore in no position to counter what I am proposing,' said Pushkin.

'I propose that we act in concert,' continued Pushkin.

'Both of us hack into the American databases just as we have done in the past, shut down their electrical grid which will paralyse their banking system, communications including military installations allowing us the opportunity to launch an attack,' suggested Pushkin.

'I propose that we use North Korea to launch ballistic missiles,' said Pushkin.

'We both know that Kim Jang-un has developed nuclear missiles and that way we stay on the fringes and are not directly involved,' he continued.

'We can smuggle nuclear weapons into North Korea to support what they already have and secretly set them up without the American imperialists even knowing,' smirked Pushkin.

Xiu Jaoping raised his eyebrows with his forehead creased and seemed very surprised and concerned at Pushkin's suggestions.

'So what you are saying is that we use North Korea as a pawn and don't care about that country and the consequences they will suffer?' questioned Xiu Jaoping.

'Precisely,' responded Pushkin.

Xiu Jaoping was concerned by Pushkin's suggestion as the Chinese economy is heavily reliant on trade with the USA.

A war with America would not only destroy trade between the two countries, but will most certainly lead to a full scale nuclear war and the end of life on planet earth pondered Xiu Jaoping.

'Our weather scientist have mapped out the potential radiation fallout from a retaliatory strike from the USA on North Korea and the model shows that the radiation will drift west over Japan towards the USA,' said Pushkin.

'Both our countries will suffer a minimal effect of any radiation fallout,' continued Pushkin.

'Good Lord, you must be fucking kidding,' said President Trent, not known for swearing.

'I cannot believe these two bastards,' stated the President.

'They look you in the eye when you meet with them and butter couldn't melt in their fucking mouths,' said the President as they continued to watch.

Pushkin stated, 'timing is critical and I believe that we can coordinate this in a three month time frame and catch these imperialists unawares.'

An hour later Barnaby extracted the USB after the Russians and Chinese had wrapped up the meeting.

President Trent turned to face his aides.

'What do you propose gentlemen?' asked the President looking directly at Vice President Tippence.

'Well Mr. President, I think we need to call a summit with these two and lay it squarely on the table that we are fully aware of what they are planning to do,' advised Vice President Tippence.

'Let's call their bluff Mr. President because we simply cannot allow them to continue down this path,' said the Vice President.

'This simply cannot happen Mr. President,' reiterated the Vice President.

'Looking at the Secretary of State Neville Pompello the President asked, 'what's your thoughts on it Nev?'

'Extremely dangerous situation.' 'I tend to agree with the Vice President, which is to call a meeting and lay it fairly and squarely on the table,' stated the Secretary of State Neville Pompello.

'That way they will know that we are fully aware of what they are planning,' continued the Secretary of State Neville Pompello.

'Mr. President, we cannot afford to sit idly as this has serious consequences for the world at large,' emphasised the Secretary of State.

'This is extremely serious Mr. President and we need to confront this maniac as a matter of urgency,' stressed the Secretary of State.

'What's your take on it Mike?' asked the President turning to face his National Security Advisor.

'I think we should prepare our country and our allies for a possible war Mr. President,' replied the National Security Advisor Michael O'Rourke.

'We need to be ready to strike at a moment's notice Mr. President,' continued Michael O'Rourke.

'Barnaby, what's your opinion?' questioned the President.

'Well Mr, President, I think we could have our forces conduct mass exercises with our allies in the South and East China seas in concert with South Korea, Japan and our allies in NATO which has two distinct advantages to it,' said Barnaby.

'Firstly we would have massed our troops as well as troops from our allies close to their borders, which will send a very clear message to Pushkin and Xiu Jaoping not to carry out their plan as we would be on high alert and ready to strike right on their doorstep,' continued Barnaby.

'Secondly, we will be ready to strike in an instant if need be Mr. President,' said Barnaby.

'OK gentlemen, let's wrap this up for now and meet again the day after tomorrow at 10.00 a.m. in the situation room,' said the President.

'This is absolutely confidential and is to be kept amongst the five of us only,' stated the President emphatically.

'No leaks gentlemen,' ordered the President.

Standing to indicate that the meeting had ended, the President said, 'I will convene a meeting of our National Security Council and Joint Chiefs of Staff to be included in this meeting for the day after tomorrow and I stress, do not whisper a word of this to anybody.'

As they left the situation room, the President turned to Barnaby and said, 'follow me Barnaby, I need to have a private minute with you.'

'Certainly Mr. President,' replied Barnaby.

Barnaby followed the President to the Oval Office and the President waved him to a chair opposite his desk.

'OK Barnaby, what do you really think?' questioned the President.

'It's clear to me that Pushkin and Xiu Jaoping are hesitant to get directly involved from the outset, however it appears that their strategy is to get North Korea to launch a tactical nuclear strike and take the blame for it,' said Barnaby.

'They know that we would retaliate and are prepared to offer North Korea as the sacrificial lamb,' continued Barnaby.

'It is clear from the comments made by Pushkin that he may not be planning to launch his own nukes to attack us as an option because that would result in an all-out war.' 'We will need to be prepared for any contingency Mr. President,' stated Barnaby.

'I very much doubt that he would use this option as he is fully aware that a counter strike will lead to a full scale nuclear war which will mean the end of life on earth,' stated Barnaby.

'Pushkin is a sly bastard and I think he may well have planned an alternative Mr. President,' said Barnaby.

'God knows sir, one can simply not trust him,' continued Barnaby.

'We know he has a bevy of mistresses and I do believe that he would want his infidelity to continue until he can no longer lift his bat,' Mr. President.

The President afforded himself a smile at Barnaby's comment.

'So Mr. President this is what I think we should do,' he went on to say.

'You have an up and coming summit with Kim Jang-un of North Korea scheduled to take place in Vietnam within the next two weeks,' continued Barnaby.

'Keep that meeting on schedule and we will take care of Kim Jang-un and the heirs to his throne, which are his sisters Kim Yang-jong and Kim Yul-song,' said Barnaby.

Take care of them thought the President staring at Barnaby with a creased forehead and raised eyebrows.

'How the hell will the CIA take care of those three?' asked the President.

'Eliminating all three opens up the avenue for a military coup led by General Du-Ho Cha who as we know harbors a more conciliatory stance towards the west, thus we will have eliminated three birds with one stone and effected a regime change, whilst securing North Korea's nukes, negating that part of Pushkin's plan,' continued Barnaby.

'I doubt whether Pushkin and Xiu Jaoping would launch nukes on their own and start a full-scale nuclear war as they know the consequences thereof, however we need to be prepared,' said Barnaby.

'So what are you suggesting you do with Kim Jang-un and his sisters?' enquired the President leaning forward in anticipation.

'Mr. President, I cannot divulge what I am proposing as any knowledge of this would incriminate you,' said Barnaby.

'You need to stay right out of this Mr. President and trust that I will not let you down,' continued Barnaby.

'What do you think the consequences of eliminating one world leader and the heirs to his throne would be?' asked the President.

'No comment Mr. President, you need to be assured that the CIA will deliver as we have always done sir and I can assure you that we will not fail,' stated Barnaby.

'If you are planning to eliminate a world leader, that would cause a worldwide outcry of condemnation and the world will most certainly blame us for it,' stated the President.

'How on earth would you eliminate all three without it looking like an assassination?' questioned the President.

'Best you don't know Mr. President, however be sure that the world will not be able to prove that the USA was responsible,' said Barnaby.

'Hmm, I will need to think long and hard about this and the risk it poses for myself and my administration and I will give you an answer after the up and coming meeting,' said the President leaning back in his chair.

'Too much at stake here and we cannot afford to make any mistakes at all,' continued the President.

With that the President stood, took Barnaby's hand and bid him farewell.

'See you at the meeting the day after tomorrow,' said the President.

Chapter 12

Hotel Ankor

Russia

Victor Portnorsky had been entrusted by Pushkin to lead the Russian security detail and he visited the hotel where the conference would take place a day before the meeting.

He flew from Moscow to the Russian/China border city of Blagoveshchensk in Russia, the venue for the meeting between Pushkin and Xiu Jaoping and met with the hotel manager stating that he wanted to inspect the venue and conduct a security check.

He asked to be left alone to conduct his security checks stating that it needed to be done privately.

The manager cleared the conference room of all workers who were busy setting up the conference table giving Victor complete privacy to roam about unaccompanied.

Studying the position of the conference table and where the leaders would likely be seated, he skirted around the table gazing up at the various air vents.

Victor then retrieved a long ladder that was leaning against a wall and proceeded to remove every air vent around the room checking the inside of each ventilation shaft thoroughly.

It would appear to any person viewing the CCTV camera footage that he was conducting a thorough search of all the air vents in the room.

This procedure had taken forty five minutes and any person monitoring the closed circuit CCTV would have lost interest as it seemed very mundane and seemed to take forever.

He purposely left the air vent situated above the conference table to last.

The vent was situated slightly towards one end of the conference table allowing for an excellent view of where he believed the leaders would be seated.

Having checked all the air vents in the room, he finally made his way towards the remaining air vent, removed the cover and pretended to check the inside of the shaft whilst carefully extracting a mini camera fitted with an offsite remote recoding feature from the sleeve of his suit jacket.

He quickly fitted it deep into to the shaft of the ventilation duct, ensuring that it was pointing towards the area where he believed the leaders would be seated and replaced the air vent cover.

The position he had chosen was not visible to the naked eye as it was attached to the darkened wall of the aluminium ducting and he took great care to position it securely, hoping that the images would capture both leaders.

He later tested it and was pleased to see that it worked and that he had installed it correctly.

Luck was on his side as the footage later revealed that he had placed it in a perfect position capturing clear images of both the leaders.

A day later Pushkin arrived by helicopter at 12.00 noon and his security detail hustled him into the Aurus Senat limousine the Russian version of the limousine called the beast that the American President uses.

Victor rode shotgun in the front seat of the limo from the airport at Blagoveshchensk in Russia to the Hotel Ankor in the city.

Xiu Jaoping and his delegation arrived a little after 2.00 p.m. and he too was hustled into the Hongqi, the Chinese version of the US beast.

Security agents from both countries had flown their Presidential Limousines to Blagoveshchensk ahead of the meeting.

Sweeps of the room had repeatedly been done by both the Chinese and Russian security including the air vents a number of times. Victor took a calculated risk that they would not sweep the air vents yet again.

A lot hinged on this, but he was confident that the camera fitted with audio sound would in fact work and not be discovered, however if discovered, he would no doubt be arrested and jailed, so he prayed that it would not be discovered.

Making a show of it, he personally swept the ceiling area around all the air vents with a high tech detector with a hidden activation switch in full view of all the Chinese and Russian security personnel.

He carefully meandered his way around the room sweeping each air vent mere minutes before the meeting between Pushkin and Xiu Jaoping was due to begin.

As he approached the air vent where the hidden camera was positioned, he positioned his body facing away from both groups of security agents blocking their view of his hands and deactivated the remote.

Keeping his eyes fixed on the ceiling, both groups of security agents seemed to follow his gaze towards the ceiling following the detector as it swept over the last air vent.

Victor reactivated the remote once he was clear of the vent.

He needed to be ultra-cautious not to be caught.

Notwithstanding the fact that the remote was not likely to beep anywhere near the camera until the camera was switched on, he simply could not risk anything going wrong.

There was too much at stake.

Victor was able to activate the camera from the remote in his pocket when both leaders were seated.

He had hidden the recording device in his room that would capture the footage and audio on a USB stick which he would later pass onto the CIA.

Having been privy to numerous meetings that Pushkin attended and to secret information discussed at these meetings, Victor was now deeply concerned that his boss Pushkin and Xiu Jaoping were about to start a nuclear war and his dream of living a life of freedom was slipping away.

He always harboured the belief of living in a peaceful world.

Chapter 13

Monte Carlo

Monaco

Jon stared at the plaque on the embassy wall.

It read-"Liberty is Freedom-Ability to do as one pleases," inscribed on it.

Yeah right, he thought to himself as the door swung open with Stan and Capitaine Petit entering, offering their hands in the usual greeting as they approached.

'Hello Jon,' said Stan taking his hand in a firm grip.

'Hi Stan,' replied Jon.

'Monsieur Jones, bonjour,' hello Mr. Jones, said Capitaine Petit.

'Good to see you again,' said Bastienne.

'Bonjour Capitaine,' replied Jon.

Best remember my assumed name he reminded himself yet again.

Stan pointed to seats around the table as he made his way towards the head of the table.

'Well, we have information on an ISIS fighter that we have been trying to find for a number of years,' said Stan.

'Recently some information on the whereabouts of Daler Yasim came to light when our intelligence sources intercepted a communication between a Saudi businessman by the name of Rahul Hadad and Mr. Yasim,' stated Stan.

'From what we have been able to find out about Mr. Hadad, is that he has a very successful construction business based in Riyadh and has been financing terrorism for some time,' continued Stan.

'He, like many other wealthy Saudi's, hate American's and our allies and harbors the belief that Islam should rid itself of westernised Christianity and punish us for occupying their holy land,' said Stan.

'Daler Yasim had disappeared for years and had gone to ground until this recent communication which we intercepted between himself and Mr. Hadad,' continued Stan.

'From what we have been able to glean, it appears that Mr. Hadad has a gripe with the Royal family of Monaco due to the fact that his bid to build a lucrative multibillion dollar exhibition centre in Monte Carlo was rejected,' stated Stan.

'It appears that Mr. Hadad believes that his bid was rejected because he is a Muslim,' said Stan.

'Our intelligence sources discovered that Mr. Hadad had arranged to kidnap the heir to Monaco's throne, namely Prince Jaq and use him as a pawn to get Prince Raineri to change his mind and award the lucrative contract to his company, namely the Saudi Development Corporation,' commented Stan.

'The CIA shared the information with the French Police, who in turn shared it with Prince Raineri,' said Stan.

'Prince Raineri asked the French for assistance and this is how Capitaine Petit and the CIA got involved,' continued Stan.

'I have asked Stan to second you to this mission as you are experienced with an excellent track record and that you of course, are French,' interrupted Bastienne.

'So, we believe that Yasim has recruited two other jihadists namely, Uzair Wali and Fawad Hashim and that they will enter Monaco on a private luxury yacht posing as crew members,' said Bastienne.

'Princess Charlotte has insisted on her children living a normal life as far as possible.' 'Not only do they attend a normal government school, but she also wants them to associate with commoners and has allowed her son to attend a birthday party for a school friend on Saturday,' stated Bastienne.

Bastienne reiterated, 'as stated previously, these three terrorists intend taking Prince Jaq hostage at a friend's party which he will attend and use him as a pawn to force Prince Raineri to reverse his decision and award the contract to Saudi Development Corporation.'

'Our intelligence believes that they intend using a three man party to carry out this mission by posing as delivery men at the party, then take Prince Jaq captive and make their way to the yacht and set sail immediately,' continued Bastienne.

'I have arranged for a 10 man party which includes Stan, you and myself to fly to Monte Carlo tomorrow morning and have rented two adjoining apartments at Twenty One Monte Carlo, an apartment block with views of the harbour,' said Bastienne.

'We will set up in one of the apartments that is relatively close to where the party will be held at the Casino and monitor the terrorists every move from there,' stated Bastienne.

'Our team will consist of six French Special-Force Operatives, Stan, you, a designated driver namely Pierre Du Champs who happens to be an ex rally driver and myself,' continued Bastienne.

'I have arranged for a luxury yacht to be available for our team to use as well as a high powered tender and we will position the hired yacht close to the luxury yacht that the terrorists will use,' said Bastienne.

Having discovered the plot to kidnap Prince Jaq, Bastienne had contacted the palace in Monte Carlo and was eventually patched through to Prince Raineri.

He briefed the Prince on the threat of a possible kidnapping of his son Jaq and whilst, the Prince was initially weary of Bastienne's plan to allow someone to deputise and pose as Prince Jaq, he relented after Bastienne had briefed him on the plan to capture the terrorists.

Prince Raineri was extremely concerned about the safety of all the children, particularly the young lad that was to pose as Prince Jaq's body double as well as the trauma that this young lad may experience.

'Prince Raineri had chosen not to alert his chief of police and had placed all his trust in the French authorities to deal with this threat and any future threat that the Principality may face in the future,' continued Bastienne.

The Principality of Monaco had never faced a threat in the past and the police and security establishment had been set up to deal with day to day policing matters and traffic control.

The Principality is the world's second smallest sovereign state, after the Vatican City and has a very limited military capability that depends almost entirely on France for defence.

There is no standing army and all law and order duties are the responsibility of police.

The next morning Jon reported to the embassy at 0800 hours and was ushered into the basement where a black Jeep SUV awaited his arrival.

Agent's d'Avray and Van Der Jong greeted Jon with a warm handshake as he jumped into the rear seat.

Turning to face Jon and taking his hand in a warm greeting, agent d'Avray said, 'so off to Monte Carlo on holiday today.'

'Yeah right, I wish boys,' replied Jon.

'Airport please driver, my private plane's waiting for my arrival,' continued Jon.

'Aye Aye captain,' replied agent Van Der Jong as he meandered his way out of the basement and joined the early morning traffic on their way to Paris Le Bourget airport.

As they approached the hanger, Jon noticed Stan, Bastienne and the French Special Force Operatives loading their gear into the Lear Jet.

He bid agents d'Avray and Van Der Jong farewell, jumped out of the SUV, retrieved his gear from the cargo compartment and joined Stan and Bastienne at the foot of the staircase of the Lear Jet.

Jon offered a courteous 'good morning gentlemen,' as he took Stan and Bastienne's hands.

Bastienne introduced the team to Jon and a couple of minutes later all boarded the Lear Jet with Jon making his way up the stairs at the rear.

The Co-Pilot greeted him in the usual manner as he entered the belly of the jet, 'welcome aboard, long time no see Mr. Jones,' he offered.

'Hi my friend, we meet again and this time I brought some guests along,' added Jon.

Continuing he said, 'hope you kept my plane in a pristine condition as I want to impress my friends,' he said.

'Yes sir, all in order,' replied the Co-Pilot.

The Co-Pilot retrieved the staircase and moments later they taxied towards the runway, turned onto the runway with the Pilots engaging full throttle and they were amongst the clouds a few minutes later.

Jon once again stared at the passing landscape as they climbed to altitude and he announced to all on board that he would serve the team drinks and hors de' oeuvres as they all settled in for the short haul flight of one hour and twenty minutes to Monte Carlo.

The announcement was greeted with loud cheers of anticipation that something special would be served by this self-designated flight attendant.

An hour later the Co-Pilot announced their impending arrival into

Monte Carlo startling Jon back to reality from his stupor.

Having taxied to a secluded part of the airport, the team disembarked, loaded their gear into two SUV's and departed for the apartments rented by Bastienne.

The two SUV's made their way through the usual heavy traffic of Monte Carlo and entered the basement of the apartment block, making their way to the two reserved parking spots near the elevator.

The team unloaded their gear from the SUV and rode the elevator to the top floor of the apartment complex and entered one of the apartments that had an-inter leading door.

Prince Raineri had arranged prepayment for the rented apartments and total secrecy ensuring that the team's arrival remained unnoticed as they rode the elevator to the two apartments allocated to them on the top level.

Bastienne had flown to Monte Carlo two days previously and met privately with Prince Raineri at the Palace and the Prince confirmed that he had arranged for someone to deputise as Prince Jaq's double at the party.

Having met with the parents of the youngster chosen to deputise as Prince Jaq, Prince Raineri was reminded of the remarkable resemblance the two had in common.

The youngster's father was a distant cousin to Prince Raineri.

In fact the two could almost pass as identical twins. Whilst, the parents of the youngster were initially very weary of allowing their son to be used as a double for Prince Jaq in such a dangerous operation, they relented after having heard what Bastienne had planned.

It was imperative that this type of terrorism be nipped in the bud as other terrorist organisations may also attempt to kidnap members of the Principalities Royal Family.

Jon allowed himself a quick glance at the sweeping views in front of him before joining the team and unpacked his gear.

Stan and Bastienne set up and tested their communications equipment. Satisfied that all the equipment was functioning normally, they made their way to the harbour posing as tourists seeking the luxury yacht that the terrorists intended using, eventually locating it anchored a short distance from the harbour entrance.

Using a pair of binoculars, Bastienne read out the name, 'Neptune, there you are,' he whispered.

Having identified the yacht that they had rented for the mission, Stan and Bastienne made their way towards the mooring and boarded it. Stan commented on the name as they boarded, 'Sea Hunter, that's rather appropriate,' he said as he turned to face Bastienne.

They went about checking the sea worthiness of the vessel ensuring that it had a full tank of fuel as well as the sea worthiness of the tender which was a rigid hull inflatable fast boat with twin 450R racing motors.

Bastienne had split the team into three groups of two and instructed one group to loiter around the jetties and the second team to position themselves at a coffee shop on the promenade with a view of the Neptune.

The designated driver was instructed to familiarize himself with the various roads leading to and from the Casino and the third group was to meander in and out of shops along the promenade and tail any people coming ashore from the luxury yacht.

None of the teams encountered any people coming ashore from the luxury yacht that afternoon.

Next morning Stan and two French Special Force Operative team members boarded the Sea Hunter that they had rented posing as a group of tourists and set sail, anchoring near to where the Neptune had dropped anchor.

They cast fishing lines making it look like a few rowdy mates enjoying each other company.

This gave them the opportunity to conduct video surveillance twenty four seven and record the terrorists every move on board the yacht.

Stan noted that there appeared to be seven people on board which included the three terrorists that would most likely carry out the kidnapping, a Captain, two further crew members and one other unidentified person.

Bastienne, Jon, four French Special Force Operatives and Pierre the designated driver rode the elevator to the basement and loaded their gear into the SUV, jumped in and made their way to the casino.

Bastienne had rented a delivery van for the operation and dropped Pierre off at the truck hire company en-route to the casino and had arranged for printed stickers with the wording-Monte Carlo Fresh Produce on it that could be stuck on the side of the rented delivery truck.

He had arranged for two Special Force Operatives to pose as cleaners going about the daily chores cleaning windows and mopping the floor around the entrance to the Casino.

Bastienne and Jon would pose as waiters designated specifically to the party for Prince Jaq's friend.

One Operative would pose as a chef in the kitchen busying himself with mundane chores in case the terrorists used the kitchen as an escape route into the rear laneway and one Operative posing as a concierge and position himself at the entrance to the hotel.

Bastienne wanted to be as close to the action as possible in order to ensure that the operation was a success.

No room for error.

Bastienne had covered all the exit routes and thought that the terrorists may use the kitchen or goods receiving loading dock as a possible escape route evading any possible hotel security personnel on duty in the hotel.

Bastienne's ear piece crackled to life as all operatives reported in.

Stan was the first to confirm that a tender carrying three people had departed the yacht Neptune and was heading towards the jetty.

Bastienne contacted the agent posing as a concierge and alerted him that the terrorists were on the move, then contacted Pierre the designated driver who was instructed to seek a parking for his delivery van close the good receiving door in the laneway near to the kitchens back door and refuse bins area.

He was convinced that the terrorists could possibly use that avenue as an escape route.

A short while later the guests started arriving with parents bidding their respective children farewell at the entrance and the children were then escorted to a private function room within the casino by hotel staff.

A security detail consisting of three police officers drove up to the entrance at the casino and immediately surrounded the youngster posing as Prince Jaq as he exited the limousine and made his way into the hotel.

The Special Force Operative posing as a concierge notified Bastienne that Prince Jaq had arrived and that he was being escorted to the function room.

A band was playing light music and all of Prince Jaq's mates greeted him with a handshake and hug as he entered the private function room and were totally unaware of the fact that the person posing as the Prince was in fact a double.

A short while later a delivery van pulled up at the main entrance to the hotel and two of the terrorists posing as delivery men unloaded some parcels placing them onto a trolley and wheeled them into the hotel.

The Special Force Operative posing as the concierge was notified that the delivery were surprise gifts for the host with compliments from the Palace.

The concierge went about checking the contents of parcels and put the parcels through a scanner and satisfied that the contents posed no danger, allowed the two terrorists to proceed to the function room indicating the way.

The two terrorists meandered their way through the afternoon throng of people towards the private function room and he immediately notified Bastienne that the terrorists had arrived and were making their towards the function room.

The terrorist driver then drove his delivery van towards the rear of the hotel, backed up into the laneway towards the goods receiving door, parked and waited.

Bastienne's earpiece crackled to life again as Pierre reported that a van had parked outside the goods receiving door and confirmed that he was watching the terrorist drivers every move in his side rear view mirror.

Bastienne's belief that the terrorists could possibly use this avenue to exit the complex was confirmed and he instructed Pierre to back his truck up towards the goods receiving dock and block the van's exit, thus neutralizing the possibility of an escape by the terrorists.

Pierre backed his truck into the laneway, exited the vehicle and went about unloading some cartons onto a trolley for delivery and wheeled the trolley to the goods receiving door and rang the doorbell. He waited for the good receiving person to open the door and entered.

The van that the terrorists were using was parked behind him and a quick glance confirmed that the driver had become extremely agitated.

A few minutes later Pierre emerged and stored his trolley in the rear of the delivery vehicle and as he climbed into the cab, he once again caught a glimpse of the driver in the van parked behind him in his rear side view mirror.

He pretended to go about reading his delivery manifest and could see that the driver was becoming very edgy.

The party was in full swing with the youngsters dancing to the hip hop music.

Prince Raineri had insisted that he did not want the capture of these terrorists to turn into a gun fight and stressed that he wanted the French Police and their Special Force Operatives to do everything in their power to avoid a shootout.

He also wanted to avoid any media coverage.

Walking towards the function room earlier, Jon, turned to face Bastienne and whispered, 'you know that you cannot arrest and charge these people because it will cause a diplomatic row and the Saudi's will demand their release,' he said.

Continuing Jon said, 'in fact they will most likely impose an oil embargo on France and Monte Carlo that will have a devastating effect.'

Bastienne merely nodded, then added, 'yes I know.' 'Don't worry I have a solution.'

Bastienne and Jon had positioned themselves on the inside of the swing doors in the function room ensuring that they would not be seen as the terrorists opened the door and entered.

A short while later the two terrorists opened the door and entered the function room pushing the trolley.

Bastienne and Jon immediately fell in behind them as they started towards the centre of the room where the young lad posing as Prince Jaq was positioned.

Bastienne and Jon both jabbed their Glocks fitted with silencers firmly against the sacrum at the lower base of both terrorist's backs and ordered them to turn around and make their way back to the door.

Jon leaned forward and whispered into Daler Yasim's ear, 'if you make one wrong move, Mr. Yasim, I will kill you, you piece of shit.'

Bastienne then instructed both terrorists to make their way out of the function room and indicated towards a passage leading away from the function room.

As they rounded the passage corner and out of sight of any prying eyes he ordered them to lie face down on the carpet and Jon frisked them for any hidden weapons and disarmed them.

Jon cuffed both terrorists with Flex cuffs and bound their mouths with duct tape, then pulled them to their feet and instructed both terrorists to make their way along the passage towards the goods receiving dock.

Bastienne ordered Pierre to arrest and detain the terrorist driver, cuff and gag him and load him into the rear of his own delivery van.

Pierre exited his delivery van and approached the terrorist driver with his manifest in hand asking for instructions to get to a certain suburb of Monte Carlo and as the driver looked at the manifest, Pierre pointed a Glock to his temple and ordered him out of the van.

He cuffed the driver with Flex cuffs and gagged him with duct tape.

He then frisked and disarmed him and bound his feet with duct tape, picked him up and loaded him into the rear of his own delivery van.

Jon and Bastienne directed the two cuffed terrorists towards the goods receiving door and exited, then bound their feet with duct tape and hoisted then into the rear of the delivery van alongside the terrorist driver.

Bastienne ordered all Operatives to the laneway and they joined Jon in the back of the delivery van taking up positions near the rear doors with guns pointed in the direction of the three terrorists.

Bastienne jumped into the passenger's seat and Pierre pointed the van into the daily traffic heading in a north easterly direction towards a remote site away from the hustle and bustle of Monte Carlo.

The youngsters were bopping to the beat of the music and were completely unaware of what had just transpired.

Stan and the two Special Force Operatives donned their wet suits, goggles and scuba gear, slid off the port side of the Sea Hunter and swam underwater towards the Neptune that was anchored some three hundred yards away.

As they approached the Neptune, both Operatives removed their scuba tanks and passed them to Stan and slipped gently aboard the yacht ensuring that there was minimum rocking of the yacht as they boarded.

This ensured that anybody on board would not be alerted to any sudden movement of the boat.

Both Operatives with goggles on and holding their guns fitted with silencers made their way into the main cabin and rounded up the three people on the lower deck, cuffed and bound them with duct tape around their mouths, then instructed them to lie face down on the floor.

One Special Force Operative then bound their feet with duct tape.

Having seen that the three people on board were now securely tied up, Stan cautiously lofted the two scuba tanks onto the swim platform rear deck, removed his own tank and placed it on the rear platform and climbed gently aboard.

Stan put the barrel of his Glock against the Captain's head and asked him where the fourth person was.

Wide eyed and very scared the Captain indicated with his head that the fourth person was in the master cabin.

Stan silently made his way to towards the master cabin, pushed the door slightly ajar to ensure that the coast was clear and entered.

He could hear the running water of the shower and made his way towards the side of the cabin ensuring that he remained hidden and waited patiently until the person had finished showering.

A couple of minutes later the person showering turned the taps off and as he opened the shower door feeling for a towel he glimpsed the vision of a man in a wet suit with goggles on and a gun pointed directly at him.

'Mr. Hadad I take it?' stated Stan.

No response from the naked man staring rigidly at Stan who instructed him to dry himself and wrap the towel around his waist and with his Glock positioned firmly against the back of his head pushed him in the direction of the main cabin.

Entering the main cabin Mr. Hadad was astounded to find all three crew members lying face down, gagged and cuffed on the floor.

One Special Force Operative cuffed him, bound duct tape around his mouth and feet then placed him alongside the other crew members lying face down on the floor.

Stan double checked that all four were securely cuffed with the Flex cuffs, then made his way to the rear platform, donned his scuba tank and slipped back into the water.

He swam back to the Sea Hunter and once aboard signalled with a flashlight for Special Force Operative to start the Neptune's motor and set sail on a southerly course towards the horizon.

He fired up the motor of the Sea Hunter that they had hired and set sail at a forty five degree angle away from where the Neptune was sailing and followed the coast line towards the east finally anchoring offshore at the designated spot and waited patiently as the sky slowly changed to from a crimson reddish orange to purple marking the coming night.

The Neptune sailed for three hours and was well out to sea with no view of the landscape of Monte Carlo before the Special Force Operative killed the motor allowing the yacht to drift on the current.

Around twenty one hundred hours Stan noticed two flashes of light from a torch and boarded the tender, ensuring that nobody was walking on the beach, he headed towards the shore.

Bastienne, Jon and the four Operatives dragged the three terrorists towards the tender, lifted them on board and jumped in. Stan immediately pointed the tender in the direction of the Sea Hunter and minutes later all were on board.

They hoisted the tender into position on the rear platform and secured it, then Stan raised the anchor plotting a course towards the Neptune and set sail.

'Nobody knows that we have captured this lot so I think we need to get rid of them,' said Jon turning to face Bastienne.

'You think just like me Monsieur Jon.' 'You must come and work for us my friend,' said Bastienne.

'Some day maybe,' replied Jon, his mind wandering back to the gorgeous Luitenant Johnston.

Around midnight Stan could see the navigation lights of the Neptune drifting in the open ocean and pointed the Sea Hunter towards it.

He slowly pulled up alongside the Neptune an hour later and tied up alongside.

Bastienne, Jon and the four Operatives then picked up the terrorists involved in the attempted kidnapping of Prince Jaq and transferred them one by one to the Neptune and jumped on board.

Bastienne ordered all the Special Force Operatives to leave the Neptune and make their way back to the Sea Hunter, ordering them into the engine room and to remain there until further instructed.

Jon attached weights to the feet of all of the captives who were wide eyed and mumbling as best they could pleading for mercy.

Bastienne and Jon removed all their valuables, wallets, keys and any identification papers in their possession.

'Don't want any of the team to witness what we are about to do,' said Bastienne.

'No need to jail these pieces of shit, just need to get rid of them,' continued Bastien.

Ignoring their pleas, Bastienne and Jon then dragged each terrorist and the crew to the port side of the Neptune and threw them overboard.

He and Jon set the table for dinner displaying seven plates, knives and forks.

Anybody eventually finding the drifting yacht would assume that the guests had taken a dip in the ocean and that the yacht had drifted away from them on the changing tide and that they were unable to get back.

Bastienne then fixed a course for the Neptune towards Algeria and set it on autopilot at eight knots.

He and Jon jumped into the water and swam to the Sea Hunter.

Stan, watched as the Neptune sailed towards the African coast, turned to Bastienne and said, 'thanks for not making me a part of the final solution, which therefore exonerates me from any future prosecution.'

Bastienne ordered all the Special Force Operatives onto the main deck and turned to face them he simply said, 'good riddens.'

Continuing he said, 'we have enough terrorists in our prisons that get preferential treatment, best food and accommodation at the tax payer's expense.'

Looking at all present, Bastienne said, 'cela n'est jamais arrivé,' this never happened.

Continuing he said, 'comprenez vou?' Do you understand?

'Do I have each and everyone's word that you will never discuss this with anybody ever again?' questioned Bastienne.

All nodded in agreement and shook his hand.

The Sea Hunter set sail towards Monte Carlo with three Operatives taking the first three hour watch whilst the others all found a spot to bed down and get some rest.

The second shift took over at zero three hundred hours.

Around zero five hundred hours the Sea Hunter made its way into port and berthed at the reserved jetty. The crew packed up their gear disembarked, rendezvoused with the Pierre and made their way back to the rented apartment.

Bastienne called the Palace and arranged to meet with Prince Raineri later that afternoon and the Palace confirmed an appointment with Prince Raineri at seventeen hundred hours.

'So Bastienne, your mission was successful I see,' said Price Raineri.

Bowing his head in respect, Bastienne replied, 'Yes Your Serene Highness, I am pleased to confirm that the mission was successful and that the youngster posing as Prince Jaq, all the children and the staff of the Casino had no idea of what had happened.'

'I am interested to know what you did with the terrorist's?' inquired Prince Raineri.

'Well, Your Serene Highness, with respect Sir, I think it's best that you do not know, thus you can never be implicated or questioned in the future,' said Bastienne.

'I see,' replied Prince Raineri nodding.

'I am particularly pleased that there wasn't a need to have an old fashion western style gun fight and that you managed to ensure that not only did the staff of the hotel, but also the general public or the media even get an inkling of what took place,' said Prince Raineri

'Princess Charlotte and I are most grateful,' said Prince Raineri.

'Please pass on my sincere thanks and congratulations to your team for an excellent job,' continued Prince Raineri.

As the Prince rose to bid Bastienne farewell, he took his hand in a firm grip and once again thanked him personally on behalf of himself, Princess Charlotte and the family of the youngster's parents that allowed their son to deputise for Prince Jaq.

They are most grateful that their son came out of the experience unscathed.

Early the next morning the team packed their gear into the two SUV'S and made their way to Monte Carlo airport and boarded the Lear jet and flew back to Paris.

Staring at the passing landscape below, Jon's thoughts drifted back to the operation and he pondered about the Captain and the two crew members of the Neptune.

He came to the conclusion that whilst they may have simply been hired as a charter and not involved in the actual kidnapping plot, he was convinced that they would have become involved whether they liked it or not.

That convinced him that they were collateral damage and that Bastienne could simply not allow them to go free as they would have exposed the entire operation.

Yes, he thought to himself, wrong place, wrong time, you suffer the consequences.

Chapter 14

War Games

South China Sea

Sitting at his desk, the President swivelled in his chair to face the large south facing Oval Office window and staring at the gardens he thought to himself, this is one massive gamble.

President Trent felt himself physically age and wondered what past President Kennedy must have felt like during the Cuban missile crisis.

Have to admit that it is one option worth taking the risk on as the stakes here are far too horrific to even contemplate he thought to himself.

Vice President Miles Tippence, Secretary of State Neville Pompello, National Security Advisor Michael O'Rourke and the Joint Chiefs of staff were all seated and stood as President Trent and Barnaby entered the situation room two days later.

'Good morning gentlemen, please be seated,' said the President.

'You all know Barnaby Heathcott the Director of the CIA?' he asked as he made his way to his seat at the head of the table.

'Barnaby offered a courteous, 'good morning gentlemen,' and took his seat next to the President.

'First and foremost, I would like to stress the need for absolute confidentiality in this meeting,' confirmed the President.

'I have total trust in each and every one of you to abide by the confidence I have in you and not to discuss anything you learn from today's meeting with anybody, including all the people around this table, senior staff in your respective offices, any family members, friends or mistresses you may possibly have secretly hidden somewhere,' said the President.

General Melvin Mitchfield, the Chairman of the Joint Chiefs of Staff offered a sheepish glance towards Barnaby Heathcott the Director of the CIA, as it was well known to Barnaby that he was having an affair with this assistant.

A feint smile creased Barnaby's face as his eyes met General Mitchfield's, confirming his knowledge of the affair.

Turning towards Barnaby the President said, 'right gentlemen this is what we have,' and nodded to Barnaby to insert the USB into the monitor and roll the footage.

The screen lit up with images of Pushkin and Xiu Jaoping settling into their seats with their respective entourages beside them.

They watched the footage in silence. After the footage had concluded and Barnaby had switched the television off and the lights back on, all were shocked by what had just transpired.

The President addressed the room.

'As you have just seen, we have a major problem' stated the President emphatically.

'Time is not on our side,' continued the President.

'Your opinion please General,' said the President turning to look at General Mitchfield.

'Well Mr. President, we have the ability to destroy any nukes launched against us or any of our allies, thanks to President Reagan,' confirmed the General.

'We have constantly updated and modified our satellite capabilities and may I add that we have successfully tested their capabilities over past decades,' stated General Mitchfield.

'So I believe that we can destroy any intercontinental missiles carrying nukes launched against us or any of our allies,' continued the General.

'The trajectory of an ICBM is that it would travel outside of the earth's atmosphere and the effect of destroying a nuclear missile in space, is that there would be no mushroom cloud visible nor any blast wave,' said the General.

'We conducted a series of tests code named Project Fishbowl and part of the project included a project called Starfish Prime in 1962, when we detonated a 1.4 megaton nuclear bomb approximately 250 miles above the earth's surface,' continued the General.

'The results of that test in 1962, were not only an intense outpouring of heat and light but high-intensity radiation in the form of gamma rays and X-Rays as the blast interacted with the earth's magnetic field,' said the General.

'So Mr. President, destroying nukes in outer space will have a very detrimental effect on the earth, however significantly more advantageous than having a nuke explode on earth,' continued the General.

'If they in fact launched nukes, we would destroy all their satellites using lasers installed on our own satellites.' 'This was implemented by President Reagan known as Star Wars, thus neutralising all their communication systems, effectively totally blinding them,' explained the General.

'We had best ensure that any nukes they launch do not make it past their borders and that we do everything in our power to ensure that this never happens Mr. President,' said General Mitchfield.

Total silence fell over the room with all present staring resolutely ahead considering the consequences of this type of action.

'Imagine if we destroyed multiple nukes in space,' said the General.

'God knows what the consequences of that would be,' continued the General.

'Possible black out of the sun which would have a drastic effect of life on earth leading to starvation within weeks of an event such as that,' stated the General emphatically.

'Of course a ballistic missile is a completely different matter entirely as it travels within the earth's atmosphere, however these are short range and our most recent intelligence has confirmed that the North Koreans have developed ballistic missiles with capabilities of reaching our shores,' stated the General.

'They can launch these type of missiles at sea as they now have the naval capacity to do that,' said the General.

'But Pushkin and Xiu Jaoping may in fact offer the North Koreans assistance, so we would need to be on our toes to avoid that possibility,' stated the General.

The room fell silent once more as the men around the table took time to process the information.

The Secretary of State spoke next.

'Well Mr. President, we had best ensure that this does not occur, because God forbid, if one or more of those nukes make their way onto the earth's surface, no matter where it lands, it will have a devastating effect on humanity,' said the Secretary of State.

'If we launch a retaliatory strike, that will be the start of a nuclear war and the end of the world,' continued Neville Pompello.

All looked at the President to take the lead.

'Anybody else have any suggestions?' asked the President.

'Can the CIA play a part in de-escalating this or even take steps to eliminate any possibility of this occurring at all?' asked Michael O'Rourke, the National Security Advisor, turning to face Barnaby Heathcott.

'I can assure you that Director Heathcott will examine every possible way to help avoid this,' said the President.

'I believe that we should immediately prepare for massive military exercises in South Korea, Japan and the Philippines including our NATO allies in these war games,' said General Mitchfield.

'We have been planning a massive military exercise scheduled for a year from now, so I suggest that we fast track this to take place with immediate effect,' stated the General

'Yes I agree,' responded the President.

'Gentlemen, as you all understand, this is highly classified and I again stress that there is to be no interaction with each other around this table, nor with your staff and advisors, family or friends or anybody else,' continued the President.

'Act normally and keep this to yourselves,' stressed the President.

'If we have a leak on this, from anybody in this room, I will not only fire you, I will have you jailed for life,' stated the President emphatically.

'I want your personal guarantee starting with you Miles,' who verbally gave his personal assurance.

The President looking each person in the eye went around the table and everybody present verbally gave their personal assurance of complete confidentiality.

'OK gentlemen, I have your word so let's wrap up the meeting and we will reconvene a week from today at 2.00 p.m.' said the President.

'In the meantime, start preparing for the war games General,' said the President looking at General Mitchfield.

The President stood and all stood in respect as he departed the room. On his way out he asked Barnaby to follow him.

The remaining people sat back down in total silence and simply stared ahead and at each other in silence for some time, before getting up and leaving the situation room.

Entering the Oval Office, the President turned to face Barnaby and said, 'this has dire consequences for the world Barnaby.'

'I need you and your team to somehow find an alternative,' stated the President emphatically.

A week later Barnaby met with the President an hour before the meeting was scheduled to begin with the President offering Barnaby a cup of coffee.

'I hope you have conjured up some sort of an ironclad plan to sort this mess out Barnaby?' asked the President.

'Yes Mr. President, I am convinced that the plan I have in mind will work and lead to a de-escalation of the crisis at hand,' said Barnaby.

'Right Barnaby, give it to me chapter and verse then,' said the President.

'I can't divulge what I have in mind Mr. President, as knowledge of this will implicate you and your administration and lead to your impeachment and worldwide condemnation,' explained Barnaby.

'Dammit Barnaby, I cannot be kept in the dark on this as there is way too much at stake here,' said the President with a raised voice.

'Sorry sir, but this way you can deny any knowledge or involvement in what is being planned Mr. President,' continued Barnaby.

'I simply cannot divulge this plan to you Mr. President and I am asking you to trust that I will deliver a favourable outcome,' said Barnaby.

'Continue with your scheduled meeting with Kim Jang-un in a couple of weeks time and leave the rest up to me sir,' Barnaby went on.

'This is risky and you want me to trust that you will be able to successfully carry out whatever it is that you are planning in complete secrecy?' questioned the President.

'That's correct Mr. President,' replied Barnaby.

The President entered the room at precisely 2.00 p.m.

'Good afternoon gentlemen, please be seated,' said the President.

'Right, does anybody have a recommended solution to this problem?' asked the President.

The Secretary of State replied. 'I think that you and I should confront Pushkin and Xiu Jaoping as matter of urgency and lay it squarely on the table Mr. President.'

The President pursed his lips in anger at what Ivan and the Chinks were planning.

Looking at the General, the President asked, 'what's your take General?'

'We should immediately arrange for the war games with South Korea, Japan, India, Philippines and Taiwan to take place supported by NATO,' stated General Mitchfield.

'This will need to occur within the next few weeks in the South and East China seas, starting with a massive naval display and a huge contingent of ground and air forces to be deployed in South Korea, Japan and the Philippines,' said the General.

'We will move a number of squadrons into the area and they will be involved in various air to air combat missions as well as supporting ground forces,' continued the General.

'I know that this is short notice, however I believe that it has a two-fold message for the Russians and Chinese,' stated the General.

'Firstly we can test our war footing readiness at a moment's notice giving the Russians and Chinese a very clear message of our readiness and secondly we will have mustered a huge force close to the Russian, Chinese and North Korea borders sending them a distinct message,' said the General.

'I am due to meet with Kim Jang-un in a week and I intend keeping that meeting in Hanoi and will not let on that we have any inclination of what Ivan and the Chinks are planning,' said the President.

'Any suggestions Barnaby?' asked the President.

'No Mr. President, I think that we need to wait and see what the outcome of your meeting with Kim Jang-un yields and I have to agree with the Secretary of State's suggestion, that you should possibly consider confronting Pushkin and Xiu Jaoping,' said Barnaby.

'I am also in favour of the proposal by General Mitchfield to conduct a war games exercise in the South and East China seas within the next month,' continued Barnaby.

Nodding, the President looked at Barnaby full well knowing that he had conjured up an alternative plan.

'Is there anything that you would like to add Mike? Questioned the President.

'We need to fully brief our allies and be prepared for a possible war with Russia and China Mr. President,' said Michael O'Rourke the National

Security Advisor.

'Things are scary and can get ugly very quickly indeed and possibly the end of life on earth may be closer than we think,' said Michael.

'Gentlemen, let's put the General's proposal into play and arrange a massive war games theatre with our allies in the South and East China Sea, with assets in the air, on land and in the sea in South Korea, Japan and the Philippines,' said the President.

'I have scheduled a video conference with allied world leaders for later this evening and will brief them on the serious scenario facing us at the moment,' stated the President.

'Thank you gentlemen, I again stress the importance of complete confidentiality in this matter,' said the President.

'As they say in German, ruhig,' quiet, reiterated the President.

'I will convene another meeting in the near future to update you of all developments and General can you speak with all your allied commanders right after I have spoken to all their leaders later this evening,' said the President rising from his seat.

Later that evening the President had a scheduled video conference with various world leaders.

All world leaders had been briefed by the various USA ambassadors in each country.

Each world leader was notified of the need for absolute confidentiality and that President Trent would meet with them on a secure video conference later that evening.

World leaders were expressly told that they were to be the only members of their respective governments that were to be present.

As the President convened the video conference with all the world leaders present, one by one the various world leaders responded to President Trent's cordial greeting with courteous responses.

President Trent had chosen a select group of world leaders namely the G7 consisting of the Canada, France, Germany, Italy, Japan and the UK, however included Australia, South Korea, Taiwan and the Philippines.

'Good evening Chancellor Mohr and gentlemen,' offered the President.

'As stated by our ambassadors, this meeting is highly classified and anything said here this evening, must be kept totally confidential,' said the President.

'I have decided to only disclose what I am about to tell you at this time due to the classified nature of what I am about to say,' stated the President.

'It has come to our attention that Pushkin and Xiu Jaoping met secretly on the Russian/China border city of Blagoveshchensk in Russia recently,' continued President Trent.

'We have it on good authority that the Russians and Chinese are planning a possible tactical nuclear strike on the US as well as certain other targets around the globe,' stated the President.

Pausing for impact, he continued, 'they intend using North Korea as a pawn in this and launching ICBM's or Ballistic nuclear missiles from there,' said the President.

All the leaders were deadly silent.

'How creditable is your intelligence Mr. President,' enquired Borden Jacobson the Prime Minister of the UK?

'It is rock solid,' confirmed President Trent.

'As you know, I have an up and coming meeting with Kim Jang-un in a weeks-time and I intend keeping that meeting on schedule,' said President Trent.

'I will not in any way let it be known that we know what the Russians and Chinese are up to,' continued the President.

'So this is what I am proposing,' said the President.

'We all commit to war games in the South and East China seas, within the next month and yes I know that this is extremely short notice but it will be a good dress rehearsal to test our preparedness for any threat that we may face in the future,' continued President Trent.

'I suggest that we have huge land based forces stationed in South Korea, Japan, Taiwan and the Philippines conducting these war games which will give the Russians, Chinese and North Koreans a very clear message,' continued the President.

'This threat has come about because of the measures we have all taken to move manufacturing away from China that has had a disastrous effect on their economy as well as the sanctions we all have imposed on Russia,' stated President Trent.

'They believe that our economies are in such disarray from the effects of the COVID 19 virus that has swept the world which offers them an opportunity to strike,' stated President Trent.

'I reiterate that our intelligence has it on record that they are planning a nuclear strike on the USA and some possible other strategic locations around the world,' said President Trent emphatically.

'Using North Korea as a pawn in this, they believe that any response coming from us in the USA against North Korea will not have a detrimental effect on them as any nuclear radiation will waft over South Korea, Japan and towards Australia and the USA, thus minimising any serious effect on both China and Russia,' continued the President.

'Ladies and gentlemen, we all know what a nuclear strike means to the world at large,' said President Trent.

'Clearly the USA will retaliate and we all know the consequences of that escalating into an all-out nuclear war, which will lead to annihilation of all human, animal and plant life on earth,' said President Trent candidly.

'I understand that I am asking you to participate in these war games at very short notice, however it has a double edged advantage for all of us,' continued the President.

'Again, it will test our ability to respond to a world crisis in record time and mobilise our troops immediately and secondly it will give both Pushkin and Xiu Jaoping a very clear message not to even consider doing what they are planning,' reiterated President Trent.

'As you are aware, we all have committed to military exercises a year from now, however I am suggesting that we bring forward those exercises to take place within a month,' stated President Trent.

'I am suggesting that the heads of the military in each country form a joint command centre to coordinate and plan the execution of the war games as a matter of urgency within the next day or two,' said the President.

'I will instruct our Joint Chief of Staff General Mitchfield to take the lead on this and to coordinate the Joint Chiefs of Staff of all our countries and get these war games started ASAP,' stated President Trent.

'I will order our sixth fleet to sail for the South and East China seas within a week from today and will order two other Battle Group fleets to join them within the next month,' continued President Trent.

There was an eerie silence from all leaders present, until finally Borden Jacobson the Prime Minister of the UK stated.

'What guarantee can you give us that this is not another Iraq fiasco Mr. President?' questioned Prime Minister Jacobson.

'With respect Mr. President, if what you are saying is true this could mean the end of humanity so you and your Secretary of State need to do whatever it takes to avoid this catastrophe and I am available to offer any support you may need,' pressed Prime Minister Jacobson.

'Thanks Borden.' 'I have tried to contact Pushkin on a few occasions to set up an urgent meeting, however he has not taken my calls nor has he attempted to return them, thus clearly he believes that his option to launch an attack is his best strategy,' said President Trent.

Continuing, President Trent said, 'we all know that there is civil unrest and anarchy in Russia and he has resorted to draconian measures to deal with that.'

'Monsieur Président, with respect sir, we in France are very suspicious of intelligence you may have because this is now a matter of life and death and we really cannot afford another Iraq, Syria or Afghanistan scenario,' said the French President Emile Macon.

'I have personally viewed the intelligence and I can assure you that it's authentic and credible,' said President Trent.

'Mr. Präsident, we in Germany are also very sceptical of your intelligence services,' stated the German Chancellor.

'I would like to reiterate our stance, which is that we share President Macon's concern and would like to view the intelligence you have on this threat,' said the Chancellor of Germany Amelia Mohr.

'I can assure you all that this is a very real credible threat as I have been personally been shown the evidence and simply cannot share this sensitive information with you as it will compromise certain informants,' reiterated the President Trent.

'I am again asking that you confine this matter to your own security advisors and military chiefs in the strictest confidence only and we cannot let this become public knowledge as that would cause mass panic,' stressed President Trent.

'So I reiterate that this needs to be classified and confidential,' continued the President Trent.

'I understand that the media will be all over this when we start mobilizing our forces and I am positive that they will be highly suspicious of any military activity that will take place, so once again, I would like to stress the importance of secrecy in the way you deal with the press,' stressed President Trent.

'I hope that the war games will give the Russians and Chinese a very clear message that they should abandon their idiotic idea,' emphasised President Trent.

'Well Mr. President, we clearly only have one choice, which is to support you as the alternative is unimaginable, so I am committing to these war games and I will immediately meet with our military chief and instruct him to cooperate fully with General Mitchfield,' said Prime Minister Jacobson.

Immediately all leaders followed that lead and committed to participate in the war games exercise.

'Time is of the essence friends,' reiterated President Trent.

'I fully understand that putting our military on a war footing albeit under the disguise of war games exercises, will result in mass panic worldwide, so we need to negate speculation that an attack by the allies on Russia and China is imminent,' stressed President Trent.

Repeating his earlier comment, President Trent said, 'I can assure you that this is a very real threat as I have personally been shown the evidence and I am again asking that you confine this matter to your military chiefs and security advisors only,' reiterated President Trent.

'I understand that the media will be all over this when we start mobilizing our forces and I am positive that they will be highly suspicious of any military activity that will take place, so once again, I would like to stress the importance of secrecy in the way you deal with the press,' repeated President Trent.

'Thank you all for your participation and we should convene again the day after tomorrow at the same time at which time, I hope that your military chiefs will have met with General Mitchfield,' said President Trent.

'We urgently need to deploy our forces to the area with a huge contingent of ground forces, a naval armada and air forces to the South and East China seas,' said President Trent as he bid all leaders farewell.

All leaders met with their respective security advisors and military chiefs the next morning informing them of a mass mobilisation of ground, air and naval forces to conduct warfare games in the South and East China Sea.

They stressed the need to be ready for deployment within two weeks and reiterated that this is merely a military exercise that will take place within a month and is in no way a preparation for war.

Chinese whispers made its way to the media who reported the massive world war games exercise to take place in the South and East China seas and on land in South Korea, Taiwan, Japan and the Philippines.

Confirmation of the authenticity of the planned war games was born out by massive military activity in the participating countries.

The following day, General Mitchfield contacted all the military commanders of each of the countries on a secure video stream and laid out the plans for the mass mobilisation of troops, massive air force display of supremacy and a naval armada showcasing their military might.

Having planned a similar military exercise for a year hence, General Mitchfield sought each commanders input into the revised plan and timetable.

All the commanders had almost finalised their plans for the planned war games exercise that was to have been conducted a year later, thus were very well advanced in their organisational planning and now simply had to implement it within a month rather than a year in advance.

'Gentlemen, thank you for your time,' stated General Mitchfield as he started the secure video conference.

'Our leaders have really thrown a spanner in the works, however as we now all understand the serious nature of the decision they took, it is appropriate that we all proceed with this as if it was the real thing,' continued General Mitchfield.

'I would like to reiterate what President Trent stated to your leaders, that this is merely a military exercise and not a preparation for war and for all of us to confine this to our most trusted military commanders,' said General Mitchfield.

Chapter 15

Red Dragon Hotel

Hanoi

Rafael found himself back in Barnaby Heathcott's office at Langley.
'Hello Rafa,' said Barnaby.

'Bonjour Director,' replied Rafael.

'Hope you had a good trip young man?' inquired Barnaby.

'Thank you sir, I did,' replied Rafael.

'What I am about to tell you is highly classified so I am taking you into my confidence and trust that you will not let me down,' stated Barnaby.

'You cannot speak to anybody about this at all and I stress nobody,' continued Barnaby.

'Yes sir,' replied Rafael.

'I have spoken to a friend of mine who heads up MacaBurgers and have arranged for you to do a week's intensive management training at one of their stores in Illinois,' said Barnaby.

'After you have completed the training, you will fly to Hanoi in Vietnam and report to the local MacaBurgers store based in Hang Bai Street, a few minutes from the Metropolis Hanoi Hotel and pose as the head chef sent by their head office to check on quality control,' continued Barnaby.

'You will be on duty when our President meets with Kim Jang-un, the Korean leader in two weeks,' said Barnaby.

'The USB stick you got from Victor Portnorsky in Zurich revealed the possibility of a nuclear strike from North Korea on the USA and may even include targets elsewhere around the world including France,' said Barnaby.

Rafael stared at Barnaby in silence.

Raising his eyebrows Barnaby stated, 'hence the importance of confidentiality.'

'Absolutely sir, I fully understand,' replied Rafael.

'You will take charge of the kitchen at MacaBurgers in Hanoi when you get there before the summit takes place,' said Barnaby.

'The manager at the MacaBurgers store is expecting you and fully understands the need to have the most experienced chef that has a security clearance on duty when these two leaders meet,' stated Barnaby.

'We are unsure, however believe that Kim Jang-un may order burgers for himself and his two sisters who will accompany him on this trip.'

'He simply loves the taste of MacaBurgers and you will receive a special package delivered for your attention on the morning of the meeting,' said Barnaby.

'There will be nine patties within the carton, vacuum sealed and they will be located in the middle of the large pile of patties,' continued Barnaby.

'Look for the pile of patties with the tiny black dot in the corner of the wrapping as these are the patties we want you to use for the burgers that Kim Jang-un and his sister may order,' emphasised Barnaby.

Continuing Barnaby said, 'below the wrapped patties you will find a small plastic container that will contain a special clear liquid.' 'Once you have cooked the meat patties, squirt some of the liquid onto each patty ensuring that nobody sees you doing this and that none of it finds its way onto your skin.'

'President Trent will order a salad wrap so ensure that you make his meal first or change gloves if you make his meal after having made the burgers,' said Barnaby.

'Do not touch the patties at all whist preparing them or after they have been made and clean the grill thoroughly after having prepared the meals without drawing attention to what you are doing,' said Barnaby

'Ensure that you have gloves on at all times and should Kim Jang-un not order burgers from MacaBurgers, I want you to personally destroy the patties safely without any trace,' stated Barnaby emphatically.

'The liquid that you squirt onto the patties and the patties itself will contain a poison that will kill a human within one month of consumption,' Barnaby went on.

'You will use the alias of Liam Brown for this mission,' stated Barnaby.

'Yes sir,' replied Rafael.

Here we go again Rafael thought to himself, better remember that name he reminded himself.

'You have been booked into the Red Dragon Hotel which is about a half a mile from the MacaBurgers store in the alias of Liam Brown,' said Barnaby

Placing his airline tickets and the confirmation of the hotel reservation on the conference table, Barnaby rose and took Liam's hand in a farewell greeting.

'Au Revoir, et bonne chance,' good bye and good luck Liam, said Barnaby.

Liam reported to the MacaBurgers store on Hang Bai Street in Hanoi and was warmly welcomed by the manager Duc Huang. He was escorted through the premises and introduced to the various staff members.

'I would like to start with the inspection of the toilets,' stated Liam.

'Certainly, follow me,' said Duc leading the way.

Liam thoroughly inspected the male toilet for cleanliness, neatness and sanitization and using his checklist he ticked the box next to Male Toilets.

Duc ensured that the female toilet was unoccupied and led the way with Liam following.

Again, the ladies toilets were immaculate.

Clearly Duc had ensured that both toilets had been thoroughly cleaned early in the morning and most likely had one of the staff clean them on the hour.

Rafael again ticked the relevant box.

'Now I would like to view your refuse area outside the store please,' said Liam.

'Sure, follow me,' replied Duc as he led his way through the kitchen and out of the door leading to a laneway where the refuse bins were located.

Satisfied that the large wheelie bins were clean, Liam gave it a tick on his checklist and then proceeded to inspect the dining area which again was allocated a tick of approval.

'OK Duc, let's check the storage room and fridges,' said Liam and both were immaculate so both gained his tick of approval.

'Duc, I would like to observe the food preparation procedure please,' said Liam.

'Sure this way please,' as he led the way to where the chefs were busy preparing burgers for guests.

Multiple microwaves were in action and Liam noted that all chefs were dressed in the appropriate attire with gloves, head gear and masks, ensuring that the hygienic procedures were being followed correctly.

'Thank you Duc, I am satisfied that you have an excellent, clean working environment and I cannot stress enough the importance to maintain this high standard,' said Liam.

'Keep it up my friend and head office will score you out of 100 after I get back and your store will be entered into the store of the year competition,' continued Liam.

'Thank you Liam,' replied Duc.

'I will spend tomorrow observing the chefs and I am sure that head office has notified you that I will take control of the kitchen in two days-time due to the possibility of the world leaders ordering a meal from your store,' stated Liam.

'Yes my staff and I are aware that you will be on duty, just in case we do get an order for burgers from the world leaders,' said Duc.

The next day Liam arrived before the store opened and inspected the chef's working bench area for cleanliness and observed the pre-meal process.

'Bonjour,' hello offered Liam in his French accent.

He donned his French chef's outfit consisting of a white double breasted jacket with knotted cloth buttons, chef's checkered pants with a hounds tooth pattern and a white toque blanche tall pleated cylindrical-shaped hat that had him looking every bit like an executive chef.

The attire was not consistent with chefs clothing at MacaBurger stores, however as the company Head Chef, it was appropriate that he wore the executive chef's attire and looked the part.

The staff responded with cordial and respectful greetings.

'OK, today I will observe what you are all doing and tomorrow I will run the entire kitchen,' said Liam.

'I believe that Duc has notified you of what is taking place here in Hanoi, Oui,' yes? Questioned Liam.

Assuming his duty as an executive chef from MacaBurgers head office, Liam spent the day observing activities in the kitchen offering instructions on some minor issues.

The day seemed to drag on forever as he observed the activities in the kitchen.

A day later, Liam arrived early once again and got set up for the possibility of an active day.

Shortly after his arrival a delivery arrived with various commodities including buns, meat patties, vegetables and salads in a refrigerated courier van.

Liam supervised the goods receiving process and opened the carton containing the meat patties, pretending to inspect it he noted the tiny black dot on a bundle in the middle of the carton.

He lifted the shrink wrapped patties and noticed the small plastic container hidden below.

He resealed the carton with packaging tape and notified all chefs not to touch that particular carton which he placed on the top shelf in the fridge.

The day's activities continued normally and around 12.00 noon a group of six people arrived at the store and asked to see the manager.

Liam noted the arrival of two policemen accompanied by what appeared to be secret service agents from North Korea and America and did not in any way look at them, rather kept his focus on the kitchen activities.

Duc approached Liam and notified him of the order for three triple cheese burgers with fries and a salad wrap and he went about preparing three chocolate milkshakes and a fruit juice.

Having taken a new pair of rubber gloves from the box as the policemen and agents entered the store, Liam retrieved the box containing the bundle of patties from the fridge and identified the bundle with the black dot on it and put the plastic container into his pocket then proceeded to prepare the burgers.

One North Korean and one American agent entered the kitchen and positioned themselves close to where Liam was preparing the burgers observing his every move.

The other agents and policemen positioned themselves strategically around the store.

Liam made the wrap first and then proceeded to cook the patties on the grill.

He took great care to position himself between the grill and the agents and went about squirting the liquid onto the meat patties after they had been grilled.

He finally completed the order a few minutes later placing the order into an esky that the agents had handed to Duc earlier.

Liam removed his gloves and placed the plastic container into one of the gloves and then placed that glove into the other.

Having paid Duc the required amount, the agents then made their way out of the store and into a SUV and sped off in the direction of the Metropolis Hanoi Hotel.

The arrival of the policemen and secret service agents caught the attention of the staff and many were observing their activity, which gave Liam the opportunity to quickly place the discarded gloves into a plastic bag he extracted from his pants pocket.

He then went about cleaning the working area without drawing attention to what he was doing.

Liam remained on duty for a further three hours and mid-afternoon notified Duc that he had completed his inspection and taking Duc's hand congratulated him on a very well run store.

Liam changed from his executive chef's attire back into his every day clothing.

'Duc, I think that you and your store will definitely be in the running to win the best store award,' said Liam.

'Excellent presentation, thank you and congratulations,' continued Liam.

'Head office will no doubt let you know how you fared in the competition in due course,' said Liam

Bidding everybody farewell Liam made his way to the exit and with a wave of the hand, turned and left.

Liam dropped the plastic bag containing the plastic patty wrapping, plastic container and gloves he had in his pocket into a bin as he made his way back to the Red Dragon Hotel.

He collected his suitcase from the concierge, jumped into a cab and left for the Hanoi International airport.

Back to Rafael Dujon when I get back to the States he reminded himself.

Waiting for the boarding call for his flight back to Washington Dulles International Airport, Rafael was watching the news on CNN when the anchor crossed to the reporter at the Metropolis Hanoi Hotel with footage of Kim Jang-un and his entourage enjoying lunch with President Trent.

The reporter proudly announced that Kim Jang-un and his sisters had chosen the MacaBurgers speciality of triple cheese burgers and fries for lunch with President Trent opting for a salad warp.

Images of President Trent and Kim Jang-un continued to play across the screen with the reporter hailing the summit as historic.

Rafael merely gave himself a slight nod and proceeded to board the flight.

Flight time was 20 hours and 21 minutes, so he made himself as comfortable as possible in economy class for the long flight back to the States.

As Rafael sat back in his seat and reflected on the activities of the past couple of days, his mind once again wandered back to Lieutenant Johnston.

What a stunning lady, he thought to himself.

Really wanted to hold her in my arms and put my hands on her bare backside.

Rafael enjoyed the meal and a few drinks and watched a couple of movies before falling asleep.

He was woken from a deep sleep by the overhead dinging sound of the fasten seatbelts sign as it illuminated.

The Pilot announced that they were on their final approach into Washington Dulles International airport and that he should have passengers disembarking through gate D16, thanking the passengers for choosing to fly with American Airlines.

As they taxied towards the gate, Rafael wondered what the next assignment would be and cleared customs.

As he exited the international arrivals area agent Conte fell in beside him.

'Hello Rafa,' said agent Conte.

'Oh hi Wilfred,' replied Rafael.

'Long time no see my friend,' continued Rafael.

'How can I get a cushy job like yours my friend?' asked Rafael.

'If you only knew my friend,' replied agent Conte.

They made their way out of the international arrivals hall and into the waiting SUV, with agent Marcel Rodrigues waiting patiently in the driver's seat.

'Hi Marcel,' said Rafael as he jumped into the rear passengers seat.

'I take it that we are on our way to the club?' questioned Rafael.

'Yep the boss is waiting for you my friend,' said Marcel as he merged with the traffic.

'How was Hanoi?' asked agent Conte.

'Crowded my friend,' replied Rafael.

Rafael sat back and stared at the passing scenery as they drove towards Langley and once again his thoughts drifted back to the gorgeous Lieutenant Johnston.

Can't get her out of my mind he pondered.

God how I would have loved to take her in my arms and make love to her he thought to himself.

Marcel presented his identification card to the guard in the security booth at the gate to Langley and was waiived through a short while later.

He pulled up at the entrance to the main building and both agents turned to face Rafael, bidding him farewell.

'Au Revoir, see you guys later,' said Rafael.

'Cheers,' said agent Conte.

Rafael retrieved his suitcase from the rear of the SUV and waved them farewell as he entered the main building and through the usual security procedure.

He was greeted by Miss Marple on the other side and led to Directors private elevator.

A few moments later the elevator stopped on the top floor and Miss Marple showed Rafael to the Directors door.

She announced Rafael's presence indicating the way.

'Hello Rafa,' said Barnaby rising from his desk and offering his hand in a greeting and pointed to a chair at the conference table.

'I trust that all went as planned young man?' enquired Director Heathcott.

'Yes sir, all according to plan,' replied Rafael.

'If I may ask sir, what exactly was in those patties and the plastic container?' asked Rafael.

'Well as you know we have a huge problem with the possibility of the Russians and Chinese using North Korea to launch a nuclear strike against the USA and possibly other targets such as France,' said Barnaby.

'I have taken you into my confidence and trust that you will never discuss this with anybody ever, even in retirement,' stated Barnaby looking directly at Rafa.

'Yes sir, I am aware of the threat that you mentioned before I left for Vietnam,' said Rafael.

'With the assignment successfully concluded, I can reveal that the patties contained a certain substance called Polonium and a cocktail of other deadly poisons as did the plastic vial which will kill any person that consumes it within a month or two,' said Barnaby.

'Polonium is the same poison that the Russians used to kill Alexander Litvinenko in London and mixed with the other lethal poisons in the plastic vial, ensures that it is deadly,' said Barnaby.

'Using the exact amount of this poison, will prolong a person's life for a month or two after it has been consumed and it will appear that the Russians killed Kim Jang-un and his sisters,' explained Barnaby.

'This will result in a regime change in the next month or two,' continued Barnaby.

'We can only hope that we can influence the regime change before the Russians and Chinese put their plan into action,' said Barnaby.

'Now then, I want you to fly back to Paris, take a week off, soak up some sun and visit your parents,' said Barnaby

'You need to report to Stan at the embassy a week from today at 12.00 noon,' continued Barnaby.

'You will fly back in the Gulfstream returning to Paris which is leaving in two hours from now and assume the alias of Jon Smith as you have done in the past,' stated Barnaby as he rose from the table shaking Rafael's hand in a farewell gesture.

'Congratulations on a job well done Rafa,' stated Barnaby.

'Agents Conte and Rodrigues are waiting for you and will drive you to the airport at Biglers Mill, where the Pilots are expecting your arrival,' continued Barnaby.

'Remember that silence is the order of the day Rafa,' said Barnaby.

Looking at Rafael Barnaby said, 'again, make sure that you do not speak of this again ever in your life.'

'Do you fully understand?' asked Barnaby.

'Yes sir, you have my word,' said Rafael.

'Good, because if ever it comes out, it will implicate myself, the CIA and you personally, so it's in your best interest to bury this secret forever,' emphasised Barnaby.

'Have a safe journey young man,' said Barnaby as they parted company.

Chapter 16

Acadia Saint Germaine Hotel

Paris

Rafael jumped into the rear seat of the SUV.

'Bloody hell guys, we cannot continue to meet like this,' said Rafael.

'Long time no see,' said agent Rodrigues looking at Rafael in the rear view mirror as he pointed the SUV towards the exit of the Langley complex.

'So you are going back home?' asked agent Conte.

'Oui,' yes replied Rafael.

Rafael settled comfortably into the seat for the short drive to the airport near Biglers Mill his mind drifting towards his parents and brother who he was looking forward to seeing again.

Rafael found himself staring at the oncoming traffic as they drove to the airport at Biglers Mill which passed quickly.

Exiting the vehicle, Rafael bid the two agents farewell and made his way into the hanger where the Pilots were readying the Gulfstream Aerospace G700 for take-off.

The Co-Pilot offered his usual greeting at the door.

'Hello Mr. Dujon,' he offered as Rafael entered through the door.

'Hi, we meet again,' said Rafael.

'Glad to see you have kept my plane clean,' continued Rafael.

'Yes sir.' 'Make yourself comfortable,' offered the Co-Pilot, retrieving the staircase and closing the door.

'Dinner's in the warmer whenever you feel like eating as well as some cold beers,' said the Co-Pilot turning and making his way into the cockpit.

'Thanks my friend,' responded Rafael.

Rafael stowed his belongings in the locker near the door and made his way to his usual seat on the port side.

Just as Rafael got seated the Pilots taxied towards the runway, accelerating and they were up and away a few minutes later.

Alone again and travelling in style he thought to himself.

Must be the reward for a job well done he pondered.

As they reached altitude Rafael, got up and made his way to the galley seeking a cold beer and returned to his seat, lounging back he sipped his beer all the while staring at the scenery below.

A while later Rafael returned to the galley and extracted a meal of fillet steak and vegetables from the warmer, found another cold beer and made his way back to his seat.

After dinner he put his feet up on the ottoman, took a deep breath, appreciating the need to surprise his parents and brother the next day.

He was looking forward to relaxing on the beach and with that he drifted off to sleep.

Rafael had fallen into a deep sleep and the dinging sound of the announcement by the Co-Pilot alerted Rafael to the need to buckle up for landing as the plane was on the final approach into Paris Le Bourget airport.

A short while later he felt the slight thud of the tires touching and screeching on the tarmac and watched as they taxied towards the CIA's hanger noticing the black SUV parked to the side of the hanger door waiting for him to disembark.

The Co-Pilot bid him farewell as he exited the plane.

'Au revoir Monsieur Dujon,' offered the Co-Pilot.

'See you next time,' said Rafael.

Never got to see the Pilot he reminded himself.

'Make sure you keep my plane clean,' quipped Rafael again as he disembarked from the aircraft.

'Hi guys, good to see you again,' said Rafael as he assumed his usual rear passengers seat.

'Likewise replied,' agent Richard d'Avray.

Touching the driver agent Van Der Jong's shoulder, agent d'Avray said, 'you remember Alex?'

'Yes I do, hi Alex,' said Rafael.

The agents had been instructed to drive Rafael to Charles de Gaulle airport and they made the trip in relative silence with Rafael checking his ticket.

His mind wandered back to his parents and how his family would react if they knew what he did for a living.

The driver parked the SUV at the entrance to the domestic terminal and Rafael was quickly out of the rear passenger door, collected his suitcase from the rear compartment and bid both agents farewell.

'See you boys,' he said as he departed.

Rafael made his way to the domestic check in counter and presented his booking to the lady manning the desk for the flight to Nice International airport.

The young ground attendant handed him his boarding pass and Rafael made his way to the gate and waited for the boarding call, which came some thirty minutes later.

The television in the departure lounge was playing repeat footage of the meeting between President Trent and Kim Jang-un with President Trent, praising Kim Jang-un.

The reporter stated that no agreement had been reached regarding the dismantling of nuclear arms, however President Trent stated that he was optimistic that a deal would be struck in the near future.

The footage ended with visions of Airforce One taking off from Hanoi International Airport.

Rafael boarded his flight, made his way to his window seat and settled in for the one and a half hour flight to Nice.

He was woken from his slumber by the dinging sound of the overhead fasten your seat belt sign an hour and a half later.

Rafael was quickly out of the terminal and into a cab and on his way to his parents apartment block.

His brother Pierre was manning the front desk and looked up to see Yonti entering through the front door.

'Yonti,' said Pierre smiling as he walked round from the reception desk offering his hand in a greeting.

'Quelle surprise,' what a surprise, said Pierre.

Yonti reminded himself to use his real name.

All these aliases are making me totally confused Yonti thought to himself.

Shaking Pierre's hand and giving him a hug, Yonti made his way towards the kitchen.

'Bonjour Mama,' said Yonti as he entered the kitchen.

'Oh mon,' oh my, said Yonti's mother looking up from the stove where she was busy preparing a sauce for dinner.

'Dieu, tu m'as manqué mon fils,' God I missed you my son, said his mother hugging him tightly.

'Me too mama, where's papa?' asked Yonti.

Just as he asked the question his father appeared in the kitchen doorway.

'Mon fils où étais-tu,' my son where have you been? Asked his father Marcel.

'So good to see you all,' said Yonti.

'So why have you not called?' asked his mother Brielle.

'Sorry mama and papa, I have been all over the world and you know the time zones make it difficult to be able to pick the right time to call,' said Yonti.

'Yeah droite,' yeah right, replied his father.

'Well it's terrific to see you Yonti,' said his mother.

Yonti unpacked his clothes in his room and made his way down to reception, asking his brother if he needed any help.

'Yes thank you Yonti, I have a few minor chores for you to attend to,' replied Pierre.

'Aucun problème,' no problem, replied Yonti and he went about tackling the few chores his brother had asked him to do.

It was clear that his father Marcel had handed over the responsibilities of running the business to his brother Pierre.

Yonti was pleased for his brother and to see that he seemed well entrenched in the family business, because he was not coming back to this lifestyle.

Yonti somehow felt he did not belong there anymore and made an excuse to leave a couple of days early.

He changed his flight and booked into the Acadia Saint Germaine hotel located in Rue des Saints-Pères which was near Café Floret, Stan Noble's favourite café in Paris.

Yonti bid his parents and brother farewell and caught the early morning flight to Paris a couple of days later.

Having checked into the hotel Acadia Saint Germaine and unpacked his belongings, Yonti found his way to Café Floret, ordered a Latte and was staring at the people chatting as the traffic passed noisily nearby.

The café opened in 1880 and was situated on a corner making it popular with locals and tourists alike.

A beautiful lady suddenly appeared alongside him, 'Bonjour Monsieur Yonti Barre,' she said pushing her sunglasses onto the top of her head.

Standing Yonti replied, 'Oh my Lord, hello Lieutenant Johnston, I did not recognise you out of uniform,' he said.

Looking totally bewildered, Yonti continued in his husky French accent, 'wow, you are as beautiful as a flower in full bloom.'

Blushing slightly, she assumed a seat next to Yonti.

Lieutenant Commander Johnston offered, 'please call me Claire.'

'Well what a surprise,' said Yonti.

'Fancy bumping into you here,' he continued.

'How's married life treating you?' asked Yonti.

'Well that's another story altogether really,' said Claire.

'Believe it or not, I caught my husband cheating on me during our honeymoon,' continued Claire.

'That was the end of the marriage, so I packed up and left immediately, returned to Paris, annulled the marriage and returned to my maiden name,' said Claire.

Brilliant thought Yonti to himself.

'Oh wow, what an idiot your ex-husband was to cheat on such a beautiful lady,' said Yonti.

'That calls for a celebration,' said Yonti signalling to a waiter to bring them a bottle of Dom Peignoir champagne.

Clinking glasses Yonti toasted, 'à votre santé mon beauté,' cheers my beauty, in his best French accent.

Blushing openly Claire leaned over and gave Yonti a kiss on the cheek.

'How did you know where to find me Lieutenant?' questioned Yonti.

'Well it's Lieutenant Commander now actually,' said Claire.

'Oh wow, I am so sorry I did not know,' said Yonti.

Clinking glasses, Yonti said, 'that's fantastic, congratulation on your promotion ma beauté.'

'So how did you know I would be here or is it merely a coincident?' questioned Yonti.

'I knew that you would come here if you were in Paris, so I took an off the cuff guess,' replied Claire.

Raising his glass and taking a sip of champagne, Yonti said flirtatiously, 'well to be truthful I am really pleased to see you.'

Yonti realised that Claire must have been tracking his every move since he returned to France and wondered if she had possibly been monitoring his every move since she annulled her marriage or perhaps even ever since he joined the CIA.

The CIA seems to know a person's every move he thought to himself.

Suddenly there was loud banging noise as a car careered along the sidewalk towards the corner where Yonti and Claire were seated crashing into chairs and tables as it headed directly towards them.

People were diving for cover and scurrying to get out of the way avoiding being run over.

Yonti grabbed Claire and threw her through the doorway entrance of the café, then jumped towards the curb as the car careered towards him.

Spinning around he lifted his leg and extracted the Glock from his ankle holster, aimed and took two quick shots at the driver through the side window as the car passed by.

The first shot shattered the passenger window and the second shot was aimed at the driver's right temple which found its target leaving the driver slumped forward with his head coming to rest on the steering wheel.

The car careered out of control over the road and crashed into a lamp post 30 yards from where Yonti had been standing.

In an instant, Yonti was at the driver's door and opened it confirming that the driver was deceased. He then made his way back to the café seeking Claire through the throng of people that had gathered at the entrance to the café.

People were staring at Yonti in amazement.

Yonti pulled Claire into his arms, hugging her tightly he said, 'désolé ma beauté, j'espère que je ne t'ai pas blessé.' sorry my beauty, I hope I didn't hurt you, said Yonti.

Yonti could feel Claire shaking visibly with tears running down her cheeks as she snuggled into his embrace. He hugged her tightly.

Looking towards the gathering crowd of people, Yonti thought, that was a close call.

An instant later, a gun man opened fire with an AK 47 at patrons that had gathered on the sidewalk. Yonti once again pushed Claire into the café and was back onto the sidewalk running towards the assailant with his Glock aimed directly at the armed man dressed in traditional Muslim style clothing, screaming Allah Akbar, God is great.

The assailant noticed Yonti running towards him, dodging left and right to avoid the smashed furniture on the sidewalk with blistering speed as he closed the gap like a cheetah chasing its prey, which did not give the gunman enough time to direct his weapon onto him.

Yonti aimed at his head, squeezed the trigger and popped off two quick rounds in succession on the run, killing the assailant instantly.

Yonti instantly kneeled down beside the assailant feeling for a pulse confirming that he had killed him, which was obvious as the pool of blood increased around his head on the side walk.

Standing over the dead gun man Yonti moved the AK 47 away from the body with his foot and kept his foot on the weapon whilst looking up and down the sidewalk ensuring that there were no more assailants lurking close by.

People had gathered around the injured people trying to offer any assistance possible and the wailing sound of sirens announced the arrival of the gendarmerie, the French police and ambulances.

Yonti quickly put the Glock into the back of his pants as the police approached whist keeping his foot on the AK47. The police approached with weapons drawn and aimed at directly at him.

The police soon realised that he was not a threat and secured the area.

Yonti turned and made his way back to the Café in search of Claire, who seeing him approach ran into his arms.

Now visibly shaking, tears streaming down her cheeks, her mascara smudged on her cheeks, Claire put her arms around Yonti and whispered into his ear, 'Je ne veux pas te perdre,' I do not want to lose you.

Claire went on, 'deux appels rapprochés en une journée, il faut y aller,' two close calls in one day, we have to go, she said.

Yonti and Claire made their way through the crowd of people who stared in their direction with admiration for what he had just done and made their way towards the Academic Saint Germaine Hotel where Yonti was staying.

Yonti wondered how the hell the gendarmerie and television crew got there that quickly.

As they entered the hotel foyer, the daily broadcast on the television was interrupted with the news of the attack near Café Floret and the reporter giving a detailed analysis of the tragedy that had taken place shortly before.

Waiting for the elevator, Yonti and Claire watched the reporter giving an in depth report of the incident on the television in the lounge area.

'A mad man has driven a vehicle onto the sidewalk knocking over chairs and tables with people diving for cover,' said the reporter.

'Fortunately he did not drive over or kill anybody,' continued the reporter.

'An unknown man had intervened, shooting and killing the driver of the vehicle before he was able to claim any lives,' stated the reporter.

Continuing the reporter said, 'a few moments later an assailant armed with an AK 47, shot multiple people some 30 yards from Café Floret and it appears that four people have lost their lives.'

'These two terrorist incidents appear to have been connected,' said the reporter.

'The heroic citizen that shot and killed the driver of the car and then took chase down the sidewalk killing the assailant with the assault rifle is nowhere to be seen,' said the reporter.

'A number of people have been injured and are being treated,' said the reporter.

'Many have been rushed to hospital as we report this incident,' she continued.

'I can confirm that four people have died from bullet wounds fired by the assailant with a further six people being attended to and taken to hospital with severe injuries, some believed to be life threatening,' said the reporter.

'Clearly this is a terrorist attack and we have a hero that has saved multiple lives somewhere in the crowd,' continued the reporter.

'It appears that this man is either an off duty police officer or some sort of a security agent,' said the reporter.

'We have just uncovered footage of the heroic actions of the mystery person that killed the driver and the gunman taken by one of the patrons at Café Floret which we will bring to you shortly,' continued the reporter.

'We don't know who this man is, but he is truly a national hero,' said the reporter.

'Fuck, I hope they do not have a clear picture of my face,' said Yonti.

'I have lied to my parents and brother about my job,' he continued.

'They believe that I am an investment banker based in the USA,' said Yonti.

Claire snuggled up into Yonti's arms with her head leaning on his chest as they rode the elevator in silence.

Yonti retrieved the Glock from the back of his trousers and removed the spare magazines from his pocket placing them on the side table next to the bed.

He opened the bar fridge and extracted a bottle of Chardonnay, opened it and handed a glass to Claire who was seated on the bed with her feet tucked under her buttocks.

'Je te regarde ma pétale,' here's looking at you my petal, said Yonti.

Claire took a sip, stood and put her glass of chardonnay down on the bedside table and embraced Yonti, kissing him passionately, she started unbuttoning his shirt, undoing his belt and unzipping his fly all the while holding him in a tight embrace with one hand.

Yonti undressed her, almost ripping the clothing from her body as they stood naked hugging each other in a loving embrace.

Yonti whispered in his husky French accent, 'voulez-vous faire l'amour,' do you want to make love?

'Oui, prenez-moi,' yes take me, replied Claire.

Yonti swept her off her feet and placed her gently on the bed.

Their lovemaking started gently at first, increasing in rhythm and intensity as she reached multiple orgasms.

Lust took over with no time for foreplay, which would come later, he just needed to be inside her and place his hands on her buttocks as he had dreamed of so many times before.

Having finished their love making, Yonti switched on the television and to his horror, images of himself dodging the car on the sidewalk and shooting the driver as well as killing the assailant with the AK 47 were being aired.

The images had been taken by a patron at the Café and passed onto the Television Station.

Dear Lord what are my parents going to say, Yonti thought to himself.

His mobile rang an instant later.

'Hello Rafa, is Claire with you?' asked Stan.

'Yes sir, I'll put her on,' said Yonti handing his mobile phone to Claire.

Bloody hell, I'm Rafael again he reminded himself.

'Hello Stan,' said Claire.

'God, I'm glad to hear your voice and that you are safe,' said Stan.

'Thanks,' offered Claire.

'Here's Rafa,' she said handing Yonti his mobile phone.

'Rafa, well done, that was a heroic deed young man,' said Stan.

'Sadly a few people have lost their lives, however you have saved dozens of lives,' continued Stan.

'I look forward to catching up the day after tomorrow,' said Stan.

'Au revoir, good bye,' he said and disconnected the call.

Yonti and Claire just lay there watching the reporter continue with her report of the incidents.

I am indebted to the CIA for its training which reminded him of a comment made by the Director of the CIA, Barnaby Heathcott, thought Yonti.

Barnaby had said, the training you will receive, will adequately arm you with the necessary skills to counter any threat you may encounter.

Hundreds of hours of weapons training had honed his skill to perfection, both on the run or in a stationary position.

His grouping had been immaculate in all categories which is why he did not hesitate to take the head shots.

Suddenly his mobile phone rang again.

'Oh fuck it's my father,' said Yonti.

'What they hell am I going to tell him,' he said out aloud.

Best try to deflect it as best possible he concluded.

'Bonjour Papa,' said Yonti.

'Bonjour Yonti, I have you on speaker and your mother and brother are alongside me,' said Yonti's father Marcel in an agitated voice.

'What on earth are you doing shooting and killing people my son?' asked his father.

'Don't lie to me either,' said his father emphatically.

'Papa, I cannot speak right now, but I promise I will call you later,' said Yonti.

'Au revoir papa,' good bye father and he hung up.

God I hope he won't be angry with me hanging up the way I did Yonti thought to himself.

I wonder how I should break the news to my parents and whether they will understand or even accept what I do for a living he pondered.

Yonti ordered room service meals as they wished to avoid any scrutiny and after having eaten, they made passionate love for the second time that night.

Yonti's gentle touch seemed at odds with his career as an assassin and a ruthless CIA agent. His soft nature was in contrast with what he did on a daily basis.

He was a skilled lover and using his experience quickly found her G-Spot with his tongue and using his middle finger he drove her to multiple orgasms.

She finally pushed him off and proceeded to take his penis in her mouth and orally stimulate him.

Yonti expertly positioned her on top of himself in the sixty nine position and both went about orally pleasing each other until he swung her around and moved her towards his feet inserting his penis into her vagina and let her mount him in the reverse cowgirl position with her head facing his feet.

What a beautiful body he thought to himself.

Yonti moved her into the dog style position and continued to pound her vagina in ever increasing pulsating movements.

Finally he flipped her expertly around allowing her to straddle him whist caressing her breasts and felt himself ejaculate.

She reached a final orgasm and begged him to stop.

'I'm spent,' she whispered.

Sweet Jesus, thank you for making my wish come true, Yonti thought to himself.

I have always dreamt of holding that bare arse in my hands.

I promise sweet Jesus, that I will come to church at least once a year he thought to himself and reward you for what you have done.

Satisfied that his performance was outstanding, Yonti thought to himself.

What a dangerous weapon I've got, red hot my friend!

Chapter 17

Khasan

Russia

President Trent entered the situation room and all present stood as he made his way to his seat.

'Please be seated,' said the President.

Looking at General Mitchfield, the President asked, 'so General where are we at with the war games?'

'Well Mr. President, we have started deploying troops from all of the allies you have met with and should have all our assets in place within the next two weeks,' replied the General.

'We have three naval battle strike groups sailing towards the South and East China Seas as I speak and each strike group consists of an aircraft carrier, two guided missile cruisers, two destroyers, one frigate, two submarines and a supply ship,' continued the General.

'I have ordered a further two nuclear submarines to deploy in the area and I can confirm that the United Kingdom and France have also deployed naval assets and collectively a further four nuclear submarines,' stated the General.

'In total we will have a total of twelve nuclear submarines deployed and scattered around the South and East China seas Mr. President,' replied General Mitchfield.

'We have moved three squadrons of stealth B-21 long range bombers to the area and have based a squadron in South Korea, Japan and the Philippines,' said the General

'I have assumed overall command with the full support of our allies and we will have all troops on the ground within the next week or two,' continued the General.

'Excellent General,' said the President.

'I want Pushkin and Xiu Jaoping to get a very clear message,' continued the President.

'We have noticed that the Russians and Chinese have started moving assets towards their borders with North Korea as they must fear an invasion is imminent rather than the war games we have announced,' said the General.

'I intend speaking with our other allies shortly and if the threat escalates I will put our country on a war footing, however will wait before I order a move to DEFCON 3,' said the President.

'If this threat does become a reality or if Ivan and the Chinks make any false moves, we will need to be ready,' stated the President emphatically.

'We will meet every day at 10.00 a.m. in the situation room gentlemen,' said the President.

'My meeting with Jang-un yielded nothing, however I used the opportunity to praise him in order to cast a shadow of doubt on the plans that he and his close friends have devised,' continued President Trent.

'Anybody else have anything to add?' questioned the President.

Nobody offered a comment with most having accepted that a military show of force may deter the Russians, Chinese and North Koreans from executing their plan.

Standing, the President brought the meeting to an end and asked Barnaby to follow him.

Entering the Oval office the President pointed to a seat on the couch, 'please be seated,' said the President.

'OK Barnaby, what exactly did you do in Hanoi?' asked the President.

'With respect Mr. President, I cannot disclose any details sir, because I cannot implicate you in anything we did,' replied Barnaby.

'We have been tracking the movements of Pushkin, Xiu Jaoping and Jang-un and I can confirm that these three have a meeting scheduled in two weeks-time in the city of Khasan which as you know is located near the tripoint on the Tumen River where the borders of Russia, China and North Korea converge,' said Barnaby.

'The CIA has secretly developed a high altitude stealth drone which we are busy testing at this time Mr. President,' said Barnaby.

'This drone has the ability to carry counter missile ordinance capable of destroying missiles launched by an enemy and has a ceiling height of forty thousand feet and a range of two thousand nautical miles,' continued Barnaby.

'We could deploy this in South Korea close to the border with North Korea and have it over the launch site if North Korea launches any missiles,' said Barnaby.

'We have one drone operational that has been put through extensive testing and a two under construction at this time.' 'Each drone can destroy six nukes as they are launched from the enemy's own back yard,' continued Barnaby.

'So what have your early tests revealed?' questioned the President.

'Positive results which gives us an excellent alternative option Mr. President,' said Barnaby.

'That's impressive,' stated the President.

'And you are absolutely sure of its stealth and accuracy?' questioned the President.

'Yes I am Mr. President, I have personally witnessed the drone in action and the classified nature of this means that the military does not know it exists Mr. President,' stated Barnaby.

Looking at Barnaby in amazement, the President said, 'you people at then CIA are truly secretive.'

'OK Barnaby, keep me fully up to date with everything,' said the President.

'Oh, by the way, were any of your people involved in that recent incident in Paris?' enquired the President.

'Yes Mr. President, the person that eliminated both terrorists is one of our own,' replied Barnaby.

'Please pass on my thanks and congratulation,' said the President.

'I would like to meet him some day,' offered the President.

'Will do Mr. President,' replied Barnaby.

The meeting ended with the President standing and taking Barnaby's hand.

Barnaby returned to Langley and went about analyzing the data and footage results of the recent tests of the stealth drone's performance.

Simply have to make sure that this does not fail if it's ever called into action, thought Barnaby.

Chapter 18

La Villette

Paris

The next morning Yonti and Claire rode the elevator to the ground floor in the Academic Saint Germaine Hotel and as they walked through reception towards the exit, Yonti noticed a well-dressed Arabic looking gentlemen seated facing them. He appeared to be reading a newspaper in the corner of the lounge.

Keeping his eyes fixed on the man as they walked towards the exit, Yonti noticed that he continued reading the paper as they made their way towards the exit.

The training he had received and the experience he had developed in the field had honed his sensors to be aware of his surroundings at all times.

As they exited the hotel on their way to breakfast, Yonti noticed a van parked close to the hotel's entrance.

Two men suddenly appeared behind them and one had jammed a gun into Yonti's back and the other had a hand around Claire's mouth pushing her towards the van.

As the kidnapper forced Claire towards the van, Yonti dropped his body, turned instantly in a half circle, twisted around positioning himself alongside the assailant and using his hand deflected the gun away from his back towards the hotel window.

All done with lightning speed in order to minimize the possibility of being shot.

This was a move he had learned on his way to becoming a first Dan in Martial Arts.

In the movement Yonti caught a fleeting glimpse of Claire in the hotels window whose eyes were stretched wide open with fear.

Twisting his body, he placed one leg behind the assailant and threw him to the ground all the while deflecting the gun away from both Claire and himself.

Two shots rang out hitting the window and shattering it before Yonti had wrestled the gun from the assailant and shot him twice in the head with his own gun.

Yonti noticed a movement in his peripheral vision coming from the hotels entrance and dove to his left as a shot was fired in his direction.

The assailant was the well-dressed Arabic man that was seated in the lounge reading a newspaper who then ran and jumped into the rear of the van through the open side door as the van sped off down the road.

It was then that Yonti realised that he had been hit on the top of his left shoulder next to his neck.

The bullet had missed any bones and main arteries, however damaged the thoracoacromial artery which is a branch of the axillary artery and is located at the top of the shoulder that divides into 4 branches serving the shoulder and upper chest.

The brachial artery travels down the upper arm and is a continuation of the axillary artery.

Blood oozed out of the wound.

Prompt surgical intervention would be essential to ensured that any damage would be minimal.

Another inch and it would have lodged in his neck and killed him.

Still holding the assailant's gun, he crouched on one knee, aimed at the van that was speeding down the road and was about to fire when a car screeched to a halt alongside him with the rear door open. Stan shouting for him to jump in.

Yonti jumped into the car as the van turned the corner ahead and looked at Stan.

'What the hell are you doing here?' Asked Yonti.

It was then that Yonti noticed Capitaine Bastienne Petit of the DGSE', the French equivalent of the CIA and the British MI6 in the front passengers seat.

'Hello Jon,' offered Bastienne without turning as they sped towards the corner where the van had just turned.

Dear Lord, I better remember my name is Jon he reminded himself.

The driver was an ex rally driver and floored the accelerator in pursuit of the van, beeping his horn to warn pedestrians and other vehicles to get out of the way.

Handing the assailants gun to Stan, Jon said, 'We need to get these fucking bastards.'

'They've got the love of my life in that van,' shouted Jon.

Leaning forward Stan noticed the blood stain on Jon's shirt coming from his left shoulder.

'Fuck me, you have been hit,' said Stan

Staring ahead Jon did not answer.

Jon positioned himself between the two front seats and stared ahead at the van they were following.

The driver swerved numerous times to avoid pedestrians and vehicles all the while closing the gap between the van and themselves.

Suddenly the car that they were travelling in crashed into a vehicle exiting from a parking spot and came to a screeching halt.

Jon watched in horror as the van rounded the corner ahead. He was quickly out of the car, retrieved his Glock from his ankle holster and ran down the street after the van, with people scurrying to get out of his way.

Pedestrians stared in shock at Jon as he ran bleeding down the road.

As he turned the corner he saw the van disappear around another corner and he continued running all the while praying that the van would be held up in traffic.

Sprinting in the direction that the vehicle had taken he came to the realisation that his pursuit was in vain.

Panting and out of breath he placed his hands on his knees with the Glock firmly gripped in his right hand.

With his head raised looking in the direction that the van had driven he stood upright and pushed a passing biker off his motor bike and jumped on, revving the bike he continued the pursuit of the van.

With the van now completely out of sight, Jon had no idea which possible direction it had taken and he eventually pulled up on the curb and heard the wailing sound of sirens of the gendarmerie in pursuit with the whirling sound of a helicopters blades audible in the distance.

Bleeding more profusely due to the exhaustive activity of the last few minutes, Jon felt light headed and needed to sit on the sidewalk for a moment.

A short while later Stan found him and instructed the driver to pull up alongside the sidewalk. Stan and Bastienne stood over him and helped him to his feet.

'Dammit,' shouted Jon.

'Why the fuck did this happen when I have just found the love of my life,' he screamed.

'I want to take these fucks and skin them alive,' shouted Jon.

Stan removed his shirt and tore strips off then pushed it under Jon's shirt trying to stop the flow of blood.

Leaning over him, Stan took Jon's face into his hands.

'Focus Jon,' he said.

Jon could feel himself getting dizzy from the loss of blood and as his head slumped forward Stan caught him and slapped him rather heavily on the cheek.

'Stay with me Jon and listen carefully to what I have to say,' said Stan.

'Bastienne and I have been tracking these terrorists since the incident at Café Floret yesterday as we believed that they were part of the cell that had attacked and killed the people in the street,' said Stan.

Jon's head slumped forward again and Stan propped him up lifting his head said, 'we need to get you to a hospital right away.'

This statement got Jon's attention and with his glassy eyes he tried desperately to focus on what Stan had said.

Lifting his head again Stan said, 'Jon, look at me.'

Jon, tried his best to focus and whilst most of what Stan was saying seemed muffled, he made out Stan's next few words.

'We have been tracking these bastards that's why I cut my call short when I called to check on Claire,' said Stan.

Slapping Jon hard on the cheek again Stan said, 'est-ce que tu comprends,' do you understand?

Jon merely looked at Stan with a stare of hopelessness until Stan said the following.

'Bastienne has been monitoring the activity of this cell and in particular the van used in this kidnapping today and has been tracking it since yesterday's attack at Café Floret,' continued Stan.

'We know that this van followed you and Claire to the hotel and believed that this van could possibly be used to somehow kidnap you and Claire,' said Stan.

'Bastienne and I were parked down the street monitoring the driver of the van who we believed was the remainder of the terrorist cell,' continued Stan.

'Clearly this van was to have been used as a getaway for the bastard who had shot and killed the people on the sidewalk,' continued Stan.

'Look at me, dammit Jon and listen carefully to what I have to say,' said Stan forcefully.

'We followed the terrorist in the van to the hotel and Bastienne walked towards the van after it had parked outside the hotel and stopped to piss against a lamp post in full sight of the driver in the van which caught his attention.' 'I walked around the van and attached a GPS tracker under the fender so we know exactly where that van is right now,' offered Stan.

'Est-ce que tu comprends?' do you understand? Said Stan aggressively.

'Trust me,' pleaded Stan.

This caught Jon's attention and he seemed able to focus.

'We need to get somebody to pick you up and get you to the hospital,' said Stan.

He started dialling an agent when Jon grabbed the mobile phone out of his hand.

'No,' shouted Jon, 'I must do this rescue myself,' he insisted.

Stan helped him to his feet and placed his left shoulder under his right armpit with Bastienne alongside him assisting. They made their way to the car which was badly dented from the collision with the vehicle exiting the parking spot earlier, however still able to be driven.

Stan assisted Jon into the rear passenger seat and moved Jon's shirt slightly exposing the entry wound. He went about trying to stem the flow of blood coming from Jon's shoulder.

Jon grimaced with pain, clenching his teeth he reminded himself of the need to try and stay alert.

Suddenly the other rear passenger door opened and in hopped another person pushing Stan towards the middle of the rear seat.

Jon trying his best to clear his vision made out the vivid image of his friend Joseph Diamond the Mossad agent from London.

Leaning slightly forward Jon looked at Joseph and said, 'what the fuck are you doing here?'

'Well I have been tracking this cell from London to Paris and now find myself in the good company of Stan, Bastienne and yourself,' said Joseph.

'God you Mossad guys are good,' said Jon in a rather slurred manner.

'Better believe it my friend,' said Joseph.

'Wouldn't miss the fireworks for all the tea in China,' replied Joseph.

Bastienne had his laptop open and was monitoring the location of the van on the GPS he had attached to the underside of the fender of the van.

The monitor indicated that the van was parked in La Villette, a suburb on the outskirts of Paris.

Giving the driver directions they made their way towards the location of the van and Stan accessed a satellite image of the surrounding area, giving them an excellent overview of where these terrorists were located.

The driver parked half a mile away in a secluded spot with a view of the eight storey apartment block and Stan turned to Jon offering him his hip flask.

'There Jon, here's some medicinal medicine my man,' said Stan.

Jon took a swig of whisky and felt the burning warmth enter his body. A few swigs later Jon began to feel alive again and his vision became more focused.

'Gods own water,' murmured Jon to himself.

Turning to Stan, Joseph asked, 'so who the fuck is Jon'?

'Long story,' said Stan, with Bastienne looking somewhat bewildered as well.

Bastienne called a contact who arrived shortly after in a van with a Vinola Water Company logo printed on the sides.

They transferred to the van with all the modern electronic gear and immediately got to work listening for any possible communications coming from the apartment block.

Jon point blankly refused medical attention and was determined to free Claire and had become aggressive at the mere suggestion by Stan that he and Bastienne could take care of freeing her.

'Don't fucking ask me to go to hospital again,' demanded Jon.

'Give me some more whisky,' demanded Jon.

Finding his humour returning, he said, 'makes me frisky.'

'I personally want to kill those fucking bastards,' said Jon.

'OK, we need to focus and monitor where these bastards are,' said Bastienne.

'Let's all don the bionic ear listening earphones and point your parabolic antennas at the apartments and listen for any chatter,' instructed Bastienne.

'Stan you take the top level, Joseph you take the level below that and I will take the third level from the top,' instructed Bastienne.

'Jon, if you are feeling up to it, you take the next level down from me,' continued Bastienne.

'Point the antenna in the direction of the apartments and listen for any chatter,' said Bastienne.

These antennas are sophisticated with a range of three miles and were only available to the French authorities.

All the trackers are being recorded with people interpreting everything that is picked up and said in the apartments.

Jon found it most frustrating and felt absolutely helpless, questioning Bastienne whether the GPS tracker that Stan had placed under the van's fender was in fact intact and working.

'Oui, these bastards have parked the van in the basement parking,' said Bastienne.

With his earphones attached, Stan leaned forward and lifted Jon's shirt and went about injecting him with a small dose of morphine he found in the medical kit.

Bastienne was a real professional and thought of the need to pack a medical kit in the case of an emergency.

Bastienne had been issuing orders through the communications network in the van and as Jon felt the morphine take effect, the pain dissipated a little and he took another swig of whisky.

He knew that he should not mix the scotch with the morphine, however it made him feel human again.

A few minutes later, Bastienne said that he had some chatter on his headset.

It was coming from the floor that he was monitoring. The third floor from the top and was from the apartment in the middle which had one of the curtains drawn to one side.

Everybody focused on the apartment and Stan and Bastienne trained their binoculars onto the apartment, however could barely make out some blurred movement behind the sheer curtains.

Bastienne counted the number of apartments from the right hand side, 'its three levels down and the fifth apartment from the right,' he said.

'The one with one curtain pulled halfway across the window,' reiterated Bastienne.

Bastienne's earpiece came alive and an interpreter confirmed that the voices were that of Arabic speaking people and a couple of voices were encouraging their fellow terrorist to hurry up and fuck her.

Everybody had eyes on it and Jon estimated that the large bay window was around fifty feet below the top of the building.

Bastienne continued to monitor the muffled conversation coming from the apartment and continued to bark instructions into the communication system.

It was clear that he had activated the Strike Force who had gathered in the basement of the building hidden in amongst the refuse bins away from view ensuring that they would not to alarm residents.

Jon asked for a 200 yard rope that could be used to abseil down the side of a building to be placed on the roof of the building and to his surprise Bastienne stated that this had already been done and was placed on the bottom step of the staircase.

'Bien joué,' well done, said Jon.

The driver of the van started it and drove towards the rear of the building and out of sight.

Stan looked at Jon and said, 'you are in no condition to attempt anything.'

'Says who Stan?' said Jon staring at him.

'Watch me,' said Jon as he jumped out of the van and made his way towards the staircase, picked up the rope and taking three steps at a time proceeded to climb to the top floor.

Claire had been stripped naked and was tied to the bed.

Her arms and legs spread wide and bound tightly against the four corners of the bed and her mouth taped closed with duct tape.

She stared wide eyed and petrified at the man now undressing in front of her as it was obvious that he was going to rape her, then allow his comrades in crime to do the same and then most likely kill her.

She fought to break free as he undressed at the foot of the bed while his comrades cheered him on, waiting patiently for their turn near the bay window.

Jon had reached the roof a short while later and was startled when his friend Joseph appeared alongside him out of breath.

'Jesus, you move like a leopard about to strike its prey, albeit a little out of breath,' offered Jon.

'Got to watch your back my friend,' said Joseph, gulping for air.

They quickly went about securing the rope to a pole on the roof with Jon pulling and tugging it, leaning backwards with his full weight on the rope that was looped around his body to ensure that the knot that they had tied was secure.

Will be one hell of a fall to my death if this knot comes lose thought Jon.

Jon extracted his Glock from the rear of his trousers, slightly cocked the weapon to ensure that there was a round in the chamber, doubled checked that the safety was off and returned it to the rear of his pants.

He reminded himself that he had not fired a shot earlier.

Jon quickly laid out the rope on the floor running it from the pole to the edge of the building, looped it around and ran it back towards the pole, then looped it once more and ran it back to the edge of the building.

He left the remaining rope in a pile next to the loops.

He quickly paced from the pole to the edge of the building where the rope was looped, then back towards the pole and back again and calculated that three times the length of the looped rope would measure some fifty feet. He picked the rope up at that point and twisted it twice around his calf and body just as Joseph asked him, 'what the hell are you planning?'

Jon walked to the edge of the building and peered downwards to ensure that he was directly above the apartment window three stories below and made the decision to be slightly short of the target and slightly above where he needed to be rather than too far down which would mean he would miss the target altogether.

He concluded that as he fell and realised that he was a little high he could relax his grip and his momentum would let him slide down the rope a little until he was in line with the window.

Tricky because he would need to make the adjustment within a millisecond or face the possibility of missing the target altogether, but he had no other choice. He only had one chance at this and simply could not get it wrong.

Jon ran back to the pole and felt the top of his shoulder. The pain had eased and felt numb thanks to the morphine shot.

His shirt was stained with blood down the left hand side and he convinced himself that this was the only way to free Claire.

'What the hell are you planning?' asked Joseph again.

He hoped that his estimate of fifty feet from the top of the building to the bay window was accurate as he simply had to get it right.

Jon checked the twisted rope around his leg and looped his hand and arm around the rope, then stepped outside of the line of the ropes that he had measured lying on the ground ensuring that he had a tight grip on the rope he replied, 'watch', as he ran at full speed towards the edge of the building maximising the distance he could achieve away from the building as he fell towards the ground.

Like a long jumper in the Olympics.

Jon had calculated that with such a short run he could possibly get to around 30 feet from the side of the building if he ran at full speed and jumped off the edge and tumbled towards the ground.

The rope unravelled following Jon and snaking along the ground towards the edge of the building as he ran towards the edge and descended towards the ground.

As he dropped towards the ground he twisted his body around in flight so that his feet faced the window and braced himself for the jolt when the rope had reached the distance to the target.

Jon released his grip slightly allowing him to slide down an extra yard as he neared the window. He had to be precise for the entry through the bay window.

Joseph jumped to avoid being tripped by the rope rapidly snaking towards the edge of the building and ran to the edge, leaning over he saw Jon crash through the bay window feet first shattering the glass.

'Sweet Lord in Heaven, please ensure he made it,' he mumbled as he gathered himself and ran towards the staircase.

'Fucking mad man,' Joseph murmured to himself as he ran down the stairs.

'Aller ordonné,' go ordered Bastienne into the two way radio, which was the order to the strike force to ascend the staircase to the apartment on level five.

Jon smashed through the window feet first with glass shards scattering in all directions and crashed into two of the kidnapper's standing near the bay window causing them to be catapulted towards the bed and tumble into their accomplice preparing to rape Claire.

In an instant Jon rolled, turned sideways extracting the Glock from the rear of his pants and shot the man left standing near the bay window, then turned and shot the two terrorists that had been catapulted towards the bed trying to get to their feet, shouting, 'fuck you.'

The terrorist preparing to rape Claire was the same Arabic looking person that was seated in the lounge of the Academic Saint Germaine hotel reading a newspaper that shot Jon in the shoulder.

He pleaded for mercy as Jon shot him twice between the eyes shouting, 'fuck you, you Arabic piece of shit.'

Jon quickly ran to the bed and pulled the bedcover over Claire as he was aware that Bastienne's strike force would enter moments later.

The banging sound of the strike force using a metal baton to bash down the door was evident as Jon shouted to them in French, 'iv'e les a tués,' I've killed them.

A moment later the Swat Team entered the apartment guns at the ready to find Jon standing at the edge of the bed and four dead bodies on the floor.

Bastienne and Stan pushed their way into the room followed moments later by Joseph.

'Sweet Jesus in Heaven Jon, that was some move,' said Stan looking at Jon's bleeding face.

'C'est sorti d'un film de James Bond,' that's out of a James Bond movie, said Bastienne.

'Fucking awesome, what a move my man,' said Joseph.

Pointing towards the door, Jon said, 'Gentlemen, if you please, Claire would like to get dressed.'

Looking at both Claire and Jon Stan said, 'thank the good Lord that you are both OK,' as they made their way out of the apartment.

Jon untied Claire and removed the duct tape from her mouth.

She stood naked crying uncontrollably in his arms.

'Shh, Mon pétale,' Shh my petal, whispered Jon into Claire's ear as he pulled her tighter into his arms.

'You are safe now,' said Jon.

'Let's get you dressed and get out of here,' said Jon.

Naked and stepping back, careful not to stand on the broken glass shards on the floor, Claire stared in horror at Jon's blood stained shirt and the blood on his face from the shattered glass of the window he had crashed through moments before.

She dressed quickly, picked up her handbag which the kidnapers had placed on the sideboard in the room and put her shoulder under Jon's right arm, as they made their way out of the apartment towards the elevator.

Claire smiled and thanked the Swat team as they passed.

As they exited the elevator, Jon collapsed falling to the ground and Claire tried her best to hold onto him, screaming for help.

Stan, Bastienne and Joseph were at his side in an instant with Bastienne barking orders into a two way radio.

Moments later an ambulance pulled up and the paramedics were quickly attending to Jon putting him onto a stretcher and transferring him onto a trolley which they quickly wheeled to the ambulance.

Claire jumped in and sat alongside Jon as the paramedic went to work.

The ambulance sped off siren wailing in the direction of the hospital.

Watching the ambulance disappear in the distance Bastienne turned to Stan and Joseph and said 'quel putain de mouvement,' what a fucking move.

'Oui, aurait rendu James Bond célèbre,' yes would have made James Bond look famous, continued Bastienne.

'Fucking mad man,' commented Joseph.

Stan, Bastienne and Joseph stood motionless staring in the direction of the ambulance as it disappeared around the corner.

The ambulance pulled up at the American Hospital of Paris located in Neuilly-sur-Seine, in the western suburbs, with trauma surgeons ready to go to work on Jon.

The paramedics quickly wheeled him into emergency and Claire was stopped from following him and guided to a waiting room where she sat in the corner and burst into tears shaking uncontrollable as she recalled the earlier horror.

A nun offered Claire a bunch of tissues, 'ici madame,' here madam, she said.

Claire looked up with tears streaming down her cheeks and offered, 'merci beaucoup,' thank you very much.

A nurse brought a cup of coffee to Claire and offered some support.

'God will take care of him,' reassured the nun.

'Thank you very much sister,' said Claire.

She sat with her head in her hands for what seemed like hours, when eventually one of the doctors gently touched her on the shoulder.

As she looked up he said in broken English, 'all's well, but he has lost a lot of blood,' said the doctor.

'I am pleased to say that the bullet did not hit any main artery or bones and there will be minimal damage,' said the doctor.

'The loss of blood stemmed from one of the minor arteries having been severed and luckily for him he got to the hospital in time, because of the loss of blood, he possibly would have died soon,' explained the doctor.

'He is extremely lucky,' continued the doctor.

The doctor added, 'another inch towards the neck and he would be dead.'

'It took some time to remove all the glass shards from his body,' stated the doctor.

'We have given him a blood transfusion and he is resting now, so you can sit next to him for a while, but I ask that you do not disturb him until he wakes up,' continued the doctor.

Turning to leave the doctor said, 'he is a very lucky man.'

'Merci docteur je suis reconnaissant,' thank you doctor, I'm grateful, said Claire feeling the tears start to well up in her eyes again.

Claire was shown the way to Jon's room, entered and sat down alongside the bed sobbing quietly to herself.

She held his right hand and laid her head gently onto his hand while saying a silent prayer of thanks to her maker.

Hours later Claire had fallen asleep with her head placed sideways on the bed facing Jon and still holding his hand and was awoken by Jon moving his hand to the top of her head.

Startled, she lifted her head and felt the tears well up in her eyes again, stood up and gently hugged him cupping her hands on both sides of his cheeks.

'Thank God,' she said as she kissed him passionately.

'I thought that was the end for me and as I lay on that bed and thought of you,' she said.

Sobbing uncontrollably with tears streaming down her cheeks Claire said, 'you are like a cat with multiple lives, please God they never run out.'

Using his real name she said, 'I love you and don't want to lose you Yonti.'

Yonti turned his head towards her and looking at her through slit eyes, felt some tears well up in his eyes.

'Je veux passer le reste de ma vie avec toi ma beauté,' I want to spend the rest of my life with you my beauty, he whispered.

'Do you have my gun and magazines?' he asked.

'Yes, they're in my bag,' replied Claire.

She took his mobile phone out of her bag and put it on the side table next to the bed.

Nodding his thanks, Yonti's thoughts drifted to his parents for a fleeting moment, reminding himself that he promised to call them again.

What am I going to say to them he thought.

Chapter 19

White House

Press Conference

President Trent entered the situation room and all stood as a sign of respect.

'Please be seated,' said the President.

'I have spoken to all our NATO allies and all are aware of the threat that we and possibly they are facing and all have agreed to join the war games immediately,' said the President.

'Whilst many were unhappy that we have withheld the information regarding this threat, they all understood the reason I did not involve them in the beginning,' continued the President.

'The media are all over this so we need to be very careful in what we say or in any media releases,' said the President.

'As I understand it Ivan and the Chinks have recently met with Kim Jang-un at Khasan at the tripoint on the Tumen River and we have noted that they have moved assets to their borders with North Korea,' stated the President.

'They are therefore clearly worried about our war games and may possibly want to implement their plan sooner rather than later, which adds to the urgency,' continued the President.

Barnaby had briefed the President earlier in the day and turning to face Barnaby, the President asked, 'so Barnaby, you believe that Kim Jang-un may not be well?'

'Yes Mr. President, we have been monitoring all three leaders and whilst he appeared at the recent meeting between these leaders, it is believed that he took ill sometime after that and was flown to Moscow for treatment,' said Barnaby.

'Our intelligence sources have indicated that he was flown to the Clinic Hospital in Moscow and is undergoing treatment,' repeated Barnaby.

'I cannot confirm why he was admitted, however we are trying to get more information at this time,' offered Barnaby.

'We believe that both his sisters are in Pyongyang, however neither have been seen,' stated Barnaby.

'Well that may cause the Russians and Chinese to move up their timetable, so I hope sanity prevails with this lot, however due to the state of their respective economies which is far worse than ours, I am not convinced at all,' said the President.

'I have tried to set up a trilateral meeting with Pushkin and Xiu Jaoping, however neither have retuned my call, so it's clear that are not interested in meeting with me and one must therefore assume that they are planning to implement their idiotic plan,' continued the President.

'General, please give us an update?' asked the President.

'Well Mr. President we have started the war games and are in the process of moving additional assets into place with aerial combat missions currently underway in the South Korean peninsula,' stated the General.

'We will have all ground forces involved within the next couple of days in a simulated invasion of South Korea, Japan and the Philippines,' said General Mitchfield.

'What is our preparedness with our nukes?' asked the President.

'We have placed them on high alert and in a holding pattern Mr. President, awaiting further instructions from you sir,' said the General.

'As you are aware, I have to face the media later this afternoon and I will undoubtedly be grilled on why we have placed our nukes on an alert status,' said the President.

'Going to be tricky trying to explain that one,' continued the President.

Turning to the Secretary of State Pompello, the President asked, 'what's the latest Nev?'

'Well Mr. President, I'm due to meet with the Russian foreign Secretary Lacrov a week from today and I intend bringing up this matter which hopefully will lead to a de-escalation of tensions,' said the Secretary of State.

Looking at the National Security Advisor, the President said, 'OK, and what's your read on it Mike?' asked the President.

'Very dangerous situation no doubt Mr. President,' replied Michael O'Rourke.

'We may need to consider taking this matter to the United Nations if the Secretary of State has not been able to get Lacrov to convince Pushkin to alter course,' he continued.

'I believe we need to be ready for a possible world war and we all know the consequences of that Mr. President,' said Michael.

The President cut the meeting short with all present standing in respect as he departed the room.

As he departed, he reminded all that they would meet the next day at the same time.

Later that afternoon the President faced the press.

A barrage of questions followed, questioning the President why the sudden war games were being conducted and whether the country and the world at large was preparing for war.

Holding his hands up, the President said, 'there is no threat to the USA or the world at all, we are merely testing our preparedness without giving our forces much notice in order to test their ability to mobilize at a moment's notice.'

Continuing the President made every effort to deflect prying questions from the media repeating what he had said earlier.

The reporter from CNN pushed the President further.

'Mr. President, why the need to place the country's nuclear warheads on an alert status?' asked the reporter.

Got a leak somewhere thought the President silently to himself.

'This was done to test the preparedness of our forces at a moment's notice,' stated the President.

'Let me remind you, that God forbid if ever we faced the real threat of a possible nuclear attack, we would need to be ready to destroy any nuclear weapons in flight and be able to retaliate in an instant,' continued the President.

'In a nuclear attack there is no time to twiddle your fingers or hesitate,' stated the President emphatically.

'You need to act swiftly,' continued the President.

'Time would be critical in that type of situation, hence the fact that we are testing our preparedness,' said the President.

'So ladies and gentlemen, please be assured that we are not going to war nor do we intend declaring war with North Korea, the Soviet Republic or China at all,' stated the President emphatically.

'I remind you that I recently met with the North Korean leader and whilst the pressing issue of nuclear weapons was discussed, no agreement has been reached on them disarming,' stated the President.

'I am confident that the talks will yield positive results in the future,' continued the President.

The questions kept coming thick and fast and each time the President deflected it to mere war games, however the media were suspicious.

Albeit that the President and other world leaders kept on assuring the media and their citizens that the war games were primarily focused to assess their preparedness, the media at large were not convinced at all.

'When I recently met with Kim Jang-un the supreme leader of North Korea, the meeting went extremely well and we are continuing the dialogue of convincing them to disarm and I am confident that those talks will yield results in time,' said the President turning to leave and ending the meeting.

The media sensed that there was more to these war games than had been disclosed.

As the President turned to leave a reporter from Aljazeera shouted out, 'Mr. President, I have it on good authority that there is something serious going on and that the USA is preparing for war with Russia and China,' he said.

Turning to face the reporter the President said, 'I don't know where your source has gleaned that information from, but I can assure you that the war games that the USA and NATO are involved in, are merely testing our ability to respond to any threat quickly,' as he made his way out of the room.

Chapter 20

Bastille Day

French Riviera

The news channels werc re-running the story of an incident at an apartment block in La Villette on the outskirts of Paris where an eye witness said that there was a police raid on an apartment.

Police have confirmed that four terrorists had kidnapped a lady and that all terrorists had been killed by police with the lady having been freed unharmed.

The eye witness said that one policemen seemed to abseil down from the roof and crash through a bay window into the apartment.

Lying in the hospital bed Yonti was watching the afternoon news two days after his daring escapade when Stan, Bastienne and Joseph walked into his room.

'Well, well how the hell are you doing this morning Jon?' asked Stan.

Here we go again, must remember my name is Jon, Yonti reminded himself.

'Bon jour my friends,' replied Jon.

'Long time no see boys,' continued Jon.

'Bon sang, c'était un mouvement Jon,' geez that was some move Jon, said Bastienne.

'Really something out of a James Bond movie,' continued Bastienne.

Turning to face Stan, Joseph asked, 'so who the hell is Jon?'

'That's his second name my friend,' replied Stan.

'Yeah right, I'll get it out of him sooner or later,' said Joseph unconvinced.

Reaching inside his jacket pocket Stan extracted his hip flask and offered it Jon.

'Some of Gods holy water for you,' said Stan.

'Johnny Blue my friend,' continued Stan.

'I believe it makes you frisky,' added Stan smiling.

'Thanks, I could use a swig of that,' said Jon.

A moment later Claire walked in.

'Hello gentlemen,' said Claire.

'I have not had the opportunity to thank you for saving my life,' she said.

Looking and pointing to Jon, Stan said, 'not quite true, that honour belongs to James Bond over here.'

'Yes a very daring entry,' said Claire and kissed Jon on the cheek.

'I'm extremely happy you were not hurt physically Claire,' said Stan.

Hugging Jon, Claire said, 'Merci beaucoup mon bel homme,' thank you very much my handsome man.

'You saved my life,' continued Claire.

Having gone to the hotel earlier and packed his meagre belongings into his suitcase, she booked him out of the hotel paying the bill and took his possessions to her apartment, unpacked them neatly in preparation for his discharge from hospital.

Looking at Bastienne, and Joseph Stan said, 'well I think it's time for us to get out of here.'

Turning to Jon and Claire Stan said, 'I want you both to take two weeks off, so see you at the embassy a fortnight from today at 12.00 noon Jon.'

Sweet Jesus, here we go again 12.00 noon, Jon thought to himself.

All three bid Jon and Claire farewell and left.

Claire, unpacked a new shirt, a pair of jeans and shoes from the bag she had brought with her and laid them on the bed.

'Best get dressed my sweetheart,' said Claire.

'Thank you my petal,' said Jon.

Hugging him tightly, Claire said, 'tu es mon héros,' you are my hero.

Taking his face in both hands she kissed him passionately.

'Je t'aime mon pétale,' I love you my petal, replied Jon.

Claire had fallen head over heels in love with him.

As he got out of bed his whole body ached and a moment later he caught a glimpse of his face in the mirror.

Seeing himself in the mirror for the first time since crashing through the bay window Jon said, 'I look like someone that has been in a war.'

Using his real name Claire said, 'It will heal fast Yonti, my handsome man.'

Wish I could be posted here to the land of my birth he thought to himself.

All too bloody hard trying to remember my aliases every ten minutes he pondered.

'Get dressed and let's get out of here,' continued Claire.

Yonti wanted to book himself out of hospital the day after he was admitted, however on the doctor's orders, he was forced to stay for a second night so he was more than ready to be on his way.

They made their way out of the hospital with Jon limping and stooped over due to the pain in his shoulder and they got into Claire's car and drove to her apartment.

Yonti merely stared at the people on the sidewalks and at the passing traffic in silence.

Claire glanced his way a couple of times and decided not to start any idle chat and left him with his thoughts.

Claire parked the car in the basement garage and they rode the elevator to her apartment.

Claire had sobbed herself to sleep the previous evening as her thoughts drifted back to just how lucky she was to not have been raped by these four terrorists and then killed.

My lover is a very special person, one in a million, a tough athletic man with the softest nature and what a lover she thought to herself.

'Oh wow, this is very nice,' said Yonti as they entered the apartment.

Tastefully decorated and full of colour with well-chosen artwork that adorned the wall.

Moving into the bedroom Yonti said, 'and this is the engine room?'

'Je l'aime mon pétale,' I love it my petal, continued Yonti.

Yonti slowly lay down on the bed and opened his arms inviting Claire to snuggle in which she unduly did.

They both got undressed and both fell asleep.

Later Yonti said, 'je pense que ma baguette magique fonctionne, mais tu devras faire tout le travail ma beauté,' I think my magic wand is working, but you'll have to do all the work my beauty.'

'Regarde juste,' just watch, said Claire.

Their love making was gentle with Yonti lying on his back with a full erection, albeit that he was not able to perform in his usual Casanova fashion.

Sometime after both had caught their breath, Yonti said, 'I think we should take a drive to visit my parents.'

'I really want you to meet them, but I am concerned that they will question why I killed those two terrorists and quiz me for information about the banking job I told them I had,' said Yonti.

'I lied to my parents, something I have never done,' continued Yonti.

'I just don't know how to handle the questions that will inevitably come from them,' he said.

'I have been instructed by Director Heathcott never to disclose what job I do to anybody including my parents, so I have to think about trying to deflect the questions that will most certainly come,' continued Yonti.

A week later Claire drove Yonti to the hospital to get the stitches removed and then pointed the car in the direction of Nice, a drive of around five hundred and seventy eight miles taking around seven and a half eight hours.

Claire pulled up in front of Yonti's parent's apartment block and parked the car.

Walking sheepishly into the front entrance, Claire hugged Yonti tightly showing her support for the impending meeting with his parents.

As they walked through the door hand in hand, Yonti's father looked up and noticed his son limping. He shouted to his wife to come and see who had arrived.

'Hello papa,' said Yonti.

His father hugged him then still holding his arms pushed him slightly away and looking at his face said, 'what happened to your face and why are you limping my son?'

'I had a small accident,' said Yonti.

Looking at Claire Marcel said, 'qui est cette femme incroyablement belle?' who is this stunningly beautiful lady?

'Papa, meet Claire, the love of my life,' said Yonti.

Marcel gave Claire a kiss on both cheeks and a hug and said, 'hello Claire.'

Just then Yonti's mother appeared from the kitchen and ran into her sons arms hugging and kissing him.

'Oh mon seigneur comme c'est bon de te voir,' Oh my Lord how good to see you, she said.

She too pushed him away slightly and asked, 'what happened to your face?'

Trying to deflect the question Yonti said, 'Mama, meet Claire, the love of my life,'

Yonti's mother Brielle kissed Claire on both cheeks and hugged her.

'Pleased to meet you Claire,' said Brielle.

A moment later Yonti's brother walked in and shook his hand, 'great to see you my big brother,' and was introduced to Claire.

'Que fait une belle dame comme toi avec un homme si laid?' what is a beautiful lady like you doing with such an ugly man? Said Pierre kissing Claire's hand.

'Non, c'est moi qui suis le chanceux,' no it's me that is the lucky one, exclaimed Claire.

'It's great to see you Yonti and to meet you Claire.' 'This calls for a celebration,' said Brielle.

Marcel made his way to the bar and grabbed a bottle of Dom Pérignon and five champagne flute glasses and popped the cork.

Clinking glasses, Marcel said 'a votre santé,' cheers.

'How long are you staying?' asked his mother?

'Just a couple of day's mama,' said Yonti.

'I will need to prepare some extra food for dinner,' said Brielle and excused herself with Pierre following her into the kitchen.

Looking at Claire, Marcel said, 'you are most welcome in our home.'

'Unpack and make yourself comfortable Claire, Yonti will show you to his room,' continued Marcel.

Turning to face Yonti Marcel said, 'I look forward to hearing the full-story over dinner as well as what happened to you face.'

Following Claire up the stairs, Yonti pointed the way to his room.

Turning to face Claire he said, 'I have never lied to my parents and can't tell them what I do for a living,' said Yonti.

'Stick to your story even if it's a lie and tell them that you are a banker, after all you are banking dead terrorists you know,' said Claire.

Putting his hands together as if in prayer, Yonti silently said, 'please forgive me for the lies I am about to tell My Lord.'

Claire put her arms around him and hugged him tightly.

Brielle had made one of her specialties for dinner, a Seafood Mornay which was absolutely delicious.

'Thank you Mrs. Barre, that was absolutely scrumptious,' said Claire.

'Pleasure Claire, please call me Brielle and my husband Marcel,' she said.

Turning to look Yonti in the eye, his father asked, 'so young man, you promised to call and never did.' 'What exactly were you doing killing two people in Paris?'

The moment that Yonti dreaded had arrived.

Not able to look them in the eye, Yonti said, 'well I met Claire at the Café Floret in Paris and we were getting acquainted when all the drama unfolded.'

'I grabbed a gun and did what I thought was the right thing to do,' continued Yonti.

Not wanting to reveal that he had the gun in his possession as a CIA agent, he tried as best as he could to refocus their attention in another direction.

'I took up target shooting as a hobby and have been doing that for a long time, so luckily I had perfected my accuracy and did not miss,' said Yonti.

'Yes admirable my son, but you killed two people,' exclaimed his father.

'Well papa, would you rather I did nothing and allowed these terrorists to kill many more people including possibly Claire and myself?' asked Yonti looking his father in the eye.

'No my son, I think what you did was very brave indeed and from what I have seen on television, they are saying that you are an absolute hero,' said Marcel.

'The reporter said that she believed that the person that shot those terrorists was an off duty police officer, so are you in fact working for the French police my son?' asked Marcel.

Looking his father in the eye Yonti replied, 'no papa I don't work for them at all and I was staying in Paris overnight and wanted to surprise you and mama, but this happened so I had to meet with some people to sort things out.'

'Well my son, you are a hero and very brave,' said his mother.

'I'm very proud of you Yonti,' said his mother and leaned over and kissed him on the cheek.

'Our country needs to get rid of terrorists like these,' continued his mother.

'So what happened to your face?' asked his mother.

'I had a little accident when I fell through a window,' replied Yonti.

Both parents stared at him without commenting any further.

Turning to face Claire his mother said, 'so you two met at a Café just before the shooting.'

'Yes we did and Yonti saved my life by pushing me into the Café and out of the way of the car careering down the sidewalk,' she replied.

'He is my hero,' continued Claire.

Later that night in bed, Claire whispered to Yonti, 'well done, you handled that well without telling too many lies.'

'Oui mon pétale,' yes my petal, said Yonti staring at the ceiling.

Yonti and Claire spent time sun baking and frolicking in the sea and he slowly regained his strength.

Next day Yonti and Claire were lying on the beach watching people playing ball games when Claire turned to face Yonti.

'I feel like an ice cream, how about you?' asked Claire.

'I'm fine thanks, so don't worry about me, I will stick to water,' stated Yonti.

Claire removed her purse from the backpack and made her way towards the ice cream vendor's cart positioned at the side of the road and went about selecting an ice cream of her liking.

Yonti stood and proceeded to stretch his body from side to side arching his torso backwards when there was a sudden commotion coming from the ice cream vendor's cart.

Yonti spun around and noticed people scattering in all directions and quickly retrieved his Glock and two magazines from the backpack, cocked it and ensured that the safety was off.

He slid it into the back of his costume pants and held two magazines in his left hand as he ran limping towards the ice cream vendor's cart.

Stopping in his tracks as he noticed that two beared men had grabbed two females and had knives at their throats. One of the females was his beloved Claire.

Oh dear Lord not again, Yonti thought to himself.

The two bearded men walked backwards dragging the females with knives at their throats and made their way towards the laundromat across the road.

They positioned themselves against the laundromat window facing the gathering crowd.

They were shouting something in Arabic and Yonti could make out Allahu Akbar, God is most great.

Yonti quickly made his way to the front of the crowd and limped towards the bearded men holding the two females hostage with knives at their throats.

One of the hostage takers screamed instructions for Yonti to stop.

'Je la tuerai,' I will kill her, he shouted in French.

Yonti stopped some thirty feet from the hostage takers and knew that if ever he needed to be deadly accurate and lightning fast, it was now.

Suddenly, a police vehicle screeched to a halt close by distracting the two hostage takers.

Yonti waited for a few moments as the hostage takers seemed distracted and turned towards the police vehicle exposing the sides of their heads, he extracted the Glock from the back of his costume with lightning speed and fired two shots in quick succession at the hostage taker that had Claire in his grasp, hitting him in the temple.

He then trained the weapon onto the second bearded man within a millisecond and discharged a further two rounds into the middle of the hostage takers forehead.

The four shots were taken with blistering speed missing both females by a mere fraction of an inch.

Both hostage takers fell to the ground and both Claire and the other hostage ran towards the crowd.

People in the crowd were filming the drama on their mobile phones.

Claire ran into Yonti's arms just as Bastienne appeared from the police vehicle.

Whilst shaking with fear, she had remained remarkably calm.

She had every confidence that Yonti would save her yet again.

Turning to face Bastienne, Yonti asked, 'where the hell did you come from?'

'Always covering your back Monsieur,' replied Bastienne.

'Aren't you supposed to be in Paris?' asked Yonti.

'Oui, but duty calls and I am here,' stated Bastienne.

Yonti wondered how on earth Bastienne could have known that there would be another attack on the citizens of Nice.

People stared at Yonti holding Claire in a tight embrace, with his Glock still in his hand and started applauding his bravery as they made their way back to the beach to collect their backpack.

Yonti picked up the backpack and placed his Glock into it just as the French Police were cordoning off the area.

Bastienne motioned for Yonti and Claire to follow him towards the waiting police car and they all jumped in. The driver drove off in the opposite direction to where his parent's apartment block was situated.

Yonti's father Marcel heard the four shots and ran out of the apartment complex and down the road towards the laundromat where he thought both Yonti and Claire were sunbathing on the beach.

As he approached the crowd he noticed Yonti and Claire being ushered into a police car and driven away in the opposite direction.

What on earth is happening to our beautiful country he thought to himself?

Wasn't that long ago when a terrorist in a nineteen tonne truck deliberately drove into a crowd of people celebrating Bastille day on the same promenade where their family apartment block is situated.

Eighty six people had died on the fateful day on the sixteenth of July 2016 with a further 458 injured.

As they rounded a corner, Bastienne instructed the driver of the police vehicle to stop, jumped out gun in hand, pointing it towards the windshield of a car following them and instructed the driver to stop.

Obeying the order to stop, Bastienne instructed the driver to put his hands behind his head and the driver complied.

Bastienne watched as the police vehicle drove off and rounded a corner and waited for a few minutes allowing time for the police vehicle to disappear from sight.

He then jumped into the rear of the vehicle and instructed the driver to make a U-turn and drive back to the laundromat.

He did not want anybody to follow the police vehicle that was transporting Yonti and Claire back to his family's apartment block.

The police vehicle drove around several blocks ensuring that they were not followed and finally stopped at the rear of his parents apartment block allowing them both to exit and make their way towards the front entrance.

Yonti and Claire made their way towards the pool and had just laid down on the lounge adjustable recliner pool chairs when Yonti's father appeared with his mother Brielle.

'Good Lord Yonti, what happened?' asked Marcel.

Yonti explained to his father that Claire and another female had been taken hostage by knife wielding terrorists who threatened to slit their throats.

'I did what I had to do,' said Yonti.

'Good Lord my son, you are a very brave person,' said his mother.

'I am pleased to see that you are unharmed Claire,' said his father.

Both his parents had come to terms with the possibility that Yonti was working for the French police and did not question him any further.

Yonti turned to Claire and quietly whispered, 'I think it's time for us to pack up and leave tomorrow my petal.'

The next day Yonti and Claire bid his parents and brother farewell and they made their way back to Paris. As they drove back to Paris, Yonti turned to Claire and said, 'you know that staying with me puts you into danger.'

'Yonti, I am not going to leave you, so don't ever say that again,' said Claire emphatically.

They spent the last couple of days together mostly in her apartment in Paris venturing out for the odd meal and afternoon coffee.

Chapter 21

Military Installation Systems

Russia and China

Unbeknown to anybody except the Director of the CIA Barnaby Heathcott and Stan Noble the CIA station chief in France, Rafael having learned of the intentions of the Russians and Chinese put his expertise in computer science engineering to work.

Rafael spent hundreds of hours of his spare time on his laptop setting up algorithms and hundreds of dummy Internet accounts around the world.

He had informed Director Heathcott that he had set up a fool proof system that could not be traced and that he had hacked into the Central Processing Unit of the Russian and Chinese military installation systems and planted an encrypted instruction into each of their systems, with full access to the launch codes.

It would be impossible to trace the source of the hack as the instruction in both systems were encrypted and untraceable and he had manipulated the architecture and arithmetic logic units in both systems that perform arithmetic and logical operations altering the instructions in their computer systems.

This altered the memory used to hold instructions and data.

He had infiltrated all four functions of the Central Processing Units of both countries and altered the four strategic states within their respective systems and had setup sleepers in their respective systems and any attempt at tracing the source would be impossible as data would travel through the thousands of Internet listed accounts leading to a dead end.

They would only become active in their systems if they ever activated a launch code sequence, thus an extremely remote possibility existed of it ever being discovered.

Rafael had found a way to infiltrate the guidance system of the ICBM's and Ballistic missile systems in the Russian and Chinese systems and had managed to secretly install a destruct instruction into their systems which meant that at the time of a launch, the missile would self-destruct on the launch pad.

It was believed that this was impossible to do, however Rafael put his expertise in computer engineering to good use and had found a way to access their system protocols and insert the untraceable instruction to self-detonate missiles on the launch pad when a launch code is activated.

He used two trusted operatives in the CIA fluent in Russian and Chinese to help him interpret the two languages and decipher any codes he may encounter in their systems.

Both operatives were sworn to secrecy.

The Director had questioned Rafael whether what he had done was realistic and fool proof.

Barnaby and Stan had kept this secret to themselves as Stan was the only person that Barnaby fully trusted.

You never ever know whether we will one day need this to self-activate Barnaby thought to himself and if ever, we had better hope like hell it works.

President Trent entered the situation room for his daily meeting with the National Security Council and Joint Chiefs of Staff.

'Good morning gentlemen, please be seated,' said the President.

Continuing the President asked General Mitchfield for an update on the war games.

'Things are progressing well Mr. President,' replied the General.

'All assets are in place and the games have begun in earnest,' continued the General.

'Satellite images indicate that the Russians and Chinese have moved significant assets to the Korean border as they are assuming that an attack is imminent,' stated the General.

Everybody around the table seemed to have accepted that the war games exercise show casing the allied military power may deter the Russians and Chinese from carrying out their secret plan.

Other than the Secretary of State Neville Pompello who was still seeking to meet with his Russian and Chinese counter parts, nobody had anything further to add.

The meeting ended with the President asking Barnaby to join him in the Oval office.

'Well Barnaby, you were very quiet in the meeting,' said the President.

'Yes Mr. President, I have something very important to share with you which is unknown to our military, any members of the Joint Chiefs of Staff or anybody seated around the table and is highly classified and for your knowledge only,' said Barnaby.

'In fact there are only a few trusted people within the CIA that know of this Mr. President,' said Barnaby.

'As mentioned privately to you in the past we have developed a stealth drone that is capable of intercepting any missiles and destroying them in flight close to where they would be launched,' said Barnaby.

'These stealth drones have a ceiling height of forty thousand feet and can carry a payload of six anti-missile missiles that cannot be detected which gives us a distinct advantage over our adversaries in a time of crises,' stated Barnaby.

'We have one ready for deployment and I have arranged for it to be secretly deployed to South Korea.

We have a further two under construction at the moment that will be operational within the next twelve months Mr. President,' said Barnaby.

The President stared at Barnaby in silence until he finally said, 'how sure are you that these drones will be effective?' asked the President.

'I have personally viewed the testing of this drone in action and I can assure you that it yielded a one hundred percent positive outcome in the trials,' said Barnaby.

'However one cannot be one hundred percent sure until it is tested in a real life war theatre Mr. President,' stated Barnaby.

'This is highly classified Mr. President,' emphasized Barnaby.

'You are the only person in government that knows of this now other than Stan Noble, myself and a few CIA operatives that I trust with my life,' said Barnaby.

'So that is one option we have up our sleeve, however the realistic answer is whether we will in fact know exactly which country and where that country would intend to launch a nuclear warhead from or any other kind of missile aimed at the USA or any of our allies,' said Barnaby.

'We would obviously need to have the drones deployed close to where they would intend launching,' concluded Barnaby.

'I am impressed Barnaby,' said the President.

'Despite all the criticism we get for the huge funding to the CIA annually, I must compliment you and your team and thank you all for the excellent work you do to keep us all safe,' said the President.

'Well Mr. President, I have some further news for you sir,' stated Barnaby.

The President leaned forward in his chair with his elbow resting on his desk and his hand clasped around his mouth as he listened intently to what Barnaby was saying.

'Respectfully Mr. President, this too is highly confidential and for your knowledge only sir,' stated Barnaby.

Continuing, Barnaby stated that one of their operatives in the CIA had hacked into the missile guidance systems of the Russians and Chinese and planted a self-destruction function into their databases with full access to their launch systems that cannot be traced.

The destruction function would be activated when a launch code is sequenced within the Russian and Chinese guidance systems, resulting in the self-destruction of a missile on the launch pad.

The President stared resolutely at Barnaby as he continued.

'The agent that hacked into their systems is the same agent that was involved in the elimination of the terrorist that drove a car onto the sidewalk injuring many people and then went on to kill the terrorist that shot and killed a few people, as well as injuring a number of civilians in Paris not so long ago,' said Barnaby.

'And you say this is the same guy that has hacked into the Russian and Chinese guidance systems and did this?' stated the President.

'Yes Mr. President, he is a French citizen that we recruited a few years ago in Paris,' stated Barnaby.

'Amazing, I would like to meet this young man and personally thank him for his service to our country and the world at large,' said the President.

'Yes Mr. President I will arrange that whenever he is back in the States,' said Barnaby.

'So how the hell did he manage that Barnaby and how sure are you that they will not discover it or be able to trace it back to us and what is the probability of success,' questioned the President?

'Well Mr. President as stated one can never be one hundred percent sure until it's been tested in a theatre of war, however as far as the drones are concerned, I would rate that at a sixty percent positive outcome,' said

Barnaby.

'The reason that I am giving it a sixty percent tick is that the success of it doing what it is intended to do, is that clearly it would need to be deployed in the zone of the launch which is a lot more difficult to predict as an adversary may launch from multiple sites,' continued Barnaby.

'As far as its ability to succeed, from what I have seen, I would give it a ninety five percent tick, again one can only be one hundred percent sure in a theatre of war,' said Barnaby.

'With regard to destroying nukes on a launch pad, I would give that a fifty/fifty chance as we will never know until this is activated by the Russians or Chinese,' concluded Barnaby.

'If ever the Russians or Chinese do launch a missile or multiple missiles, I ask that you pause for a short while before giving the command to launch our own nukes in response as we would need ascertain whether our drones or what our operative activated in the Russian and Chinese systems has worked,' stated Barnaby.

'Hopefully the self-destruct sequence will work if it ever gets to this disastrous stage,' said Barnaby.

'We know that should Ivan or the Chinese launch any missiles nuclear or otherwise at us, it would trigger an all-out response from us and a nuclear holocaust will ensue and that would be the end of the world,' continued Barnaby.

'Pausing for a few minutes will give us a clear indication of whether in fact this has been successful or not,' stated Barnaby.

'Well Barnaby, if it ever gets to that I can assure you that the military chiefs will insist that we launch immediately and we better hope that our satellite capability in space can destroy any ICBM's and that your drones and what your boy wonder has done can destroy any Ballistic missiles launched,' said the President.

'Seems a hell of a risk to delay if you ask me,' said the President.

'So Barnaby, do you have any other cards up you sleeve?' questioned the President.

'No Mr. President I don't,' said Barnaby.

Standing and taking Barnaby's hand the President indicated that the meeting had ended and he thanked him for giving humanity a glimmer of hope.

Chapter 22

Le Blanc-Mesnil

Paris

Claire got dressed in her white navy uniform, tied her hair in a ponytail and looking absolutely stunning left for the embassy before Yonti had woken up.

Normally a light sleeper, Yonti was unusually lethargic and slept in.

He woke up, showered, made the bed, got dressed and hailed a cab to the embassy, reporting to the security booth on time at 12.00 noon as instructed and was met at the gate by Stan Noble.

Waving him through, Stan offered the usual courteous greeting.

'Hello Jon, I'm glad to see you looking a lot better,' he said.

'Thanks Stan, it was Gods holy water that did the trick,' replied Jon.

Walking towards the entrance, Stan said, 'we were about to have you return to Langley when all this drama happened and now we have another pressing issue.'

Having cleared security at the entrance to the embassy, Jon reminded himself to use his alias yet again.

Dear Lord, these name changes are really making me sick, he thought to himself.

They rode the elevator to basement level two and entered the conference room.

Joseph and Bastienne were chatting and both rose offering their hands in a greeting.

'Bonjour Jon,' offered Bastienne taking his hand.

'Bonjour Capitaine Petit,' replied Jon.

Turning to face Joseph, Jon said, 'not you again.'

'Every time I see you I seem to get keep getting myself into some sort of trouble,' said Jon.

'You took the words right out of my mouth my friend,' said Joseph.

'By the way guys, who the hell is Jon?' asked Joseph again looking at both Stan and Bastienne.

'I told you that's his middle name,' replied Stan.

Looking straight at Stan, Joseph said, 'yeah right I have heard that one before.'

With all parties seated, Stan turned on the monitor, inserted a USB stick and images of a man driving a truck came into view on the large screen on the wall.

'OK boys this is what we have,' said Joseph.

'We in Mossad have been trying to find this terrorist by the name of Abu Abdalla for almost two decades and recently discovered his whereabouts in London,' continued Joseph.

'We believe that he made his way from Syria to the UK via Holland using the freedom of travel method through EU countries to get to London on a false passport just before Brexit,' said Joseph.

'We have confirmation that he was the bomb maker that arranged for a suicide bomber to plant a bomb at the Sbarro pizzeria in Jerusalem in August 2001, killing fifteen people including seven children and wounding one hundred and thirty people,' continued Joseph.

'He went to ground until our intelligence picked up a communication between Abdalla and an accomplice by the name of Qudair Uddin in London recently,' stated Joseph.

'Abdulla had the bomber namely Izz Al-Din Shuheil al-Masri conceal the explosives in a guitar case and take it into the pizzeria.' 'It is believed that the bomb was remotely detonated by Abdalla,' continued Joseph.

'Izz Al-Din Shuheil al-Masri is currently enjoying the seventy two virgins promised by the prophet Mohammed,' quipped Joseph.

'Abdulla has been working as a truck driver, trucking goods between the UK and France for the past two months, hence my involvement with Bastienne, the French authorities and the CIA,' said Joseph.

'The CIA has been trying to locate Abdalla for many years as well, because we know that he was one of the bomb makers responsible for making IED's in Syria that has killed and injured hundreds of American and Allies soldiers,' said Stan.

'Mossad have confirmation that he was the bomb maker in the Jerusalem bomb attack and may be planning an attack on the US embassy here in Paris,' stated Stan.

'We believe that he is due to cross into France tomorrow some time and deliver goods to a warehouse on the outskirts of Le Blanc-Mesnil, which is around fourteen miles from the embassy here in Paris,' continued Stan.

'We will monitor his progress in the UK through the Eurotunnel from Folkestone to Calais and we will watch his every move for the 186 mile journey to Paris,' said Bastienne.

'I will set up numerous monitoring points along the way and will arrange for a customary check of documents by customs at the point of entry into France, which will give us a clear indication of where he is going,' continued Bastienne.

'The three of us will be waiting for this terrorist at his drop off point,' said Bastienne.

Looking at the three guys Stan said, 'not three, but four.'

'I won't miss this for the world boys,' stated Stan.

'OK my friend, but you do look a little old for this type of work,' quipped Bastienne.

'We'll see my friend,' replied Stan.

'Our intelligence indicates that this terrorist is extremely dangerous and may be planning some sort of an attack on your embassy here in Paris,' said Joseph.

'God alone knows what he has been up to in the UK,' continued Joseph.

Later that evening Stan, Jon, Bastienne and Joseph drove to the warehouse in Le Blanc-Mesnil in the same van they used when they eliminated the two terrorists in the farm house, posing as electricity repair men.

It was late at night and the industrial estate was deserted. Jon noted the name sign-written on the building, namely Réparations de Bombardiers, Bomber Repairs.

Seemed a rather conspicuous name for a panel beater.

Bastienne made his way to the electrical box situated at the end of the street, picked the lock and turned off the power to the warehouse.

With nobody in sight, Bastienne went about picking the lock on the door alongside the roller door, whilst Jon and Joseph set up witches hats at either end of the street with detour signs to deter anybody from driving down the street towards the warehouse.

Bastienne and Stan quickly entered the warehouse looking for a possible alarm system or CCTV cameras.

None were visible, so Bastienne went about installing two mini cameras discreetly hidden that would give them a view of the inside of the warehouse.

Bastienne and Stan went about checking the warehouse for signs of anything suspicious however did not find anything of concern.

Lots of car parts and various cars in some state of repair lying around the warehouse, typical of a panel beating shop.

Bastienne and Stan exited the warehouse, locked the door and made their way back to the electrical box and he reconnected the warehouse to the electrical grid.

Bastienne locked the electrical box door and made his way back to the van.

Jon and Joseph packed up the witch's hats and detour signs, put them in the van and they drove back to Paris.

Jon got back to Claire's apartment well after midnight and Claire was awake expecting his return.

They made passionate love with him being rather tense and aggressive during their love making that seemed somewhat desperate and domineering. Something that caught Claire's attention.

His penis thrusting in and out of her vagina at a rate of knots which caused her to have multiple orgasms until he finally rolled off Claire and lay there motionless staring at the ceiling.

Claire snuggled up to him and said, 'qu'est-ce qui ne va pas mon bel homme?' what's wrong my handsome man.

He kissed her and merely stared at the ceiling in silence.

Claire sensed the tension welled up in him and wondered whether he had a premonition that something bad was going to happen.

The next day Stan, Bastienne, Joseph and Jon drove back to the warehouse in a van with tinted windows that had all the necessary communications equipment in it depicting the French Water Company logo on it.

Bastienne was busy talking to the various monitoring stations placed along the way to check on the whereabouts of the truck being driven by Abu Abdalla.

Later in the afternoon Bastienne's mobile phone came to life with the first monitoring point in the UK reporting that the truck marked Jay Jays Freight had just passed and confirmed that the rig had a bright yellow livery towing a trailer with dark blue side tarps.

A while later, the second monitoring point reported that the freightliner had cleared UK customs and was headed into the Euro tunnel.

An hour later Bastienne's laptop lit up with an incoming email.

The email was from French customs with an attachment.

Bastienne opened the attachment and read its contents which indicated that the freight consisted of used car parts destined for the Bomber Repairs Panel Beaters in Le Blanc-Mesnil.

Comfortable that their intelligence was accurate, Bastienne waited for the last monitoring report from a position some ten miles from the warehouse.

They parked the communications van a short distance from the warehouse with an excellent view of the roller door and waited for the freightliner to arrive.

The two way radio crackled to life with an agent reporting a small accident on the road to Le Blanc-Mesnil, which was a sign that the freightliner was nearing the warehouse.

It was late afternoon when the freightliner stopped in front of the warehouse, then turned and backed in through the roller shutter door and once inside, the roller shutter door was immediately closed.

Bastienne fired up the image of the inside of the warehouse from both hidden CCTV cameras and images of Abu Abdalla greeting three people in the usual Muslim greeting of As-Salam-u-Alaikum and wishing each other peace came into view.

A short while later Abdalla drew the tarp curtains and one of the people busied himself using a forklift removing the used car bodies and pallets of car parts from the trailer.

Bastienne had a five man strike force team hidden in an old truck down the road from the warehouse and gave the order to deploy and move towards the door alongside the roller shutter door.

Joseph had made it clear that he wanted Abdalla captured alive and Bastienne had relayed the instruction to his team.

Bastienne and Stan were first out of the van and ran down the road towards the warehouse with Jon and Joseph following closely behind.

Bastienne checked the door which was locked, so he picked the lock and a moment later the strike force entered the warehouse with Bastienne and Stan following closely behind.

Jon and Joseph brought up the rear.

Taken by surprise as the door opened, the four occupants scattered in all directions as the strike force team entered the warehouse with one of the terrorists firing wildly in their direction.

The strike team returned fire killing two of the occupants as Abdalla and another person dove for cover behind a car that had its doors removed, ready for panel beating.

Jon saw a movement alongside a car which obstructed the view of the strike team and discharged one shot hitting Abdalla in the left arm as he ducked for cover.

A moment later there was a massive explosion as one of the terrorists detonated a car bomb alongside where he and his accomplice had sought shelter.

The explosion instantly killed two members of the strike team as well as Abdalla and his accomplice, blowing car parts all over the warehouse and into the air with the body of a car landing on both Jon and Joseph, who were both severely injured in the blast.

Part of the warehouse roof structure had been blown off in the blast.

Jon and Joseph were both trapped under the body of a wrecked car and were unconscious from the impact of the blast.

They lay there motionless.

The strike team had taken the full impact of the blast as they had entered the warehouse.

Stan and Bastienne were crouched behind them, however Stan was positioned to the right side of the strike team and also took the full impact of the blast as they followed the strike team into the warehouse.

An earie silence fell over the smoke filled warehouse for a few minutes, before the wailing sirens of the fire brigade and ambulances became evident as they rounded the corner.

Bastienne had thought of every possibility and ensured that all emergency services were on hand and close by in case of an emergency.

The fire brigade immediately activated their fire drills dousing any flames and worked their way through the scattered automobile parts in the warehouse looking for any surviving members of the strike force team as well as Stan, Bastienne, Joseph and Jon.

First Responders located Bastienne who was staggering around in a daze ushering him to one of the waiting ambulances, whilst others attended to the remaining wounded strike force team members and tried desperately to revive Stan and the two members that took the initial brunt of blast.

The First responders tried in vain to save the two strike force team members and Stan, however it soon became evident that their effort was in vain.

Other members of the First Responders searched for Jon and Joseph and located them amongst the rubble under the body of a car barely alive. They went about trying to stabilize them, carefully placing them onto stretchers and put them both into one ambulance which raced towards the American Hospital in Paris sirens blazing.

Three other ambulances were summons to the scene and transported the injured members of the strike force team and Bastienne to hospital.

Members of the backup strike force team secured the area around the warehouse and went about removing the two bodies of their comrades as well as the body of Stan and the four terrorists a short while later. They loaded them into the remaining ambulances which drove them to the mortuary in Paris.

Jon and Joseph had both undergone emergency operations.

Jon suffered a fractured abdomen as well as two broken ribs, a fractured pelvis and severe head wounds with possible brain damage and concussion.

Joseph had suffered a punctured lung, broken arm and leg, a minor head wound and concussion.

Bastienne was the luckiest of the four sustaining minor concussion and one broken rib.

Claire had been monitoring the raid on the warehouse and was horrified by what she saw unfolding on the monitor in front of her.

Stan had arranged for a drone to be deployed above the site and for live streaming to be available for Claire to monitor the outcome.

Claire sat in horror as she stared at the screen streaming live footage of the raid.

'Please Jesus, keep them all safe,' she prayed out aloud.

Unsure whether any of the four survived, Claire burst into tears and sat with her face in her hands sobbing uncontrollably.

Stan had died of the wounds he sustained when the bomb exploded, as his body was exposed to the right hand side of Bastienne and the strike force team when they entered the warehouse.

Claire rushed to the hospital only to be stopped by nursing staff from entering the operating theatre and was ushered into a waiting room.

'Please tell me that all four survived?' she begged the nurse.

Trying to calm Claire down the nurse said that two were in the emergency operating theatres and sadly one person had died.

'Oh God no, please don't tell me this,' she sobbed uncontrollably.

A few hours later, a doctor appeared and sat down next to Claire, who was sitting with her chin resting in her hands and her elbows on her knees. Both her hands were clasped around her cheeks, sobbing quietly to herself as she stared at the wall.

'Please doctor tell me that they will survive?' questioned Claire.

'Well, the patient I operated on was rather lucky,' said the doctor.

Claire allowed herself a slight sigh of relief praying silently to herself that it was her lover that was lucky.

'He suffered a punctured lung, broken arm and leg and a minor head wound,' continued the doctor.

'I believe that the person's name is Joseph Diamond and luckily for him the head wound is superficial and has not damaged the brain, but whilst the injury to his lung is not serious he will need time to recuperate,' said the doctor.

'He is very lucky to be alive,' continued the doctor.

'Thank the good Lord,' said Claire out aloud.

'Merci docteur,' thank you doctor, said Claire.

A nurse brought Claire a cup of coffee.

'Merci beaucoup,' said Claire taking a sip of the coffee.

Hours later Claire was staring at the picture on the wall in silence, when another doctor sat down next to her and tapped her lightly on the shoulder.

'Bon jour Madame, I'm doctor Laurent and I am sorry to be the bearer of bad news,' he said.

Oh dear God no, Claire thought to herself.

'I have to be honest with you, because I'm afraid to say that the person I operated on may not survive,' continued the doctor.

Fearing the worst and trying as best she could to prepare herself for the bad news, Claire looked alarmingly at the doctor.

'Three people died from their injuries at the scene and despite the paramedics best effort to save them, sadly they were unable to save them,' said the doctor.

'The person you may be interested in namely, Stan Noble died from his injuries,' stated the doctor.

Claire stared at him in silence tears welling up in her eyes.

Continuing the doctor said, 'sadly two members of the strike force team also lost their lives.'

'The patient I operated on has very severe injuries, cerebral edema more commonly known as swelling of the brain that causes fluid to develop in the brain as well as a fractured abdomen, two broken ribs and a fractured pelvis,' said the doctor.

'The operation was successful, however the next seventy two hours will give us a better idea of his long term prognoses as we will hopefully be able to assess if there has been any damage to his brain,' said the doctor.

'If he survives the next seventy two hours and recovers from the brain operation successfully, he will need extensive physio therapy in recovery,' stated the doctor.

'I'm really sorry to be the bearer of such bad news,' said the doctor.

'I believe his name is Jon Jones,' continued the doctor.

Claire simply stared at the doctor finally offering, 'merci docteur,' thank you doctor.

'He is in recovery now and is heavily sedated,' continued the doctor.

'I don't normally allow people to see patients right after major surgery such as he has had, however I will make an exception for you Lieutenant Commander,' said the doctor looking at Claire's insignia's on her lapel.

'You can sit with him for a few minutes, but I ask that you only stay a short while,' said the doctor.

'The nurse will take you to ICU, however I reiterate and ask that you only sit with him for a short while,' said the doctor standing and handing Claire over to a nurse.

'Au revoir Lieutenant Commander, the nurse will take you to ICU,' said the doctor as he turned to leave.

'Merci docteur,' thank you doctor, replied Claire.

A nurse brought Claire some more coffee and sat with her for a few minutes.

Claire followed the nurse to ICU with tears streaming down her cheeks and she sat alongside her lover and put her hand over her mouth to subdue the noise of her sobbing uncontrollably.

Claire stared at the oxygen tube in his mouth and the maze of wires and electrodes coming from his body, then turned her attention to the monitor that was monitoring his vital signs seeking assurance that he was still alive.

The constant peeping sound of the monitor gave a small degree of comfort that he was still alive.

'Sweet Jesus, why?' Claire asked silently.

She held his hand, stood up and kissed him lightly on the cheek.

'S'll te plaît, ne meurs pas sur moi mon bel homme,' please don't die on me my handsome man, said Claire aloud.

Bastienne was held for observation for a few hours, eventually got out of bed and got dressed with great difficulty, picked up the crutch and booked himself out of hospital.

Before leaving the hospital, Bastienne enquired where Jon was and a nurse pointed him in the direction of the ICU ward.

Bastienne hobbled down the passage on one crutch towards the ICU ward where Jon was located and entering found Claire sitting alongside Jon's bed.

'Bon jour Lieutenant Commander,' said Bastienne.

'Bon jour Capitaine Petit, please call me Claire,' she said.

'OK, Claire please call me Bastienne,' he replied.

'How's my friend doing?' asked Bastienne.

'Not well, I pray that he will pull through,' responded Claire.

Not wanting to stay and see Jon in that condition, Bastienne said, 'I can't stay but I will pray for him later tonight,' as he turned and bid Claire farewell excusing himself.

'Au revoir,' good bye, he said as he left.

A short while later a nurse appeared and notified Claire that it was time to leave.

Claire reluctantly rose, kissed Jon's hand and left the ICU ward making her way back to her car and drove back to the embassy.

She knew that she had to get a hold of herself as she entered the embassy with multiple people offering their sympathy and support.

'Thanks everybody.' 'I am deeply sorry to tell you all that Stan has been killed in the explosion,' said Claire.

Embassy staff stared at Claire in disbelief, many with their hands cupped over their mouths.

'Stan, Jon and Joseph a Mossad agent as well as a Captain from the French police by the name of Bastienne Petit raided a warehouse in Le Blanc-Mesnil,' offered Claire.

'Intelligence gathered by Mossad and by the CIA tracked down a terrorist who was the bomb maker that killed fifteen people, including seven children and wounding one hundred and thirty others in a pizzeria in Jerusalem in August 2001,' said Claire.

'The terrorist was one of the bomb makers responsible for making IED's in Syria that has killed and injured hundreds of American and Allied soldiers,' said Claire emphatically.

'All the terrorists died in the explosion,' continued Claire.

People were horrified by the news of Stan's passing, many shedding tears and frozen in shock, staring silently in Claire's direction, until one person asked, how Jon and Joseph were.

'Both Jon and Joseph are alive,' said Claire.

'Joseph has a punctured lung, a broken arm and leg with a minor head wound and concussion.' 'He will recover shortly and was very lucky,' continued Claire.

'Jon has sustained very severe injuries and the doctor that operated on him, said that he may die from his injuries and that he will only be able to get a clearer prognosis of his condition in the next seventy two hours,' said Claire.

'He has swelling of the brain, a fractured abdomen, a fractured pelvis, two broken ribs and concussion,' continued Claire.

'The doctor said that the operation was successful however he cannot say whether Jon will survive,' said Claire tears welling up in her eyes.

Turing to leave, Claire said, 'please excuse me everybody, I need to get back to my office.'

Claire retrieved Jon's mobile phone from her handbag, scrolled down seeking his parent's number, punched it into the phone and notified his parents that their son had a bad accident and was in ICU at the American Hospital in Paris and that he may die from his injuries.

Claire then called Director Heathcott and broke the news of Stan's death which was devastating for Barnaby as he had lost a very dear and trusted friend.

The next day Yonti's parents Marcel and Brielle made the trip to Paris leaving their son Pierre in charge of the family business in Nice on the French Riviera and having chatted to the doctor that performed the operation were at his bedside all day until late that night.

Still in an induced coma and unable to communicate, her son simply lay there with his mother Brielle holding his hand and not taking her eyes off him.

His father was very confused about the mysterious name of Jon Jones and quizzed Claire repeatedly about it, however to no avail.

'It's a mystery to me,' lied Claire.

'You will need to ask him when he wakes up,' said Claire.

A day later Marcel and Brielle made their way back to Nice and waited patiently to hear of any progress that their son had made.

His father had now concluded that his son was working for the French police or some agency associated with the police and was unable to speak about what he did.

Barnaby immediately flew to Paris, visited Jon in ICU and spent time with Claire and other embassy staff analyzing all the footage of the events that led to Stan's death.

He concluded that none of the intelligence indicated that there was a car bomb in the trunk of one of the cars being repaired in the panel beating shop.

Having met the doctor, Barnaby informed him of the importance to ensure that Jon survives.

Barnaby sat with Jon for a number of hours deep in thought and having said a silent prayer finally got to his feet and saluted Jon as he turned and left the ICU ward.

Further proof that the threat of a car bomb exploding outside the embassy was creditable, Barnaby reminded himself as he walked down the passage towards the doctor's office.

'This young man is an extremely important person for the future of mankind,' stated Barnaby candidly to the doctor as he and the doctor made their way towards the exit.

Barnaby made arrangements to have Stan's body flown back to the USA on board an American Airlines flight and boarded the flight himself to accompany his friend on its last journey home.

Claire visited the hospital daily and slowly saw the improvement in her lover over the days that followed. She had long come to accept his alias of Jon and the need for him to cover his tracks.

Jon eventually woke up a couple of days later and Claire broke the news of Stan's passing to him. Tears welled up in Jon's eyes as he recalled the relationship he had forged with the great man.

Claire called his parents and informed them that their son's condition had improved and that he was no longer in danger of suffering from brain damage and both parents breathed a sigh of relief.

'Merci beaucoup,' thank you very much, said both parents.

'Promettez-moi que tu le raménerez à la maison quand il sera guéri,' promise me that you will bring him home when he has recovered, said his mother Brielle.

'Oui, je vais,' yes I will, replied Claire.

Joseph had a nurse take him in a wheelchair to see his mate every day noticing the improvement in his condition daily and his own condition improved until he was finally released from hospital a week later.

The doctor that operated on Jon was extremely happy with his recovery in the three weeks since the incident, stating that his progress was remarkable in such a short space of time. Luckily, with no obvious brain damage that was undoubtedly due to the excellent physical condition he was in.

In the rare moments when Claire and Jon were alone, she lifted the blankets and slid her hand towards his penis, massaging it slowly, with Jon moaning that it was now a dead soldier and was like a flat wheel.

'Don't worry my handsome man, I will blow it up again,' quipped Claire.

'Espérons qu'il fonctionnera à nouveau,' hope it will work again, he said smiling as he regained some of his humor.

'I think you need to take a sip of God's holy water,' said Claire handing over Stan's hip flask.

'In memory of my good friend,' he said taking a sip.

Should not be doing this in my condition he thought to himself, but stuff it, it's in memory of a good friend.

Director Heathcott continued to call daily to check on his progress.

Jon found the two daily physio routines extremely taxing to begin with, however his physical strength improved day by day.

His parents called daily to speak with him and his father eventually questioned what he did for a living.

He tried in vain to shift the focus away from the line of questioning and told his father that he would tell him someday.

Having no option but to accept what his son had told him, his father never brought up the subject of his career again, believing that someday he would tell them.

Days became weeks and Jon was finally discharged from hospital.

He hobbled around and whist still in some discomfort, he recovered well over time.

Claire drove him to her apartment and once inside she put her arms around him and whispered 'Dieu merci, vous étes en vie,' thank God you are alive, she said.

Jon admired his shaven head and the scar in the mirror and complained of the odd headache occasionally in the days that followed.

He remained in good spirits and slowly but surely his condition improved.

Geez, can't have my magic wand fall asleep he thought to himself.

Hope it gets so hot that I can weld with it again, he reminded himself.

Looking at himself in the mirror, Jon whispered to himself, 'my penis is my most prized possession and sweet Jesus please make it work properly again.'

Claire had buried herself in her work at the embassy which helped take her mind off her lover.

Claire finally accessed Stan's mobile phone as his login code was known to her as his most trusted aide.

She scrolled through various emails when she saw a photograph of an encrypted message which was foreign to her.

The photograph was the most recent picture in his photo library album on his mobile phone and seemed to have been taken shortly before he left for the warehouse raid with the team, indicating that he was most likely going to attend to it when he returned later that evening.

Wonder what on earth this could be Claire thought to herself.

Best check this as it may be important she thought to herself.

Claire had a key to Stan's safe and opened it.

She removed all the documents and personal effects and laid them out on the table.

Rummaging through the pile of documents, she came across what appeared to be a conversion table and she compared the encrypted alphabet table to the photograph on Stan's mobile phone.

Claire deciphered the message and read it out to herself.

Pushkin has a plan B.

Russia has developed a new deadly chemical weapon which is a state secret and is not known to exist outside of a privileged few of Pushkin's inner circle and the scientists that developed it.

If the launch does not take place from North Korea, he will put this chemical weapon on board a commercial flight from Moscow to Washington and the Pilot will release the contents over Washington.

I wonder what launch he is referring to, Claire thought to herself.

The Pilot will overshoot the runway and declare an emergency and circle the city dumping fuel, however instead of dumping fuel he will dump this deadly poison that will filter down to earth and kill all people within a radius of fifty miles within two hours.

Claire was horrified by what she had just discovered and stared at the message for some time.

Dear Lord, I need to get this information to the Director of the CIA immediately thought Claire to herself.

Claire dialed Director Barnaby Heathcott on a secure line and informed him of what she had discovered on Stan's mobile phone.

'Good Lord,' replied Barnaby.

'Please get this message and the encrypted conversion table to me through a diplomatic pouch, as soon as possible,' said Barnaby.

'I will arrange for agents d'Avray and Van Der Jong to collect this and get it to our Gulfstream and have it flown back to Langley immediately,' said Barnaby.

Barnaby could not trust an email as electronic messages could be intercepted.

'Please expect them within the next thirty minutes,' continued Barnaby.

'Thanks and well done Claire,' said Barnaby ending the call.

Agent d'Avray reported to reception at the embassy and was met by Claire handing over a diplomatic pouch.

She said, 'take great care of this Richard as it contains some vitally important information for Director Heathcott.'

'Will do Lieutenant Commander,' said agent d'Avray as he turned and made his way back to the waiting SUV.

'Airport please driver and make it chop, chop,' he quipped to his fellow agent Alex Van Der Jong.

'Yes sir, at your service,' replied agent Van Der Jong joining the traffic and pointing the SUV towards Paris Le Bourget airport.

The agent parked the SUV inside the hanger and boarded the Gulfstream with the Co-Pilot offering his hand in a warm welcome as they boarded.

'Hi boys, welcome aboard,' said the Co-Pilot.

'Grubs in the warmer and I even have some cold beers for you hard working lads in the fridge,' continued the Co-Pilot.

Engines running the Co-Pilot retrieved the staircase and locked the door before the Gulf Stream taxied out of the hanger with the hanger door closing remotely behind them as they cleared the hanger.

The Gulf Stream taxied towards the runway, turned onto the runway and the Pilots engaged full throttle and they were up and away a few minutes later.

'I love this part of the job,' said agent d'Avary.

'Agreed my friend,' replied agent Van Der Jong as he settled comfortably into his seat.

'Not often we get to fly first class mate,' said agent d'Avray

'I will do the honors my friend so what would you like to drink?' asked agent Van Der Jong rising as they reached altitude.

'A frosty will do my friend,' replied agent d'Avray.

Both agents enjoyed their meals of roast beef and vegetables rounding the meal off with a steam date pudding.

'Great meal for a pair of hard working lads,' commented agent d'Avray.

Having enjoyed the luxury of a few beers and a couple of night caps of scotch, both agents settled in for the long flight back to Langley.

Eight and a half hours later the Gulf Stream was on a final approach into the private airport near Biglers Mill that the CIA uses exclusively.

Barnaby waited patiently for the Gulf Stream to land and watched as it taxied towards the hanger and once inside, the door opened with the staircase dropping down.

Both agents appeared in the doorway and made their way down the staircase and offered their usual greeting to the Director of the CIA Barnaby Heathcott.

'Hello boss,' they offered.

'Hi boys, hope you had a good flight and enjoyed the hospitality,' said Barnaby.

Handing over the pouch, both agents thanked Barnaby.

Barnaby thanked them and bid them farewell before turning towards the black SUV, jumped into the rear seat and they sped off with one security detail in front and another at the rear as they sped back towards Langley.

Barnaby rode his private elevator to his office on the top floor and entering through his personal assistants office said, 'I don't want to be disturbed Gizelle,' as he closed the door behind him.

Barnaby opened the pouch and laid the documents on the table.

He studied the contents and double checked the analysis that Claire had done verifying its accuracy.

God this is extremely serious he thought to himself.

He immediately dialed the White House and was put through to the President's personal assistant and notified her that he needed to see the President immediately.

A short while later, Barnaby's security detail pulled up at the security booth at the White House and were waived through.

Barnaby exited the SUV and past the security agent at the door and into the White House, accompanied by another security agent as he made his way towards the Oval Office.

The President's personal assistant tapped lightly on the door announcing Barnaby's arrival.

Rising and rounding his desk, President Trent offered his hand in a greeting.

'Hello Barnaby, what's so urgent that you needed to get here ASAP?' questioned the President.

'Coffee,' offered the President.

'Thank you Mr. President I would appreciate a cup,' replied Barnaby.

The President poured two cups of coffee offering one to Barnaby and took a seat opposite him on the couch.

'Righto Barnaby, what's so urgent?' asked the President.

'As you know Stan Noble died in the raid on the warehouse in Paris,' said Barnaby.

'Well Mr. President his aide Lieutenant Commander Johnston accessed Stan's mobile phone and found an image of an encrypted message on it that appeared to have been taken shortly before he joined the team for the raid on the warehouse in which he sadly lost his life,' said Barnaby.

Continuing Barnaby added, 'his assistant then accessed his private safe and discovered an encrypted conversion table and went about deciphering the message which had come from Pushkin's head of security, namely Victor Portnorsky.'

'Stan had recruited Portnorsky years previously when he was a lieutenant in the FSB and he has passed on valuable Russian secrets to us for many years,' continued Barnaby.

'Portnorsky was the person who passed on the USB stick with the footage of the meeting between Pushkin and Xiu Jaoping and had indicated that he wanted to defect to the west and in particular to America,' said

Barnaby.

'This will take some time to arrange and we are purposely delaying his escape as we continue to filter out more valuable information,' stated Barnaby.

'Portnorsky now has the rank of colonel and heads up Pushkin's security detail and is his most trusted security man.' 'He personally saved Pushkin's life in an assassination attempt similar to the one that nearly killed the late President Regan,' continued Barnaby.

The President sat attentively listening to what Barnaby was saying.

'Respectfully Mr. President, we need to safeguard Portnorsky's identity,' stated Barnaby.

The decoded message has indicated that Pushkin has a backup plan in case of the North Korean's not launching the nukes as planned,' said Barnaby.

The President leaned forward in anticipation of learning what Pushkin's plan entailed.

'Pushkin's backup plan is to fly a commercial airliner to Washington, have the Pilot declare a fake emergency, overshoot the runway and release a deadly poison making it seem like they are dumping fuel as they circle the city,' stated Barnaby.

'After they have deposited all the poison, they will reroute to another unknown international airport,' said Barnaby.

'The poison that will be released will kill everybody in a fifty mile radius of the capital within two hours of it being released,' continued Barnaby.

'Good Lord, what else is this bastard planning,' stated the President leaning further forward.

'The composition of the poison is a state secret and known only to Pushkin, the two scientists that developed it and a couple of his most trusted aides,' said Barnaby.

'There's simply no end to what this fucking bastard will do,' said the President.

'We will need to ferret out exactly what type of poison this is and when they intend trying to use it,' stated the President.

'Well Mr. President, I have instructed our assets in Moscow to be on the alert for any suspicious behavior and to monitor any plane scheduled for any type of maintenance in commercial hangers as well as military installations,' said Barnaby.

'We will have to be on high alert regarding all commercial flights by their own carrier and all Russian flights from international airports around the globe,' continued Barnaby.

'Well if that's the case and we are able to identify the plane, we may be forced to shoot it down over the ocean,' said the President.

'If they in fact carry this out, it will be tantamount to a declaration of war,' stated the President.

I will have to confront Pushkin directly sooner rather than later, the President pondered to himself.

'We will intercept the flight over the ocean and get the Pilot to detour and land at some remote island possibly off north Africa which will give me time to confront Pushkin directly,' said the President.

'So in theory, we may be facing numerous threats to the US and possibly other allies,' concluded the President.

'Time is not on our side Mr. President,' said Barnaby.

'Yes, very true Barnaby,' replied the President.

'Thank you for your service to our nation Barnaby,' said the President.

'I really appreciate all the work that you and all those at the CIA do Barnaby,' said the President rising to conclude the meeting.

'Do you really believe that Pushkin will do something like this?' questioned the President walking him to the door.

'Yes I think he is capable of doing something like this Mr. President,' replied Barnaby.

'Well Mr. President, my opinion is that Pushkin's threat of launching nukes from North Korea is merely a front,' said Barnaby.

'He knows that doing that would result in us retaliating in no uncertain terms and that would lead to a full scale nuclear war and the end of the world,' stated Barnaby.

'Pushkin may have suspected that we would have found out about his plan to launch nukes from North Korea which I believe is merely a front for what he really intends doing,' said Barnaby.

'It certainly looks like this could be his real plan, putting poison onto a commercial flight Mr. President,' stated Barnaby.

Taking Barnaby's hand the President said, 'thanks for your input Barnaby, please let me know of any further developments.'

Chapter 23

Novo-Ogaryovo

Russia

Sitting at his desk in his study at Novo-Ogaryovo the suburban residence of the President of The Soviet Union, President Pushkin turned to his three most trusted comrades.

'My comrades, this plan will make Washington go "Kaboom" and destroy the city and everything around it for seventy miles,' said Pushkin.

'We will render the imperialists rudderless and take control of the world,' said Pushkin.

'I want to punish them,' continued Pushkin.

Rafael once again put his expertise in computer engineering to good use and had managed to hack into Pushkin's private emails, uncovering emails between Pushkin and comrade Zotov.

He had engaged the services of an interpreter at Langley making him to take an oath to keep everything he learns from the emails confidential.

The emails revealed the name of a container vessel that Pushkin intended using.

Rafael stared at the monitor for some time and focused his attention on the name, Sea Thunder.

The vessel was owned by Sky High Shipping and mentioned a number of times in the emails between Pushkin and comrade Evgeniy Zotov, the Russian Minister of Transport.

He Googled the ships name and discovered that it was a container ship, albeit a medium sized vessel that could carry eighty forty foot containers with a capacity of eight thousand seven hundred and seven pounds per container.

The vessel is twenty years old and is rather small in comparison to today's large container vessels, therefore it was unlikely to draw any attention and had a crew of twenty people.

The next day Rafael called the Director of the CIA on a secure line from the embassy in Paris and asked Miss Marple to patch him straight through to the Director.

'Hello Rafael, what have you discovered?' Questioned Barnaby.

'Well Director, I believe that I have uncovered another plot by Pushkin,' said Rafael.

'As I understand it, he intends sailing a container ship into the Port of Baltimore loaded with high explosives, containing ANFO which is ammonium nitrate-fuel oil mixture, dynamite, nitroglycerin, PETN or pentaerythritol tetranitrate, picric acid, and TNT then detonate it whilst in port,' said Rafael.

Continuing Rafael said, 'the vessel is the Sea Thunder and is owned by Sky High Shipping, which is a Russian owned business operating out of Singapore sir,' stated Rafael.

'From what I have managed to find out, it's currently in the Russian northern Fleet Naval base port of Severomorsk,' said Rafael.

'Apparently they intend routing it from the port at Severomorsk to Singapore, load a couple of containers and then set sail for the Port of Baltimore and offload the containers that they loaded in Singapore,' continued Rafael.

'This would appear to the authorities that it is a legitimate container vessel, just going about its day to day business activities,' said Rafael.

'I believe that the stop in the Port of Baltimore will be to offload the containers loaded in Singapore and to load supplies, which I think is merely a front for what they really intend doing,' stated Rafael.

'After they have offloaded the containers, the ship's crew will disembark in stages and make their way to the airport and catch international flights to various locations outside of the USA before a timer or various timers are activated that will trigger the explosives,' said Rafael.

'The explosion will make the explosion in Beirut look like a Guy Fawkes cracker having gone off and this will result in massive damage to buildings, bridges and infrastructure as well as a huge loss in human and animal life for around seventy miles around the blast site,' continued Rafael.

'Clearly Washington falls within this radius,' stated Rafael.

'Oh my goodness, this is a very serious threat,' stated Barnaby.

'Well done, that's excellent work. Thank you Rafael and please continue to ferret out any further information possible,' said Barnaby.

Barnaby activated satellite images of the port of Severomorsk and images of a container vessel came into view on the monitor. It appeared that they were loading containers.

There would only be one way to prevent this catastrophe he thought to himself.

Barnaby called the White House and asked the President's personal assistant to arrange an urgent meeting at his earliest convenience.

A couple of minutes later the personal assistant notified Barnaby that the President would see him immediately.

Barnaby was ushered into the Oval Office with President Trent, Vice President Tippence, Secretary of State Pompello and National Security Advisor O'Rourke all offering warm handshakes.

'Well Barnaby, every time I see you its's bad news,' said the President.

'Sorry to constantly be the bearer of bad news Mr. President, however it's the nature of the business that we are in sir,' stated Barnaby.

'So what is Pushkin up to now?' Asked the President.

'We have uncovered another plot by Pushkin, Mr. President,' said Barnaby.

'It has come to our attention that Pushkin is planning to sail a container ship fully laden with high explosives into the Port of Baltimore, then trigger an explosion, Mr. President,' stated Barnaby.

The President sat on the couch with one of his elbow resting on his leg and his thumb under his chin with the palm of his hand covering his mouth.

'Good Lord, what else is this despot going to do,' said the President.

'The problem is, that we have no idea whether this is creditable at all,' said Barnaby.

'The vessel is currently being loaded at the port of Severomorsk in Russia and from what our agent has been able to glean, it will set sail for Singapore shortly,' continued Barnaby.

'It is believed that the vessel will sail for Singapore and load ten containers then sail to the Port of Baltimore, however we cannot be sure and we are currently monitoring its every move at present,' said Barnaby.

'What we have managed to discover thus far, is that Pushkin intends to fill all the containers with high end explosives and detonate them on a timer or various timers after they have docked in Baltimore,' repeated Barnaby candidly.

'This would be like a nuclear explosion and the ramifications would be, that the blast would destroy everything within a radius of seventy miles which of course includes Washington and cause a tsunami the likes of which the world has never seen,' said Barnaby emphatically.

'Sweet Jesus in Heaven, what else is this mad man going to do?' Asked the President.

'Undoubtedly, if Pushkin did carry this out, this would be a declaration of war,' stated the President emphatically.

'Barnaby, I trust that your team are doing everything in their power to ferret out if this has legs and if so, when it will sail?' pressed the President.

'It appears that they intend routing it from Severomorsk to Singapore and as we understand it, it will sail shortly,' continued Barnaby.

'As mentioned they will then load a few containers in Singapore for the onward journey to the Port of Baltimore,' said Barnaby.

'This will make it look like a normal shipment of containers between countries without drawing any attention from the authorities,' stated Barnaby.

'The ship's crew will disembark in stages and make their way to the airport and catch international flights to various locations before a timer or timers has activated the explosives,' stated Barnaby.

'Goodness me,' said the President.

Rising and taking Barnaby hand the President said, 'please do everything in your power to fully investigate this urgently,' stated the President.

'Yes Mr. President we are onto it right now,' said Barnaby.

The Vice President, Secretary of State and National Security Advisor all sat in silence as they considered the ramifications of this latest threat from Pushkin.

A few days later Barnaby again found himself in the Oval Office.

Having greeted the President and taken a seat on the couch, Barnaby said, 'I can confirm that the ship has sailed from Severomorsk an hour ago Mr. President,' said Barnaby.

Continuing Barnaby said, 'we believe that they could have loaded thousands of tons of high end explosives into the containers and as mentioned previously, if that ever exploded in port, it would be like a nuclear warhead being unleashed.'

'It would entirely destroy Washington and we estimate that it would cause a tsunami of around one and half thousand plus feet and we know what the ramifications of that would be, not only for us but for the world at large,' stated Barnaby.

'Clearly this is a realistic threat and we cannot even destroy the ship at sea, because the explosion would immediately cause a massive tsunami,' continued Barnaby.

'The ramifications would be horrific,' said Barnaby candidly.

'Thank you for the information Barnaby,' said the President.

'Please keep me fully informed Barnaby as this has dire consequences for the whole world,' stated the President.

'To quote Pushkin's exact words, he plans to make Washington go Kaboom,' said Barnaby.

'Dear Lord, how would we prevent this vessel from getting anywhere near the USA?' Asked the President.

'Well Mr. President, we would need to use Seal Team Six and land them on board the ship using the same stealth helicopters that we used when they killed Osama Bin Laden in Pakistan,' said Barnaby.

'Seal Team Six would then need to go about identifying where the remote or remotes are positioned and disarm them well out to sea,' said Barnaby.

'One would assume, that they will use a timing device or multiple devices to trigger the first explosion which of course will trigger explosions from all the other containers,' stated Barnaby candidly.

'I believe that this is our only option Mr. President,' stated Barnaby.

The President stood, taking Barnaby's hand in a farewell gesture.

Barnaby returned to Langley and buried himself at the task at hand, analysing the possible threat.

Having carefully monitored the container vessel for the past week, Barnaby watched images of it sailing into the Port of Singapore beamed onto his monitor.

Two days later, the Sea Thunder set sail for the port of the Port of Baltimore.

A week earlier, The President had General Mitchfield order one of the carrier battle groups to re-route towards Singapore.

He ordered General Mitchfield to ensure that the carrier had Sikorsky Black Hawk helicopters on board as well as seals from Seal Team Six and to position the battle group on the sea lane from Singapore to the US.

All the members of his Security Council and Joint Chiefs of Staff were seated in the Situation Room and all stood as the President entered.

'Right gentlemen, we are hopefully going to safely disarm this vessel,' stated the President.

'Barnaby, do you have a live stream for us?' Questioned the President.

'Yes Mr. President,' replied Barnaby.

A moment later the satellite feed was displayed on the monitor on the wall.

Admiral Ortez, gave an overview of their position in relation to the Sea Thunder and notified the President that the carrier battle group was sailing some fifty nautical miles south of the container vessel.

Images of seals from Seal Team Six boarding the two helicopters were displayed on the screen.

Further images beamed from a satellite at NORAD were being displayed onto another screen showing the exact position of the Sea Thunder.

Two Black Hawk helicopters took off en route to intercept the Sea Thunder under the guise of darkness as the current GMT was just after midnight and night vision images from the lead helicopter were beamed back to the Situation Room as they flew towards the Sea Thunder.

A short while later, the lead helicopter hovered above the vessel with seals fast roping onto its deck and making their way towards the bridge.

The second Black Hawk helicopter hovered above the bridge with more seals fast roping and making their way towards the crew quarters.

Vision taken from the Seal Team leader were displayed on the screen as they went about securing the bridge, identifying the Captain and first officer.

The second team of seals rounded up all the crew including those on duty in the engine room and brought them all to the bridge with the remaining seals conducting room to room searches of all the crew quarters.

Thirty minutes later the Seal Team leader reported that all twenty crew members had been accounted for.

Rafael found himself on board the Sea Thunder in the company of Seal Team Six and having identified the Captain, went about interrogating him, however the Captain stubbornly refused to cooperate.

Rafael had arranged for the team leader of Seal Team Six to move to another part of the ship so that the images displayed on his helmet cam would not be screened when he interrogated the ship's Captain.

Rafael, pulled the Captain to one side and said, 'I am only going to give you one chance to answer and if you fail to cooperate, I will then shoot you in the foot and knee.'

'Do you understand Captain?' Asked Rafael.

The Captain merely stared at Rafael and offered no comment.

Images of the crew lying on the floor were beamed on the live feed to the White House.

'One last time, where are the remote devices?' shouted Rafael.

A moment later the screen on the wall in the Situation Room went blank.

'What's happened to the live feed?' Asked the President.

Knowing why the live feed was interrupted, Barnaby said, 'I'm sure that we will have it back online soon Mr. President.'

'We must have lost the satellite feed,' continued Barnaby.

Having seen Rafael scratch his head, Barnaby knew that this was the sign to stop the live feed for a couple of minutes as Rafael was about to exert pressure on one of the captives and he did not want this to be seen and witnessed by anybody other than those in the CIA.

Barnaby had made arrangements at CIA headquarters to stop the feed for a couple of minutes as soon as Rafael scratched his head.

Barnaby said, 'I'm sure that we will have it back online soon Mr. President.'

Rafael extracted his Glock fitted with a silencer and shot the Captain in the foot.

The Captain screamed in pain.

'One more time Captain, where are the remotes,' shouted Rafael.

He whispered into the Captain's ear and repeated, 'I won't ask you again, the next time I will shoot you in the knee, do you understand?' said Rafael.

The Captain was quick to point to his first officer, 'ask him,' he said.

Rafael walked over to the first officer and without speaking, extracted an Emerson's Specwar Custom Knife from the sheath on the side of his pants and positioned the tip of the blade facing his testicles.

'I am going to cut your balls out and feed them to you and make you eat them, then I will use your ballbag as a tobacco pouch,' said Rafael.

'Do you understand?' said Rafael.

'One last time, where are the remotes?' questioned Rafael.

Just then the live feed resumed with images of Rafael, standing over the first officer were aired on the monitor.

'So what just happened?' asked the President.

'No idea Mr. President,' replied Barnaby.

'The remotes are in my quarters,' said the first officer with a petrified look on his face.

Rafael pulled him to his feet and asked the Seal Team leader to have two of his seals accompany him and the first officer to his quarters.

The Seal Team leader pulled the helmsman to his feet and ordered him to steer the ship on the same heading and ordered two seals to accompany the chief engineer to the engine room and ordered that he stop the vessel.

Having tied the first officer's hands, the two seals and Rafael made their way to his quarters.

The first officer indicated towards the sideboard drawer, Rafael opened it and found two remotes with timers in them.

That was all that was needed to remotely trigger the explosive devices in two of the containers resulting in two huge explosions that would automatically set off explosions in all the other containers.

'Who gave you the order to do this?' pressed Rafael.

'Comrade Evgeniy Zotov, the Russian Minister of Transport,' replied the first officer.

Continuing the first officer said, 'Comrade Zotov personally over saw the loading of the containers and disembarked just before we set sail for Singapore.'

Rafael grabbed the first officer by the throat and asked, 'so what were your plans when you docked in at the Port of Baltimore?'

'Our orders are to offload the containers we loaded in Singapore and then let the crew disembark in groups and make their way to the airport and catch flights out of America,' said the first officer.

Continuing he said, 'I was to be the last person to leave the ship and would set the timers to four hours ahead which would give me enough time to get to the airport and fly out.'

'After we have offloaded the ten containers that were loaded in Singapore, there would be seventy containers left on board with high explosives in them, so when they explode there would be around six hundred and nine thousand pounds of explosives going up,' he said.

'Ja, Kaboom, a very big Kaboom,' he said with a smirk on his face.

'You piece of shit,' said Rafael grabbing him by the collar.

'What's going to happen, is that I am going to tie you down and put you into one of those containers, so if you are lying to me and have some other hidden remotes that you have not told me about, you are going to go Kaboom with the rest of the containers,' shouted Rafael.

'And before you go Kaboom, I will cut your fucking balls out and make you eat them,' said Rafael.

'Do you understand, you Russian prick?' shouted Rafael.

The first officer stared wide eyed at Rafael in silence.

Rafael cuffed the first officer, pulled him up by his shirt and ordered him to point the way to the two containers that had the remote detonators in them.

Having pointed them out, he radioed the team leader and a few minutes later two seals skilled in disarming explosive devices joined them as they opened the first container situated on the lower deck.

The seals went about removing the timer and the detonator and secured the area.

The first officer pointed out the second container in the middle batch of containers and the seals repeated the same process of disarming the timing device and detonator.

Rafael turned to face the first officer and grabbed him by the testicles and squeezed as hard as he could.

The first officer screamed in pain.

'Right you fucking piece of shit, I will only ask you this once more, in which containers are the other timers and detonators,' said Rafael extracting his knife from its sheath,'

'Now I'm going to cut your fucking balls out and make you eat them you Russian piece of shit,' shouted Rafael.

The first officer, in pain with tears streaming down his cheeks said, 'I promise you that there are only these two timers and detonators on board,'

Rafael stared at him for some time and squeezed his testicles again.

'I have told you that there are no more timers and detonators,' screamed the first officer in pain.

'Rafael pulled the first officer by the scruff of his neck towards the maintenance room adjacent to the engine room.

The two seals guarded the first officer while Rafael searched for some rope and a heavy metal engine part.

He then instructed the seals to take the first officer to the upper deck and he tied the engine part to his legs that were bound.

Rafael turned to the first officer and said, 'I have warned you not to lie to me, you piece of shit.'

'Now I am going to throw you overboard and feed you to the sharks,' he shouted.

The first officer pleaded for his life as Rafael pulled him towards the port side of the vessel and prepared to throw him overboard with the heavy metal part attached to his legs.

'Good bye, you piece of shit,' said Rafael.

The first officer screamed in fear and stated, 'I promise that there are no more timers or detonators on board.'

'Please sir, believe me,' pleaded the first officer.

Rafael stared at the first officer for a couple of minutes, before instructing the two seals to help hoist the first officer and throw him overboard.

'No please,' pleaded the first officer.

'There are no more detonators on board,' screamed the first officer.

Rafael, pulled him back from the edge of the port bow and stared at him for a minute before picking him up by the collar and instructing the seals to take him to one of the containers and lock him up inside the container.

'Just to be sure that you have not lied to me, this is where you are going to stay so if it does go Kaboom, you will be the first into hell,' said Rafael.

Back on the bridge, Rafael reported to Barnaby that the two timers and detonators had been identified and that the seals had disarmed them.

The President turned to Barnaby, 'is this the agent you told me about?' he asked.

'Yes Mr. President, that's him,' said Barnaby.

The President merely nodded.

The Seal Team Leader was the first to respond.

'Mr. President, we have identified two timers and detonators in two of the containers and my team have disarmed them sir.'

'We have no guarantee that these two are the only ones on board and will now start searching all the remaining containers Mr. President,' said the Seal Team Leader.

'I expect this process to take twenty four hours sir,' continued the team leader.

'We have stopped sailing and will remain in the area until the search has been completed and will then await instructions from you Mr. President,' he said.

'Thank you and your team for saving millions of lives,' said the President.

The President tuned to all in the Situation room, 'what do you suggest I do with Pushkin?

The Secretary of State responded, 'we need to get this madman around a table ASAP and get him to stop this madness.'

'I feel that it would be appropriate if we sailed this vessel back towards Russia and set the timers to coincide with its arrival and give Ivan some of his own medicine,' continued the Secretary of State.

'However, that would make us as bad as them,' he said.

'If we in fact did do that, it would still result in a massive tsunami and kill hundreds of thousands if not millions of people and that's not the American way at all,' said Mike Pompello.

'I agree that we need to get Pushkin around a table ASAP Mike,' said the President.

Turning to face Barnaby, the President said, 'well done Barnaby.'

'Please pass on my thanks to your agent,' and then turned to General Mitchfield.

'Job well done General,' said the President.

Standing to end the meeting, the President said, 'please pass on my thanks to the Seal Team Six General and your agent Barnaby.'

Chapter 24

Zhukovsky International Airport

Russia

The President buzzed his personal assistant and notified her that he did not want to be disturbed, walked to the sideboard and poured himself a stiff scotch.

He returned to his desk, put his feet up, clasped his hands behind his head and pondered what he should do and whether trying to set up a meeting with Pushkin and Xiu Jaoping and laying it squarely on the table would solve the problem.

Desperate people do desperate things he thought to himself.

The President reminded himself that neither Pushkin nor Xiu Jaoping had returned his calls and he reflected on what the Director of the CIA Barnaby Heathcott had just told him and thought to himself, Pushkin's certainly a dangerous one.

Hmm, this is going to be tricky he thought to himself.

The President was deep in thought as he sipped the whisky from the tumbler and wondered whether this supposed nuclear attack was merely a front for what he really intended to do, which is releasing the poison over Washington.

Effectively if he did fly a commercial flight from Moscow to Washington and release this poison, the country would be leaderless and without an administration.

This would then effectively result in the country falling into total chaos which would allow Pushkin to dictate to the world at large and possibly strike with nukes.

I hope that the CIA can ascertain when Ivan intends flying this plane to Washington pondered the President.

The next day the President entered the situation room with all standing in respect.

'Good afternoon gentlemen, please be seated,' said the President.

'There has been a serious new development,' stated the President.

Looking at Barnaby, the President said, 'please bring us up to date Barnaby.'

'Well Mr. President, we have learnt that Pushkin has a plan to fly a commercial airliner from Moscow to Washington, however the flight will not carry any passengers except the Pilot, Co-Pilot and a navigator,' continued Barnaby.

'The plane will be loaded with a deadly chemical poison and the Pilot will call an emergency and overshoot the runway and whilst circling the city, he will release a deadly poison making it appear that he is dumping fuel,' said Barnaby.

'From what we have learnt, this poison is the most deadly poison that the Russians have developed to date and is top secret and the formula is only known to the two scientists that developed it and a couple of Pushkin's most trusted cadres,' continued Barnaby.

'As we understand it, this deadly poison will kill everybody and everything within a fifty mile radius within a two hour window, thus if successful, this will effectively mean that the country's administration will be eliminated and we will be rudderless,' said Barnaby.

'From what we have learned the Russians tested this poison in a remote village in Syria and within a two hour timeframe, all human, animal and plant life ceased to exist,' stated Barnaby.

'How credible is this?' asked the Secretary of State Neville Pompello.

'Well Mr. Secretary, our information comes from a highly regarded source, so I have no doubt that it is accurate,' said Barnaby.

Continuing Barnaby said, 'I believe that the threat of launching nuclear missiles from North Korea may have been a diversion for Pushkin's real plan.'

'Pushkin would know that launching nuclear missiles would bring an unprecedented retaliatory response from us and would lead to a full scale nuclear war and the end of the world,' said Barnaby.

'I don't believe that Pushkin is that stupid to get North Korea to launch any nuclear missiles nor do I believe that he would launch any nukes from mother Russia, so I believe that this is his alternative as the sanctions that we and our allies have imposed on them has severely damaged their economy,' continued Barnaby.

'Pushkin is facing increasing civil unrest in Russia with daily protests that have turned violent and we have all seen footage of the sabotage within the country and as we all know there have been rumours of a possible coup,' stated Barnaby.

'So dumping this poison over Washington and eliminating our country's administration will put him in an excellent position to dictate terms to the world and for him to continue violently clamping down on the anarchy that exists in his country,' said Barnaby.

'We have our operatives currently monitoring a maintenance hangar at Zhukovsky Airport in Moscow where the Russians currently have a Russian United Aircraft Corporation MC-21 300 airliner in a hanger,' continued Barnaby.

'This is their equivalent to an Airbus A320 that has undergone a major conversion, which appears to be in its final transformation stages from a passenger liner to a plane capable of carrying around fifty thousand pounds of liquid similar to the KC-130J refueling aircraft that our air force uses,' said Barnaby.

Everybody in the room sat in deadly silence merely staring at Barnaby in shock horror.

Secretary of State Neville Pompello was the first to respond, 'sweet Jesus, what else will Pushkin think of,' he stated emphatically.

With all present looking at the President to take the lead, the President told General Mitchfield to ensure that the air force has multiple inceptors ready at all times, as well as B52 bombers ready with nukes loaded in case we need to action a response immediately if Pushkin resorts to launching nukes.

'We also need to get our submarines ready to launch nukes on designated sites in Russia,' stated the President.

'General, this seems very credible so we need the strike group sailing in the Atlantic to position itself on a probable flight path that this Russian airliner could take,' said the President.

'If this eventuates then we may need to shoot it down over the ocean and well away from our shores,' continued the President.

'Trade winds blow away from us towards Africa, Europe and Asia so we would need to be very careful where we shoot this aircraft down and make sure that it is well away from our shores,' continued the President.

Turning to face Barnaby, the President asked, 'how long before you think this is likely to happen Barnaby?'

'I believe that it is imminent, possibly within the next day or two Mr. President,' said Barnaby.

'Right gentlemen, looks like the shit is about to hit the fan,' stated the President.

'General you have three aircraft carrier strike groups in the South and East China seas participating in the war games and one in the Atlantic,' said the President.

'Yes Mr. President, we have one positioned west of the United Kingdom on patrol waiting for your instructions sir,' said General Mitchfield.

'It is near the flight path of aircraft flying from Moscow to the USA,' continued the General.

'We need to disperse as much of this poison as possible over the sea and nowhere near our shores if we in fact do shoot it down,' said the President.

'It could possibly have serious consequences for the Africa, the United Kingdom and Europe, so I would need to consult with our allies about this matter,' continued the President.

'I want the Battle Group to be well away from any point of contact in case we do need to shoot this plane down and I don't want any of this poison filtering down to any of our naval ships, let alone make it to our shores,' stated the President.

'If possible get all shipping to move away from an intended flight path from Moscow to Washington to eliminate any possibility of this deadly poison filtering down to them,' said the President.

'And yes General, I know that this is very short notice, but as you are now aware, this is a very real creditable threat so use whatever excuse you can to get all shipping diverted away from the flight path with immediate effect,' stated the President emphatically.

'Gentlemen, we are now on the cusp of a possible disaster and cannot afford any errors,' said the President.

'Barnaby, what is the chance of us influencing a coup in Russia immediately?' questioned the President.

'No immediate possibility M. President,' replied Barnaby.

'That would take a lot of careful planning and we cannot guarantee that it would work Mr. President,' stated Barnaby.

Standing and not wanting to waste any more time, the President ended the meeting.

'Barnaby follow me please,' said the President leading the way out of the meeting.

Barnaby followed the President into the oval office.

The President walked over to the sideboard and poured two three finger tots of scotch into two tumblers offering one to Barnaby.

Clinking glasses, the President said, 'cheers, best enjoy this while we can, for God alone knows what else the despot has planned.'

Having called his wife to notify her that he would be home very late, which was an excuse and a cover for him to spend some time with his mistress, General Mitchfield told his wife that something very important had come up which needed his immediate attention and that she should not wait up for him.

Later that evening General Mitchfield lay in the bed of his mistress who was also his assistant.

Lying there facing the ceiling, his lover ran her hand over the hairs on his chest.

'You are very quiet tonight,' she said.

'What's worrying you big boy?' she asked.

'We have a huge problem that I cannot discuss,' he replied.

'OK then let's just make love,' she replied.

Hard as he tried he was unable to raise an erection so they just lay there arm in arm for an hour until he finally got up, got dressed, kissed his lover goodnight and made his way back to his office at The Pentagon.

Three days later at one thirty in the morning, Barnaby was sitting in his office when he received a coded message on his secure computer.

Dad's leaving shortly, was all that was stated on the text message.

This was the coded message notifying Barnaby that the plane carrying the poison was preparing to depart from Moscow's Zhukovsky International Airport.

Barnaby immediately called the White House and informed the security agent that he needed to speak with the President immediately.

'It's very important, please wake him up,' said Barnaby.

A short while later the President's croaky voice came on the line.

'Don't tell me Barnaby,' said the President.

'Yes Mr. President the flight is preparing to take off sir,' said Barnaby.

'I will leave immediately for the White House Mr. President,' continued Barnaby.

The President had one of the security agents call all the members of his National Security Council and Joint Chiefs of staff notifying them that they needed to be in the situation room within the hour.

Barnaby had called Rafael and Claire and instructed them to go to the embassy immediately.

He wanted Claire to be at Stan's desk in case he needed some information and for Raphael to be available in case his hacking of the Russian and Chinese missile guidance systems did not work.

All hands on deck for the emergency.

An hour later all the members of the National Security Council were present and seated in the Situation Room.

All stood as the President entered the room unshaven and still in his gown having not bothered to change with his hair uncombed.

'Good morning everyone, please be seated,' said the President.

Barnaby rose and walked over to the image beamed onto the screen and pointed at Moscow.

'We have just had confirmation that a flight from Moscow has taken off about two hours ago, so right now it's heading is on a path to Washington,' said Barnaby.

'The flight is on a heading north of the United Kingdom and the flight time is around nine hours and fifty minutes,' said Barnaby.

'I have confirmation that this is the plane that has had a major conversion to it as our operatives have been carefully monitoring it ensuring that we have the correct plane,' continued Barnaby.

General Mitchfield had contacted Admirable Gomez, the commander of the battlegroup sailing off the United Kingdom close to the intended flight path of the plane and instructed him to have three F/A-18E fighters ready for take-off on the flight deck armed with air to air missiles.

The General notified NORAD to monitor the flight path of the flight from Moscow heading towards Washington and they were updating him every fifteen minutes.

A few hours later Rear Admiral Gomez notified General Mitchfield that they had the plane on radar and were monitoring its flight path and estimated that it would pass to the north of the United Kingdom and the Battle Group in the next two hours.

Pushkin and two of his most trusted advisors sat in his study in his suburban residence and had just opened a second bottle of Stolichnaya Vodka.

Rising with all clinking their glasses, 'nah zda-rovh-yeh,' cheers said Pushkin.

'We are about to destroy the imperialists in their own back yard,' continued Pushkin.

'After that we will take the game to these Yankees and destroy them and their economy and get the rest of the world to kneel before us,' said Pushkin feeling the effect of the alcohol in his system.

President Trent, the National Security Council and Joint Chiefs of Staff sat in silence as General Mitchfield monitored the progress of the flight from a satellite feed beamed onto a screen mounted to the wall in the Situation Room.

Barnaby was speaking quietly into his mobile phone and turned to face the President.

'Mr. President, I have absolute confirmation that some form of liquid was pumped into the tank on the aircraft with people wearing heavy protective suits so no doubt this is confirmation of it being the correct flight and that it is carrying a very dangerous poison sir,' concluded Barnaby.

The President sat silently and thought of the continuing mystery concerning the whereabouts of the missing Malaysian Airlines Flight MH370 that triggered intense conversations in certain circles about whether the Boeing aircraft could have been taken over from the ground.

Evidence that the aircraft could have been controlled remotely are self-evident. The United States has deployed drone aircraft positioned all over the world to perform both surveillance and fire missions controlled by Pilots half a world away from the targets being observed and attacked by their drones.

Drones are designed from the ground up to be controlled remotely and so, it turns out, that Boeing 777's, are equipped with an emergency intervention system that would allow a remote operator to land the aircraft from the ground simply by manipulating the autopilot.

This has never been done before, according to aviation experts, but it is within the realm of possibility.

The Boeing 777 is a "fly-by-wire" aircraft, which means that all of the aeronautical functions of the plane are controlled through digital electronics, rather than hydraulic controls.

The President turned to face Barnaby and asked 'well Barnaby, what is the possibility of us taking over the controls of that aircraft from the ground?'

With all seated turning their attention to what the President had just said and waiting for Barnaby's response, he replied, 'well Mr. President, that's a remote possibility in a Boeing aircraft, however in the Russian made MC-21 300 airliner aircraft, we have no idea whether it is equipped with an emergency intervention system.'

Continuing Barnaby said, 'it would take weeks for us to investigate this possibility if not months as we would need to obtain the structural plans of the development of the aircraft, so to even make any attempt now would be a waste of time.'

The President sat back in his chair, deep in thought over what Barnaby had just said.

A few hours later the monitor lit up with a direct feed from NORAD and Rear Admiral Gomez the commander in charge of the Battle Group sailing north of the United Kingdom came into view.

'Mr. President, I can confirm that the flight from Moscow to Washington is due to pass thirty miles north of the Battle Group within thirty minutes,' stated Lieutenant General Driscol from NORAD.

Having been fully briefed by General Mitchfield earlier, Rear Admiral Gomez had given the three F/A-18 Pilots their final instructions and had ordered three fighters to be readied for immediate take off all armed with AIM 260 Joint Air Tactical Missiles.

'Rear Admiral Gomez, are your fighters on deck and ready?' Questioned the President.

'Yes Mr. President all three are ready for takeoff sir,' replied Rear Admiral Gomez.

'We will launch shortly Mr. President and we will beam images from one of our F/A-18 fighters so that you can follow the proceedings in real time,' stated the Rear Admiral.

A short while later images of three F/A-18E fighter jets came into view as they were catapulted down the deck of the aircraft carrier and into the night sky.

The President sat back in his chair coming to terms with the fact that he was about to issue an order to shoot down a civilian aircraft with three people on board which could spark a world war.

General Mitchfield confirmed that they had quietly moved from DEFCON 3 to DEFCON 2 on the President's orders a day before in anticipation of a possible retaliatory response from Russia.

Minutes later Rear Admiral Gomez was on line with images of a live stream feed from one of the F/A-18 Fighters tailing the Russian MC-21 300 airliner.

Rear Admiral Gomez confirmed that the Pilots had issued numerous instructions for the airliner to divert to the Canary Islands and land, however have had no response.

Everybody turned to face the President.

Turning to face Barnaby the President asked, 'one last time, are you one hundred percent sure that your intelligence is correct Barnaby?' asked the President.

'We simply cannot stuff this up,' continued the President emphatically.

'Yes Mr. President I am one hundred percent sure,' said Barnaby.

'We all know what this will mean if we balls this up,' reiterated the President.

'Any last minute suggestions gentlemen?' asked the President.

Going round the table, the President asked each member of the National Security Council and Joint Chiefs of Staff if they approved the shooting down of the aircraft.

Each member nodded their agreement.

'What is the probability of the poison being vaporized when the air to air missiles hits the target?' asked the President.

'Unknown Mr. President, however one can assume that possibly most of it would be vaporized on impact, so hopefully there will be a greatly reduced threat of it filtering down to shipping in the area, or wafting towards the African or European coast' said General Mitchfield.

'Final chance to change your mind anybody,' said the President.

All nodded in agreement to shoot the airliner down.

'Go,' ordered the President.

Images of the first air to air missile being fired taken from the cockpit of one of the F/A-18's was aired on the monitor on the wall.

Everybody in the Situation Room stared at the images beamed onto the screen.

The night sky lit up a short while later with a blinding white flash ten miles ahead as the missile found its target with all three F/A-18 fighter jets turning and making their way back to the aircraft carrier.

Sweet Jesus, I hope this won't start a world war thought President Trent.

'Get Pushkin on the line please,' said the President.

A few minutes later the Russian President Pushkin came on the line in what seemed to be a slurred greeting.

'Mr. President,' offered President Pushkin.

'What a surprise,' continued Pushkin.

'What can I do for you?' asked Pushkin.

'Well Mr. President we are all aware of what you have planned,' said President Trent.

'Oh and what is that' said President Pushkin.

'We know exactly what you have been up to,' stated President Trent emphatically.

'You have flown a commercial jet liner filled with a deadly poison towards Washington and intended releasing that poison over our capital which will kill everybody and everything within a fifty mile radius rendering our government leaderless,' said President Trent angrily.

Continuing in a raised voice President Trent said, 'we have just shot your airliner down.'

Pushkin shouted down the line, 'you have just killed hundreds of innocent people and this is an act of war,' he said.

'We will retaliate,' screamed Pushkin slamming the phone back into its cradle.

Chapter 25

Vyazma

Russia

Pushkin suspected that one or both of the scientist that developed the poison had somehow notified the Americans of the poison that they had developed and shouted for his personal security chief Victor Portnorsky to arrest both scientists.

Victor and his 2IC drove to their homes and arrested both the scientists immediately, notified their families to remain at home and not to contact anyone. If they did, it would have very serious consequences.

He then questioned both scientists about the deadly chemical that they had developed as they drove them back towards the Russian Government House.

Both scientists were petrified and mentioned that the poison that they had developed was the deadliest poison ever developed in Russia and was a mixture of Polonium, Botulinum, Compound 1080, Ricin, an agent known as TX20 and a compound known as VTD.

Both scientists confirmed that the poison had been tested over a remote village near the Izra district in Syria and that the results yielded a one hundred percent fatality rate within a two hour window as the deadly poison took effect. All human, animal and plant life ceased to exist in the village and to this day nothing has survived nor has anybody ever returned to the district.

Victor ordered the driver to stop in a deserted place and the driver thinking that he was going to execute them, willingly pulled over.

Both Victor and the driver exited the vehicle, pulled the two scientists out of the car and walked them towards a secluded wooded area when Victor turned and shot the driver in the back of his head.

Victor threw his mobile phone in the bushes and instructed both scientists to do the same.

He did not want the FSB to be able to track their movements.

Both scientists stared at Victor wide eyed, mouths open with fright as he untied them and bundled them back into the car telling them that he had orders to execute them.

He turned the car around and drove them back to their homes and instructed them to get their families into the car and they would flee as Pushkin would execute all of them including himself if found.

One of the scientist had two children aged eight and ten and the other had one child twelve years old.

Time was now of the essence and the two scientist quickly gathered their wives, children, some meagre belongings and laptops and squeezed into the car. Victor drove towards a warehouse near on the outskirts of Moscow.

He transferred all the people onto an old bus and drove westwards following the E-20 route towards the border with Lithuania, which is a distance of five hundred and sixty miles that would take around twelve hours.

He needed to get as far away from Moscow as quickly as possible because Pushkin would undoubtedly have the FSB and the Politsia set up road blocks around Moscow and track him down as he had not returned with the two scientists.

Taking great care to drive the speed limit ensuring that they would not to be stopped by any police on patrol, Portnorsky estimated that he would have a two hour window to get as far as possible away from Moscow before Pushkin would act.

Pushkin would be busy activating his military to retaliate for the shooting down of the airliner.

The two scientists and their families were petrified and three hours later they were nearing the town of Vyazma, one hundred and forty five miles from Moscow.

Victor slowed down a few miles from the town and turned off the main road and onto a gravel road and drove for a further eight miles towards a deserted farmhouse pulling the bus into an old barn.

Once inside Victor was quickly out of the bus and closed the barn door.

He had secretly bought this property years previously as part of his planned escape to America when the time came.

The scientists and their families debussed and made their way towards the corner of the warehouse that had some dusty old furniture scattered around in what appeared to be a dilapidated kitchen, with an array of tin foods lined up on a shelf in one corner.

Housed to one side of the barn was an old farm truck that the CIA had years previously converted into a type of tow truck with a tilt tray platform that had a hidden winch housed at the back of the cabin.

The tray had a hidden compartment under it that was thirty inches high and a small opening facing the back of the cab with a sliding door inserted into it.

The sliding door could be closed from inside the compartment when the tray was retracted back into position behind the cab and hidden from view.

The tilt tray had double tiers with side guard rails fitted to it and the first tier was able to cater for twelve head of cattle housed in a pen above the secret compartment.

Above the cattle pen where the cattle would be housed, they had fitted cross bars over the top making another tier where they were able to stack bales of hay.

When the time came to hide people inside the compartment, a person would activate the motor and the tilt tray would slide downwards at a thirty degree angle exposing the trap door and people could get into the compartment, lie down and hide.

The tilt tray is the same method used by tow trucks.

A person would then retract the tilt tray back into a level position on the truck using the hidden winch behind the cab and load twelve head of cattle into the animal pen on the lower platform that was above the hidden compartment.

Finally they would load the bales of hay onto the top level above where the cattle would be housed.

The bales of hay on the top level would make it look realistic that a farmer was transporting his live stock to market or relocating them to another farm.

Victor removed the battery from the bus and installed it into the truck ensuring that it fired up the trucks engine.

He then checked the oil, water and fuel ensuring the roadworthiness of the truck for the journey to a remote farm near the town of Smolensk.

Finally he syphoned the remaining diesel from the bus and poured it into the truck.

The CIA had arranged for an elderly farmer by the name of Vladimir Igoshin to pick the truck up at the farm and drive it to a town near the Lithuanian border whenever he received a coded message from Victor.

Victor fired up an old radio transmitter and sent a two word coded message to Vladimir instructing him to pick up the truck at the barn and load the cattle into the animal pen on the truck as well as bales of hay onto the top level.

Vladimir was an old haggard looking individual missing a number of front teeth with a wrinkled face resembling a farmer that had spent most of his years laboring outdoors.

Vladimir arrived at the barn a few hours later and greeted Victor with a warm handshake.

Victor then activated the tilt tray motor and tilted the tray downwards at a thirty degree angle and went about loading all the people into the hidden compartment, finally making his way into the crowded apartment as well.

Victor instructed the people to lie on their stomachs and rest their heads on their hands as the ride would be very bumpy.

Vladimir started winching the tilt tray back onto the truck until it was level.

The winch was securely hidden in a compartment behind the cab.

It was crowded and uncomfortable and very stuffy in the compartment and Victor asked everybody to remain calm as the cool air would find its way into the compartment when the truck starting moving.

He insisted that the scientists and their wives keep the children calm and quiet for if they were ever discovered they would face very dire consequences.

Victor promised that they would be safe when they reached America.

Vladimir opened the barn door and reversed the truck out of the barn, jumped out of the cab and closed the barn door.

He drove a short distance into the paddock, then reversed the truck to a ramp nearby and rounded up the twelve head of cattle, corralling them towards the ramp and into the animal pen above the hidden compartment.

He closed the gate at the rear of the truck after the cattle had entered the pen on the lower level, chained and locket it, then drove the truck to an open barn and proceeded to load bales of hay onto the top level.

He strapped the bales of hay to the truck and two hours later, Vladimir drove the truck towards the main road, turned and pointed the truck in the direction of Vilnius in Lithuania.

The drive to the first stop over point near the rural town of Smolensk was carefully planned and was a distance of seventy three miles.

This would be their first overnight stop.

They did not encounter any road blocks along the way and the next part of the journey would be a drive of around three hundred and fifty miles towards the Lithuanian border taking around six and a half hours.

Vladimir was careful to drive at a leisurely pace so as not to draw any attention.

He was stopped twice along the way towards the town of Smolensk and each time was waved through after the police had walked around and checked the truck.

Clearly Pushkin had ordered the police to conduct road checks on all roads leading towards the Lithuanian border.

Recruited by the CIA years previously, Vladimir was trusted to keep anything he had done secret and was handsomely rewarded.

It was an extremely uncomfortable ride for Victor, the scientists and their families lying cramped up in the hidden compartment, however the tradeoff would be the escape to the west and freedom.

Any urine and dung deposited by the cattle would simply run off the sides and not into the compartment, however the stench would be horrific, but well worth the uncomfortable ride, pain and suffering.

Earlier Victor took the time to explain to the scientists and their families that he was the head of Pushkin's security detail and that he had been sent him to arrest them.

Pushkin wanted to interrogate them and then execute them because he believed that they had somehow notified the Americans of the poison on board the airliner flying to Washington.

What Pushkin had decided to do with the poison was unknown to the scientists who both stared in disbelief having learnt what he intended to do with poison.

Victor again interrogated both scientists who confirmed that the poison was made in great quantities and transported to Zhukovsky Airport in Moscow.

Thereafter they had no idea of what Pushkin would do with the poison and were horrified to learn of Pushkin's intentions.

Early the next morning Vladimir drove towards the Lithuanian border and turned onto a gravel road some ten miles from the border and drove to a safe house in the mountains where they would stay for the night before making the trip towards the Lithuanian border on foot and crossing in a remote part of the forest.

Once over the border, Victor would call a handler with a coded message for the Director of the CIA to extract him from Lithuania.

Unbeknown to the Director of the CIA, he had brought along some human baggage.

Chapter 26

News Conference

The White House

The major television networks had been notified that the President would address the nation later that morning and all had hastily setup in the crowded Conference Room.

The President had not bothered to change and was still in his gown as he sat resolutely facing the barrage of cameras and cleared his throat.

'Good morning my fellow Americans, as you can see I am seated in the Conference Room at the White House and still in my pyjamas and gown and surrounded by our National Security Council and Joint Chiefs of Staff,' said the President as the various networks aired the live stream footage.

Not having bothered to shave and change before addressing the American people with his hair uncombed which added to the urgency of the situation confronting President Trent giving him maximum exposure.

'I was woken in the early hours of this morning by the Director of the CIA and have not had the opportunity to shave and change.' 'The Director informed me that the Russians were flying a commercial airliner towards Washington,' said the President.

'This plane has been converted to carry a payload of the deadliest poison ever developed by the Russians,' continued the President.

'We have evidence that the Russians have tested this poison over a remote village near the Izra district in Syria and that the results yielded a one hundred percent fatality rate within a two hour window as the deadly poison took effect,' stated the President emphatically.

'We have irrefutable proof that the Russian President Pushkin intended to release this deadly poison over Washington that would kill all human, animal and plant life within a fifty mile radius in two hours of the poison having been released,' continued the President.

'The Pilots had been instructed by President Pushkin to call an emergency and overshoot the runway and whilst circling Washington, they would dump this deadly poison over the city making it look like they were dumping fuel,' said the President.

'Thereafter the pilots would set a course away from America to an international destination,' continued the President.

'I gave the order to shoot this commercial airliner down and I can confirm that despite what President Pushkin and his cadres will say, we have confirmation that there were only three people on board that flight,' stated the President emphatically.

'The three people on board the flight were the Pilot, Co-Pilot and a Navigator and they did not respond to instructions from our F/A-18E interceptor Pilots to divert to the Canary Islands off north Africa and land safely which gave me no option but to issue the order for it to be shot down,' said the President staring resolutely at the cameras.

'Despite numerous efforts to get the Pilots to divert to the Canary Islands, they refused to comply which has sadly resulted in their loss of life, so their grave error of judgement gave me no option but to order the shooting down of this aircraft,' reiterated the President sombrely.

'A few days ago the CIA uncovered another plot by President Pushkin, which was that he intended to sail a medium sized container vessel namely the Sea Thunder from the Russian port of Severomorsk to Baltimore with high end explosives loaded into every container,' stated the President.

'They would load some containers in Singapore making it look like a vessel just going about its day to day activities and then the Sea Thunder would set sail for Baltimore,' continued the President.

'Once in the port of Baltimore, they would offload the few containers loaded in Singapore and the crew would disembark in stages and catch international flights out of the USA,' said the President.

'The first officer would be the last to disembark and also catch an international flight out of the USA and prior to him disembarking, he would set the timers in the containers to simultaneously trigger explosions some four hours later,' said the President.

'The result of the controlled explosions in these containers would be catastrophic and would cause total devastation and be three thousand times bigger than the bomb used on Hiroshima with a yield of some sixty megatons,' stated the President candidly.

Continuing the President said, 'the devastation would be catastrophic for all within a radius of some seventy miles of the Port of Baltimore and be like a nuclear warhead having exploded.'

'This would cause a tsunami, the likes of which the world has never seen and cause millions of deaths and the utter devastation of coastal cities around the globe with the possible loss of life in the hundreds of millions,' stated the President.

'Seal Team Six carried out a mission and boarded the Sea Thunder and have disarmed all the timers on board the vessel which is currently stationary in the Irish Sea near the United Kingdom,' continued the President.

'We have naval assets situated around the vessel which is heavily guarded by Seal Team Six and a decision will shortly be made on how we will safely remove the explosives on board,' said the President.

'It is clear that Pushkin is desperate and will do everything in his power to remain in power,' said President Trent emphatically.

'From what we have seen, the Russians have activated their nuclear missiles and we have moved our preparedness to DEFCON 1 a few hours ago, so the country is now in a state of possible war with Russia,' said the President emphatically.

'Clearly this puts us on a war footing with Russia and possibly China as the leaders of these two nations met secretly over the past three months and had planned a nuclear strike on the USA and other possible allies from North Korea,' continued the President.

'In conclusion, I am offering President Pushkin an olive branch to de-escalate the tension immediately and to meet with me in the next day or two, however desperate people do desperate things,' said the President.

If Pushkin does in fact launch any nuclear missiles, he must clearly realize that we will retaliate immediately which will undoubtedly lead to the annihilation of all living matter on earth,' said the President staring resolutely at the cameras.

'The Russian economy is in free fall due to the sanctions that the USA and other world leaders have imposed on them,' stated the President.

'As you are all aware, we have imposed sanctions on Russia's largest bank namely Sberbank and all other Russian banks that has had a crippling effect on their economy,' continued the President.

'President Pushkin has resorted to drastic measures and I appeal to him to use common sense to de-escalate tensions and retract from this dangerous position he has taken,' said the President.

'Thank you my fellow Americans.' 'I now need to end this news broadcast as I have pressing issues to deal with,' said the President standing and drawing the broadcast to an end with journalists firing questions at him as he prepared to depart the conference room.

Michael O'Rourke the National Security Advisor instructed all media present to pack up and exit the conference room immediately with people busy speaking on mobile phones, many in the room huddled over laptops and iPads.

The President, National Security Council and the Joint Chiefs of Staff returned to the Situation Room and resumed their seats.

An agent placed the Football alongside the President.

The nuclear football (also known as the atomic football) is a briefcase, the contents of which are to be used by the President of the United States to authorize a nuclear attack while away from fixed command centers.

Whilst not needed in the command center at the White House Situation Room, the Football was placed alongside him as a backup.

Michael O'Rouke the National Security Advisor turned to face the President.

'Mr. President, we need to get you and the Vice President out of Washington immediately sir,' said Michael O'Rourke.

Continuing he said, 'I have arranged for both Airforce One and Two be ready for immediate departure Mr. President.'

'We have to get both of you out of the State to a safer location,' continued the National Security Advisor.

The President sat with his elbows on the desk, the fingers of both hands intertwined with each other and the two first fingers propping up his chin as he considered what the National Security Advisor had just said.

'Yes, I think that it is a good idea to relocate Vice President Tippence, however I will remain here for the time being until God forbid Pushkin does something else,' said the President.

'To be candid, if Pushkin does launch nukes, there will be no need for me to hide in a secure location because that will be the end of life on earth,' said the President.

'So Miles, I think it is advisable that you relocate immediately to a possible safer location as a precaution, if you in fact can find one,' stated the President.

The Vice President reluctantly rose albeit that he was relieved that he and his family would be far away from Washington and followed a security agent out of the Situation Room.

As he exited the situation room, he shook everybody's hand and wished them all well.

Shortly after the Vice President had departed the Situation Room, Barnaby tapped on the table to get the attention of all the members of the National Security Council and Joint Chiefs of Staff.

'Mr. President, I have just received confirmation that our satellites have uncovered that the Russians have activated their nuclear missiles ready for launch,' said Barnaby.

The President turned to General Mitchfield and asked, 'are we loaded, locked and ready General?'

'Yes Mr. President, waiting for your order sir,' replied the General.

'God help us,' said the President.

Chapter 27

Situation Room

White House

The President turned to his aides seated around him in the situation room.

His face white with fright!

About the Author

Sid De Beer was born in Johannesburg South Africa in 1950 and is the only son of the late Sam and the late Joan De Beer.

After a successful executive management career within the office products industry in South Africa, he immigrated to Australia in 1993 at the age of 43.

Sid ended his career as the General Manager of a company within the optical industry in Australia and had successfully taken a loss making entity and turned it into a highly profitable company before retiring.

He has been married to his wife Nadine for 44 years and is the father of 3 daughters Odette, Shi-Anne and Kim and has seven grandchildren.

Sid and his wife are now retired and live in Melbourne Australia where his entire family resides.

'I live everyday like it's my last.'